"You want *three* tr
quirked upward.

Alaina grinned. "Just making up for lost time. Mason and I spent most of our holidays on research projects."

"Surely wolf biologists don't have to be in the field every minute."

She shrugged. "It varies, but Mason was determined to study wolf populations all over the world."

"Is that what *you* wanted?"

Alaina hesitated. "In the beginning I was thrilled to be part of those studies," she said slowly. "But living that way got old for me. It's one of the reasons I wanted a home base to work from this year."

"And why you want all these Christmas decorations."

"Of course. Making up for lost time, remember?"

"Then how about that one?" Gideon asked.

Alaina regarded the tree, picturing it in the cabin. "Perfect," she pronounced. As a kid she'd loved falling asleep in the light of a Christmas tree and hoped to re-create the magical feeling it had once given her.

And, speaking of magic, what was she going to do about Gideon...

Dear Reader,

On my way to school I used to pass a beautiful dog that was remarkably sweet and friendly. I called her Misty and brought her ice cubes in hot weather, which she'd play with in her enclosure and carry around in delight. At the time I didn't know much about dogs and thought she might be a husky. Then I learned she was a full-blooded Alaskan wolf, rescued as a badly injured puppy after a wildfire. I have been completely and utterly in love with wolves ever since.

Because of Misty I've always wanted to tell a story in which wolves played a central part. So *Christmas on the Ranch* gave me the chance to pit a wolf-loving wildlife photographer against a bitterly divorced rancher who might not share her enthusiasm for these magnificent animals.

I enjoy hearing from readers and can be contacted via my Facebook page, or if you prefer writing a letter, please use: c/o Harlequin Books, 22 Adelaide Street West, 40th Floor, Toronto, Ontario, Canada, M5H 4E3.

Best wishes,

Julianna

HEARTWARMING

Christmas on the Ranch

—

Julianna Morris

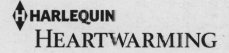
HARLEQUIN
HEARTWARMING

H HARLEQUIN®
HEARTWARMING™

ISBN-13: 978-1-335-89000-9

Recycling programs
for this product may
not exist in your area.

Christmas on the Ranch

Copyright © 2020 by Julianna Morris

This edition published by arrangement with Harlequin Books S.A.

For questions and comments about the quality of this book, please contact us at CustomerService@Harlequin.com.

Harlequin Enterprises ULC
22 Adelaide St. West, 40th Floor
Toronto, Ontario M5H 4E3, Canada
www.Harlequin.com

Printed in U.S.A.

Julianna Morris still remembers being read to by her mother in a rocking chair, wrapped in a patchwork quilt. She learned to read herself at an early age and remains a voracious book consumer on everything from history and biographies to most fiction genres.

Julianna has been a park ranger, program analyst and systems analyst in information technology. She loves animals, travel, gardening, hiking, taking photographs, making patchwork quilts and doing a few dozen other things. Her biggest wish is to have more hours in the day for everything she enjoys.

Books by Julianna Morris

Harlequin Heartwarming

Twins for the Rodeo Star

Harlequin Superromance

Bachelor Protector
Christmas with Carlie
Undercover in Glimmer Creek

Visit the Author Profile page
at Harlequin.com for more titles.

To my editor, Kathryn Lye

PROLOGUE

ALAINA WAS WONDERING if she'd missed a turn or if her GPS had malfunctioned. It felt as if she'd been driving forever.

"In one hundred feet, turn left," the electronic voice from the GPS finally intoned.

Sure enough, there was a road marked with a sign for the Double Branch Ranch. She passed over two miles of grassland before reaching the first outbuildings, then finally drove into the ranch center and parked next to a mud-splattered late model pickup.

The main house had two floors and an attic. It was solidly built from logs and surrounded by a broad covered porch. Her imagination instantly painted it with a large family and comfy outdoor furniture.

Lovely.

As Alaina opened the SUV door, a dog raced from one of the barns, barking. To some people he'd probably sound ferocious, but his ears were tilted with excitement, not aggression, and the barks were high-pitched, rather than deep with warning or anger. She'd learned a good deal about animal communication from the wildlife experts she had worked with over the years.

"Danger, come back here." A tall man strode forward to grab his collar. "Don't be afraid. He's protective, not vicious."

She stepped down from the SUV. "I wasn't afraid. Hello, Danger. You're a beauty."

Danger was mostly black and he swished his tail, his mouth open in a big doggy grin. He whined and tried to get away from the grip the man had on his collar.

"I'm Alaina Wright," she said. "Are you Gideon Carmichael by any chance?"

"That's right." He gave her hand a perfunctory shake. "Am I supposed to know you?"

"No, but I've heard about you and the Double Branch. You practice a traditional style of ranching and you're relatively close to Yellowstone National Park. I've also been told you have a foreman's house that's going unused."

A wary expression crept into Gideon Carmichael's brown eyes. "The place is more a small cabin than a house, but that's correct, it's empty most of the time. I was the foreman when I inherited the ranch, so there wasn't any need to hire a replacement. Why do you ask?"

"Because I have a business proposition. I'd like to use the hou...*cabin*, for a year. I'll provide all my own supplies, including firewood, since I understand that while the building has electricity, it's heated solely by a fireplace insert."

Gideon stared as if she'd sprouted wings and her skin had turned green. Her sister-in-law, a successful Manhattan lawyer, had suggested sending a letter first, but Alaina had wanted to get a feel for the area before committing herself, and then expedite the arrangement.

"Oh, and I'll pay you twenty-five thousand dollars," she added, realizing she'd left out the most important part. "You'd keep the money, whether I remain the whole year or not."

He cleared his throat. "Why would you want to stay at the Double Branch? This isn't a tourist location. You could rent a place in West Yellowstone or down in Jackson Hole, or even stay in the park itself. It would be a whole lot easier."

"I've been moving from one accommodation to another for the past six weeks, but I'm a wildlife photographer. Trying to be, anyhow. I can't get the photos I want with excited tourists around me, and when summer comes it will only get worse. Working from a location like your ranch could help jump-start my career. You're on the edge of an extraordinary wilderness area."

The furrows deepened in Gideon's forehead. "Except in Yellowstone or the Grand Teton, you'd have park rangers to assist if there was a problem. I employ several ranch hands, but none of us have time to look after you."

"I don't need to be looked after. You'd have no responsibility toward me beyond being my landlord," Alaina assured hastily. She handed him the envelope from Janet's law office. "Here's the paperwork, which includes a liability release for you, your ranch and your employees. If you agree, you'll receive a certified check for twenty-five thousand dollars before I move in. That would also cover payment of the electricity I'd use."

He regarded the envelope as if it were a snake threatening to strike. She'd learned that he had inherited the ranch from his great-grandfather, who'd had a reputation for being the toughest, most humorless man in this part of Montana. A man of few words, *except when he had a bee in his bonnet*, according to her source. Perhaps Gideon took after the old guy. She'd hoped that he would be more open-minded because he was one of the youngest ranchers in the area, though based on the grim look in his eyes, she'd indulged in wishful thinking.

How did someone live without a sense of humor? Laughter had been a lifeline during the worst times in her life.

"I'll take a look," he said finally. "How do I reach you?"

"My cell number is in there, or if you prefer, you can make contact through my attorney, Janet Whitcomb. At the moment I have a room at the Old Faithful Inn, so I'm not too far away. As the crow flies, that is, it's a fair drive out of the park and around to get here."

He gave her a curt nod and Alaina took it as a sign that she should leave. Danger cocked his head and let out another whine as she got back in her SUV. Perhaps they could become friends if his owner agreed to let her stay on the ranch.

Gideon Carmichael reminded her of a bull elk—stubborn, arrogant and the master of his universe. She'd have to go somewhere else if he didn't agree to her proposal, but it would be a shame. The Double Branch was the best location she'd been able to find near Yellowstone to get the photographs she wanted to become known for taking.

But one thing was sure, if he *did* agree, dealing with him would be one of her biggest challenges.

"WHO WAS THAT?" Gideon's mother asked as she stepped out on the porch.

His stepdad had passed unexpectedly a few months ago and she'd been visiting each of her children. Her doctor claimed her health was fine, but she'd lost weight and was sleeping poorly, so Gideon had asked her to stay for a longer visit at the ranch or to consider living there permanently. She'd spent her childhood summers here, so it was a place of happy memories. Surely being at the Double Branch would help.

"Son?" Helene prompted as he continued to look at a letter in the packet that Alaina had given him.

"It was a wildlife photographer who wants to live on the ranch for a year. She's willing to pay for the service, and I'd keep the money, whether or not she lasts the whole twelve months."

Helene patted his arm. "And you hope she won't."

"I didn't say that."

"You didn't have to. I learned to read your poker face a long time ago, including when you claimed your black eye came from being tackled during football practice."

Gideon grinned wryly. "You knew I'd been fighting, then?"

"I knew." She kissed his cheek. "But Stewart thought we should let it go. He was sure you had a good reason."

A tight ache grew in Gideon's throat. He missed his stepdad, though their relationship had been rocky in the beginning. Rocky? What an understatement. After his biological father deserted the family, Gideon had carried a chip on his shoulder the size of Montana. But Stewart had let time and patience do their work, and they'd grown close. Now it hurt like the devil to have him gone.

"Dad was a wise man," Gideon said. "A new kid was bullying the other students. He went after a smaller boy with his fists and I put myself in the middle."

"That sounds like you. It... I never told you how much it meant to Stewart when you boys started calling him Dad." She squared her shoulders. "Now, what can you tell me about this photographer?"

"Not much, except that she has twenty-five thousand dollars to throw around. According to the letter from her lawyer, she hopes to have everything settled by the first of June."

"You could give her credit for knowing what she wants and being willing to pay for it."

"She wants to take pictures, Mom. She claims she can't get them in the park, but people have taken millions of pictures in Yellowstone. On the other hand, if I refuse, she'll just offer the money to another rancher, so why not accept?"

Helene nodded. "At least on the Double Branch you can keep an eye out to make sure she's all right. From a distance, of course. You wouldn't want to interfere with her work."

"Having to look after her is exactly what I'm worried about. I'm too busy to keep a tenderfoot out of trouble for a week, much less a year."

"Refuse if you have a bad feeling about the situation," his mother advised.

Gideon thought about the money Alaina Wright was willing to pay. The foreman's cabin was going empty and a tenant's electrical use would be minimal. He was doing well with the Double Branch, but the extra income would add a cushion to his cash reserves. So while his instincts said to refuse, he wasn't going to.

The offer was too good to pass up.

CHAPTER ONE

ALAINA RAN THROUGH her mental checklist.

Food, fuel, camping gear, solar chargers, satellite phone, snowshoes, cross-country skis, axes, wedges…

It went on and on.

She sighed.

Inevitably there would be something she'd missed, however carefully she prepared. But there was a small town not too far away where she could get some of what she needed, including fresh fruits and vegetables, which couldn't be bought too much in advance, regardless. Ordering online was another tool she planned to use. Bozeman was close enough for occasional shopping, as well.

Her trepidation grew as she turned onto the Double Branch ranch road. When she parked in the main compound, it was a case of déjà vu as Danger ran over, barking. She got out and crouched to give him a pet. His tongue lolled to one side and his doggy smile was irresistible. Danger's dark fur, with few discernible German shepherd markings, reminded her of several wolves from Yellowstone's old Druid pack, once one of the strongest wolf packs in the park.

She looked into his golden eyes and tried to decide if any crossbreeding might have occurred. Not necessarily from the Druid pack—the Double Branch was well outside of what used to be their territory—but wolves had spread beyond the park since their reintroduction.

"You shouldn't do that," Gideon Carmichael said sharply. "I told you, he isn't used to strangers."

Alaina hid a smile. The forbidding tone in Gideon's voice obviously hadn't been sweetened by the twenty-five thousand dollar check he'd cashed. No fake smiles or pretense, which was somehow reassuring, because it meant she knew where she stood with him. Anyhow, if the ranch didn't have that many strangers visiting, he might be justified to worry how his dog would react.

"You said he was protective, not vicious, and he seems friendly. I love animals. Danger is an interesting name. Is it intended to warn visitors away?"

"I can't say. My great-grandfather named

him. I inherited Danger along with the ranch a few years ago."

"I see."

"Gideon, don't keep her standing around," an older woman scolded as she joined them. She grinned. "Hello. I'm Helene Cranston and this tall overworked cowboy is my son. You must be Alaina Wright. Welcome to the Double Branch."

Alaina instantly liked her; she was on the fence about Gideon. "Thank you. It's beautiful here. Montana is one of my favorite places."

Helene glowed. "The Double Branch used to be my grandfather's spread and it was built by *his* grandfather before him, who rode with Theodore Roosevelt at the battle of San Juan Hill in Cuba. Mr. Roosevelt didn't like being called Teddy, you know."

"That's what I've read. Did he ever stay here?"

"Oh, yes. He shot a grizzly bear, not two hundred feet from where we're standing. He and my great-great grandfather, Jonah Westcott, met in the Dakotas when Mr. Roosevelt came out from New York after the death of his mother and first wife. In one of Jonah's journals he wrote that he'd never seen a sadder man than Theodore Roosevelt, or one who tried harder to run away from it."

Alaina hadn't known about the Double Branch's historical connection to Theodore Roosevelt and now it seemed even more appropriate to have the ranch as her home base. Imagine living in a place where one of the most famous men in United States history had spent time.

Her excitement grew. This was just what she needed.

"That's amazing. Do you still have the journals? I'd love to take pictures. If it's okay," she added quickly. "I'd be careful and would give you copies."

"The journals are on loan to the town museum, along with the letters Mr. Roosevelt wrote to the family, but I can arrange for you to have access. The head of the museum board is a former beau of mine."

Gideon looked startled. "Nels Hewitt is an old beau?"

"Yes, son. We dated as teenagers when I stayed with Grandpa each summer. Nothing serious, other than him being my first kiss. It's hard for a woman to forget her first kiss. Right, Alaina?"

That was an easy question. "Right. I was

a late bloomer. Mine was my husband. On our third date."

"Oh, then you're married."

Alaina's smile wobbled. "I was. But he… We were in a car accident two years ago." Mason Wright had been the finest man she'd ever known. Despite a thirty-one year age difference, they'd suited each other perfectly. The irony was that Mason hadn't died from an age-related illness—he'd been exceptionally healthy—but from injuries inflicted by a drunk driver.

At least she'd finally stopped having nightmares about the crash. Her head throbbing. The endlessly flashing lights and sirens. Trying to help Mason, trapped behind the steering wheel. The few whispered words they'd shared before he died. Then waking up and knowing it wasn't a nightmare at all, she'd simply been reliving the most terrible moments of her life.

Helene took her hand and gave it a squeeze. "I'm so sorry. You're too young to be going through that. I lost my second husband a few months ago, but we were fortunate to have twenty-six years together. Goodness, let's not talk about it and depress ourselves. Where are you from?"

"A tiny town in coastal Connecticut. Port Coopersmith."

"I thought you were from New York City," Gideon said. "How did you end up with a lawyer in Manhattan?"

Alaina shrugged. "My husband's family is from New York. Janet Whitcomb is my sister-in-law. We've stayed close."

"Family ties are so important," Helene said. "Come inside for a cup of coffee and tell me about your work. Do you use digital or film?"

Alaina glanced at Gideon. She didn't think he'd planned to extend any hospitality to his home, which was understandable. The Double Branch was a working ranch and her presence was just a business transaction as far as he was concerned.

Still, she couldn't be rude to his mom.

"Digital," she told Helene. "Everything seems to be electronic these days, but I brought solar chargers for when I'm camping higher in the mountains."

CAMPING?

Gideon's head reeled. He'd assumed Alaina would just take short day trips around the ranch to get her pictures. But supplying herself with solar chargers meant she expected to be out for days or weeks at a time.

"How much backpacking experience do you have?" he asked.

"I was a research assistant and the team photographer on my husband's field projects. He was a wildlife biologist. We got into some fairly inaccessible locations."

"So you were with a group and not necessarily backpacking."

"If I'm not worried about my skill level, then you shouldn't be, either," she returned in a crisp tone.

"That's easier said than done. I own the Double Branch and I feel responsible for everything that happens here."

Alaina gave him an innocent look. "I signed a liability release, so you have nothing to worry about. But if I run into trouble, I'll be sure to do it on national forest land, instead of your ranch. Okay?"

"I'm not talking about liability. I'm concerned about your safety. Wilderness camping isn't the same as taking a walk around the Yellowstone geyser fields on well-maintained paths or staying in an established campground."

Alaina's chin went up and a spark of irritation flashed in her blue-green eyes. "I'll manage."

Gideon was ready to choke on his frustration. How had he gotten into this mess?

Oh, yeah, *money.*

She'd waved that twenty-five thousand dollars in his face and he'd taken the bait. Well, the terms of the agreement were clear. She wanted to be independent and that's what she would get. He'd just have to remind his employees not to let themselves be charmed into doing everything for her. On work time, that is—he couldn't prevent them from helping during their own hours. He was realistic—the combination of Alaina's shimmering blond hair and unusual eyes could turn his employees into willing marks.

His mother kept darting anxious looks between them and he gave her a tight smile.

"Alaina, please, come in," Helene urged.

"What a great house," Alaina murmured as they walked through the living room and back to the kitchen. "Is this the original home?"

"No," Gideon said. "The foreman's cabin was the first. There's electricity, but as you already know, the single source of heat is a fireplace insert."

Alaina's expression didn't change. "That's why I ordered three cords of firewood to be delivered, with more to come. The first load should have already arrived. I don't intend to be caught short. Winter in Yellowstone may be worse than surrounding areas because of its unique geology, but I know it can be bad here, too."

"The wood was dumped by the cabin. The firebox takes good-sized pieces, but at least half are still too big to fit. They'll need splitting."

Humor crept into her face. "I assumed that was likely, which is why I brought axes, a hatchet, metal wedges and a maul."

"Alaina, do you take cream and sugar?" his mother broke in.

"Black is fine."

Gideon tried to contain his impatience as the two women chatted. He'd rather be out checking the Double Branch's herds and riding fences, but he'd stayed at the ranch center to show his tenant the cabin and to ensure there weren't any misunderstandings. Now his mother was treating her as an honored guest.

Maybe it was their shared widowhood. He regretted that. The pain on Alaina's face had been very real at the mention of her husband. Embracing the wilderness might be an act of catharsis, a way to deal with her loss.

Anyway, he'd agreed to let her stay on the

Double Branch and was being paid well for the service. He needed to try putting his concerns aside and give her a chance—perhaps even do what his mother had suggested in the first place, simply keep watch from a distance to ensure she remained safe.

That might not be feasible if she hiked deep into the backcountry, but he had trouble believing it would actually happen. Backcountry camping wasn't for the fainthearted, whether you were a man *or* a woman. Few tried it alone. If Alaina was as inexperienced as he suspected, she wouldn't go far.

"Alaina, let me show you the foreman's house," he said before his mother could refill their empty cups. "The cabin is old, but my great-grandfather kept the place up, even when he didn't have a foreman living there. The walls have some insulation and the plumbing is updated."

If the improvement in his attitude surprised her, she hid it well. "I'm looking forward to seeing it. Helene, thanks for the delicious coffee."

"You're very welcome. Come over to visit whenever you like."

Gideon didn't echo the invitation, but he wouldn't deny his mother feminine companionship if that was what she needed.

"Is it all right to park my SUV near the cabin?" Alaina asked as they stepped outside.

"Of course." He thought quickly, hoping to make up for his earlier behavior. It had been churlish to make an agreement and then resent having made it. "I should ask something. Obviously there's time, but our summers are shorter than most people think. Do you have snow tires already?"

"I don't have any, but the real-estate agent in Bannister said I could get what I need through Anders Garage, so I let the owner know the make and model of my SUV. He'll order a set in July or August, and install them later."

The real-estate agent?

Gideon suddenly realized where Alaina had gotten her information about the vacant foreman's house. Nobody was sure how Rita Johnson did it, but she knew everything about everyone for thirty miles in every direction.

He cleared his throat. "In that case, you should have the tires in plenty of time. Montana allows them to be used from October to May. There's a shed by the cabin where they can be stored until needed."

"THAT'S GOOD TO HEAR."

Alaina definitely preferred a pleasant Gideon

Carmichael over the one with misgivings in his eyes.

Would he prefer her to be older and look more robust? Perhaps, but if he believed she wanted special treatment, he was dead wrong. Not that it mattered. She would be up in the mountains working most of the time and didn't require his approval. Her brothers and parents didn't approve of her plans, either, but that hadn't stopped her. She'd been coddled her entire life, now she wanted to challenge herself.

"This is it," Gideon said, breaking into her thoughts.

From the outside, the foreman's house was still a nineteenth-century log cabin with a porch that wrapped around the front and south sides of the building. Inside it was a compact home with incongruously modern features. Even the fireplace insert was a contemporary touch, with an electric fan to circulate air around the firebox and blow it into the room.

"Heat rises, so I'd recommend sleeping in the loft during the winter instead of the bedroom," Gideon said, gesturing to the staircase. "I know from experience that it's warmer up there, presuming you keep a fire burning all night. It's cold either way if you don't."

Alaina didn't intend to discuss her sleeping arrangements with a virtual stranger, so she turned and walked into the kitchen. The refrigerator was huge in contrast to the room, likely a reflection of the ranch's distance from town and the need to store more fresh foods. There was also a medium-sized chest freezer, where milk, bread and other items could be stocked for longer periods, along with a washer and dryer.

"Will this be okay?" Gideon asked.

"It's perfect. Now, I'm sure you have much better things to do with your time. Go on and I'll get settled."

He looked nonplussed, probably unaccustomed to being politely dismissed. "Of course." He took out an envelope and gave it to her. "This is a map, showing property lines, my leased rangeland and other information."

"Thanks. I'll see if the data can be programmed into my portable GPS unit."

"That should be possible. I've provided the GPS coordinates. I'll get back to work now."

She bit her lip to stop a chuckle as he walked out of the cabin.

In a way, Gideon Carmichael was just like

her brothers. They saw themselves as progressive guys of the twenty-first century, when in reality, they'd barely emerged from the cave. Even her husband had leaned too far in that direction. Mason had teased, saying it was because she looked like an ethereal princess from a medieval tale of a knight-errant, but Alaina didn't buy that excuse. With Mason, she'd also had the age difference to contend with, needing to remind him periodically that they were partners, not mentor and student.

She didn't know why the male half of her family was so impossible other than the pesky Y chromosome they shared.

But in all honesty, her mom *also* disagreed with her decision to strike out on her own instead of finding a new photographer to work with. At least the family understood why she hadn't stayed with her original mentor. He'd stolen a collection of her photographs, ones taken during field studies with Mason. She'd been forced to file a suit against him, proving that some of the photos had actually been published previously, citing her as the photographer.

Mason had left enough that she could get by, but having someone she'd respected try to take credit for her work?

Not acceptable.

Her mouth tightened. It had been a case of too much trust in the wrong person. While it wasn't the worst thing that had ever happened to her, she wouldn't make the same mistake again.

Pushing the memory away, Alaina went to the window and saw Gideon striding to a barn across the extended property. He was edgy and intense, like a wolf on the prowl.

She would need to stay on her toes during their contacts. A few minutes later, he rode out on a reddish-brown horse with Danger trotting alongside.

Hmm.

She still didn't know if she should have arranged for a horse to ride, but she hadn't seen herself taking one out in deep snow. Besides, while she could ride, she wasn't comfortable with horses. They were nice enough, but she'd broken her leg after a bad throw as a child and had never stopped being uptight around them. In return, they seemed to feel the same about her.

Now that she was alone, she stowed her fresh food in the refrigerator and then rolled up her sleeves. The current temperature was pleasant, but a cold front was predicted to move in overnight and bring snow. Getting the firewood sorted out was critical if she didn't want to huddle under blankets until the weather cleared.

The three cords she'd ordered had been dumped in piles along one side of the cabin. She soon had it sorted into neat stacks, with chunks too big for the fireplace insert closest to the chopping block. Contrary to what Gideon Carmichael seemed to think, she knew how to split wood; it had been part of the survival-and-wilderness training courses she'd taken.

The SUV was next.

She unloaded the remaining contents, deciding to use the bedroom as a studio and the loft for sleeping. Places for storage had been cleverly added in the cabin to maximize the small space, but the pantry was the best discovery. She'd ordered a shipment of freeze-dried food and other supplies for her backpacking excursions and could store it there. More would come every few weeks, along with additional staples.

"Alaina?" called a voice.

She went into the living area and saw Helene standing in the open doorway. A yellow Labrador retriever stood next to her, furiously wagging its tail.

"Hi. And who is this?" she asked as the dog dashed over, eager for attention.

"It's Cookie, my daughter's pet. Libby will be spending the summer in New Mexico and asked me to take care of him." Helene gestured to the wood by the house. "I feel guilty for letting you do all of this alone. The least my son could have done was get the firewood sorted out before you arrived."

"That wasn't part of our agreement. Anyhow, I enjoy hard work. I've spent the last several months building my upper and lower body strength." Alaina lifted an arm and flexed her muscles, then shrugged ruefully. "I'm fit, even if it doesn't show."

"I admire your determination. But you need to eat, so I brought a late lunch for us to share." Helene held up the tray she carried.

"How thoughtful."

They ate on the porch, with Alaina mostly listening as Helene told stories of her family history. It was fascinating. One branch of the family had even traveled with Daniel Boone before eventually making their way to Montana.

"It must be wonderful to know where you fit into history," Alaina said wistfully. She knew little about her genealogy.

"Part of our history isn't admirable," Helene admitted. "For example, a great-great-something uncle was strung up for stealing horses, and another was shot for desertion in the Revolutionary War. Whether they're good or bad, we can't pick our ancestors."

"True." Alaina squelched an impulse to ask more about Gideon. He had the tall, dark and inscrutable thing down to an art form. Maybe he disliked her, maybe he regretted their arrangement or maybe he just had a perpetual migraine. "You mentioned visiting the Double Branch as a kid. You didn't grow up around here?"

"No, my mother fell in love with a rancher when my grandparents took her to a rodeo in Shelton County. Mom and Dad still live on the Carmichael ranch up there and my oldest son runs it for them. Eventually it will go to him."

"You come from a real ranching tradition."

"Yes, though my daughter is studying archeology. That's why she'll be in New Mexico. She's going to be part of a new dig. My second husband was fascinated by Native American folktales and art and passed that on to Libby. Stewart was the county sheriff. Everybody in Shelton relied on him."

Alaina smiled. "One of the good guys."

"Stewart was a fine man. I just wish I

hadn't made him wait so long before accepting his proposal."

"Trust issues?"

"*Major* trust issues. Mostly in myself since I'd had such bad judgment picking my first husband. I was terribly indecisive with Stewart. Sometimes I still marvel he was so patient."

Cookie, who'd been lying on his side and snoring, flipped over and let out a low huffing sound. The sound of horses riding their direction could be heard in the distance.

Helene sat forward, concern on her face. "Alaina, you should know that Gideon has five ranch hands. One is older, close to my age, but the other four are young and single. They may hope to get acquainted."

"I'm not here for romance. And…" Alaina hesitated. Her family had been upset when she said she didn't want to get married again and tried to argue her out of it, but maybe Helene would understand. "I've had the love of my life. Now I'm focusing on my career."

Sympathy filled Helene's eyes. "My first marriage was a disaster, so it was different for me. Deep down I was relieved when Luther left for parts unknown, though my sons took it badly. I think it was hardest on Gideon. Between his biological father deserting us and his ex-wife, I doubt he'll get married again, either. Different reasons, obviously. I'll have to count on my other children for grandkids."

"I'm glad your second marriage was good."

"Stewart was one in a million. He helped to raise my boys and we were blessed with a lovely daughter. Now, you don't need to worry about the ranch hands, they're gentlemen, but I'll have my son warn them away if that would be easier."

Alaina didn't plan to ask Gideon for a single thing. He'd just see it as evidence she couldn't take care of herself.

"I appreciate the concern, but I can handle them," she assured Helene.

"All right, if you're certain. I'd better go and get Gideon's dinner started. I'm so very glad you're here."

"Me, too."

Two riders came over a rise of land as Helene stepped down from the porch. They were accompanied by several tri-colored Australian shepherds, who were energetically scampering around even after a long day. When the riders reached the cabin, Helene introduced them as brothers, Chad and Jeremy Singleton, before heading back to the main house.

The men tipped their hats in unison.

"Ma'am, you're a sight for sore eyes," Jeremy drawled. "Please let me know if there's *anything* I can do to make you feel welcome. Our bunkhouse is just a short piece down the road. You passed it driving in. Feel free to call on me day or night."

Not to be outdone, Chad pointed to the chopping block at the side of her cabin. "I'd be happy to take care of splitting any logs too big for the stove. I'll come over after dinner and take care of it in nothin' flat."

From the corner of her eye, Alaina saw Gideon had ridden up, as well. "The offer is appreciated, but I'll manage," she said firmly. "Don't let me keep you from your other work."

GIDEON RESTRAINED A LAUGH. He'd arrived in time to hear two of his employees offer their assistance to Alaina, followed by her refusal. It didn't mean she could cope on her own, just that she was going to try.

Chad and Jeremy looked disappointed. They were decent guys and living on the Double Branch offered few opportunities to socialize with an attractive woman, but they didn't argue. Her tone had been clear; she wasn't available.

"Hey, boss," Jeremy greeted him. "We didn't see any problems with the upper-elevation herds, though we found trees that bears had freshly marked. We also saw grizzly tracks, large and small. They might be from that young female we spotted last fall on the ranch boundary. She could have a couple of cubs now."

Gideon sighed. He tried to coexist with grizzly bears. They might have been removed from the endangered list in some areas, but they were still at risk with their low reproductive rates. Vigilantly riding the range helped reduce the number of cows they killed, but it didn't resolve the problem entirely.

"Stay alert," he told the two ranch hands. "I don't need to remind you how protective a mother bear can be if she thinks her babies are threatened."

"Will do."

"Have you seen any wolves?" Alaina asked, her eyes bright with interest.

Chad glanced at Gideon before shaking his head. "Not this year, ma'am."

"Please let me know if you do. They stay close to their dens when the pups are young, but there's always a chance."

They tipped their hats again and rode on.

"Alaina, do you have a particular interest in wolves?" Gideon queried, warning zig-zagging up his spine. His great-grandfather had led the local fight against them being re-introduced to Yellowstone National Park—Colby Westcott had despised wolves as much as he'd loved dogs. A number of the local ranchers still felt the same. Attitudes might be changing in some areas, but not in this small corner of the world.

Alaina smiled confidently. "I hope to get a lot of pictures. Filming a wolf pack, behaving naturally, would be an amazing opportunity. My husband studied wolves all over the northern hemisphere, but I've rarely been lucky enough to see them in the wild when I had the best camera available. Not that our field equipment was awful, but nothing like what I have now."

Gideon dismounted and tied Brushfire to the porch railing. "That isn't a good idea. I've been thinking—we have wildflowers, the mountains, valleys, all sorts of stuff for you to photograph. The ranch, for example. The name comes from two rivers joining on the property. Very, um, picturesque. Our ranch operations could be photographed, as well. I'm open to that. Branding is over, but I can take you riding to get pictures of our herds."

She crossed her arms. "This is about me backpacking and camping alone, isn't it? Sorry, but I'll choose my own subjects, thank you."

"It's just that I know how far you might have to go and how long you might have to wait. Wolves can be hard to spot. More importantly, there are risks."

"Oh, puleeeze." Alaina gave him a disgusted look. "Are you one of those people who think wolves are mindless predators who kill everything in sight?"

Gideon's head began to ache. "That isn't what I meant."

"Really? Wolves have an incredibly positive impact. They're far more important than anyone knew before they were reintroduced to Yellowstone. Have you seen the information about how much healthier the ecosystem is now that wolves are present? Their presence is even changing the shape of the rivers."

"Right. They've been really busy, working out there with picks and shovels and bulldozers. It's a big tourist draw."

Alaina's unusual eyes chilled to the color of glacial ice. "Actually, it's a natural process of restoring balance between predators and prey and the land responding. I'd explain in more detail, but you obviously wouldn't listen with an open mind."

"Let's drop the subject. I'm simply concerned about your safety. Bear attacks are also a worry. You heard what Jeremy said about the mother grizzly. We have other bears, too. And don't tell me they won't give you any trouble because you love them or something like that. Bears are bears."

Alaina touched a finger to her sternum and appeared to be tracing the outline of something beneath her shirt. "I have every intention of being careful, but I'm not concerned. Anyhow, the chance of a bear attack is what, less than one in thirty million or so?"

Gideon didn't know the statistics and didn't care. Alaina was going to make him crazy with her naive optimism about wilderness hiking. "Do you have bear spray?" he asked between clenched teeth.

"Six of the extra big bottles. I also have bear canisters and bags for food storage on the trail, along with an air horn. Once I get settled and familiar with the area, I'll leave caches of supplies in the locations where I set up observation points. It'll mean less to carry when I go out."

He had to admit she'd done her homework, or some of it, and caching supplies was a good idea. "Bear spray helps, but encounters are still risky. That includes black bears, as well as grizzlies."

"Which is precisely why I have two super-telephoto lenses and others that are less powerful. I'll show you one." Alaina disappeared into the cabin and returned with an impressive piece of equipment. "I don't *want* to get close to my wildlife subjects, because the closer you are, the less naturally an animal will behave. With this, I can be a good distance away and still capture the smallest details. Would you like me to explain how a camera works? You know, focal length, ISO, pixels—"

"That isn't necessary," Gideon broke in quickly. "But it would be best not to discuss your interest in wolves around Bannister. Most folks in this area aren't too happy about them." He stepped from the porch and untied Brushfire again. "I have chores to do in the horse barn. Do you need anything else?"

"Besides your advice?"

Heaven help him. Alaina Wright might look as if a breath of wind would blow her away, but she wasn't shy about voicing opinions and standing up for herself.

"No. Have a good evening," he muttered and led Brushfire away. At the horse barn, he looked around and saw she'd gone back into the cabin. Yet his eyes widened. He hadn't noticed it before, but the untidy piles of firewood were gone. The wood had all been stacked in the firewood racks.

His eldest ranch hand was inside the tack room and Gideon called to him. "Nate, did you help Mrs. Wright stack that firewood?"

"Nope. I just got back a short time ago. I would have offered to help later, but saw it was all done. Did you—"

"No," Gideon interrupted. "She must have taken care of it after I left this afternoon."

Nate whistled. "I'm impressed."

"Don't be too impressed. This is just her first day. We'll see how she manages when the snow is over her knees, the wind is howling and it's twenty below outside. If she lasts that long."

The ranch hand nodded and returned to work.

Gideon removed Brushfire's saddle and began grooming the stallion. He wasn't convinced Alaina knew what she was getting into, but she must be as stubborn as a mountain goat to have sorted that wood so quickly.

He was putting Brushfire in his stall when a distinctive crack echoed through the air. He fastened the stall door and stepped outside in time to see Alaina swinging her ax again. The blade sank into a chunk of wood, which split into two pieces.

Every instinct Gideon possessed told him to go over, grab the ax and do it for her. But she'd refused Chad's help, and Gideon had little doubt she'd refuse his, as well.

He frowned, assessing her skill as she continued to work. She was tentative and moved slowly, telling him that she didn't have much practice splitting wood, but she was careful and her technique and balance were all right. Still, he'd split enough logs over the years to know how long it would take her at this rate. Not only that, she was half his size and couldn't have a quarter of his strength.

His frown deepened.

Alaina had mentioned that she'd ordered more firewood to be delivered, which meant more logs to be split. Robert Pritchett had provided the first lot and would probably be the source of the next. Gideon took out his phone and found the handyman's number.

"Hey, Gideon, what's up?" Robert answered on the third ring.

"Are you delivering more wood to my place?"

"Five more cords, next Tuesday. Any problem with the first load? Some of it had knots, but no more than usual. I haven't gotten any complaints from Mrs. Wright."

"No problem I know of," Gideon hesitated, "but can you make the next one in smaller pieces? That is, all of them stove size? I'll pay the extra."

The handyman chuckled. "Is the lady having trouble using an ax?"

"Mostly I'm having trouble watching her. I keep expecting disaster. Less wood for her to split would improve my mental health. Just don't say anything. *To anyone*. I wouldn't want her knowing I got involved."

Robert chuckled. "Gotcha. See you in a few days."

Gideon disconnected and returned the phone to his pocket, feeling better about the situation.

Slightly.

CHAPTER TWO

THE NEXT MORNING Alaina woke to see a gray light coming through the loft window she'd left open to clear a lingering stale scent in the cabin. It was so chilly that her breath was fogging over the pillow.

Steeling herself, she crawled from her nest of blankets to close the window and look outside. The late cold front had moved in and snow was falling, draping the trees and buildings with a thick layer of white.

She pulled on a heavy jacket and hurried down the loft steps to light the fire, glad she'd taken the time to lay it with paper and kindling the evening before. She watched with rapt attention as the paper flared brightly, then the kindling began to burn and the larger pieces of wood last of all. Belatedly she turned on the fan that drove air around the firebox and sped heat into the room.

"Brrrr," she muttered, though it would have been worse if she'd still been camping in Yellowstone. The Old Faithful Inn was nice, but she'd only been able to stay a few days since guests with reservations were arriving. When other accommodations had dried up, she'd moved to one of the campgrounds, preferring to stay in the park, rather than drive each day from West Yellowstone or Jackson Hole.

A hint of melancholy went through her. Mason had tried to pamper her when they were in the field together, insisting she remain in her sleeping bag while he got the coffee started. It had seemed important to him, so she'd rarely refused unless other members of the team were present. And she had loved watching him move around their campsite, strong and vigorous, anticipating the day ahead. The first time she'd camped by herself, tears had poured for over an hour.

A sharp knock on the cabin door ripped Alaina away from her memories. She left the warmth from the fireplace and found Gideon Carmichael on the porch.

"Yes?"

"Just checking on how things are going. I figured you were awake when I saw smoke rising from the chimney."

The corner of her mouth twitched. "That's

what happens when you light a fire. Did Helene send you?"

His brown eyes narrowed. "Mom wanted
to know how you were doing, but I would
have come, regardless. This is your first full
day on the Double Branch and the change
in the weather must have been unexpected."

Unexpected?

Exasperation replaced Alaina's humor.
"I've spent the last two weeks camping in
Yellowstone, and have been taking pictures
there since the middle of April, so I keep a
close watch on predictions from the weather
service. On top of that, my vehicle is equipped
with a satellite radio system. I'm usually tuned
to a station that reports local conditions."

"Oh."

"Why did you agree to let me stay at the
Double Branch if you think I'm incapable of
even checking a weather report?"

Gideon crossed his arms over his chest. "I
didn't say you were incapable, but you were
busy yesterday, driving to the Double Branch
and settling in. Besides, people who don't
live here aren't aware of how unpredictable
conditions can be at any time of the year."

Alaina drew a deep calming breath and
told herself not to overreact.

"I'm fine," she said. "There's no need to

check on me from now on." Her toes curled inside the heavy wool socks she'd worn to bed. Chill air swirled through the open door, but inviting Gideon inside didn't seem wise, if for no other reason than his cowhands might see them and get the wrong idea.

"In that case, I'll go back to work."

He turned and headed toward one of the barns.

Alaina shivered and shut the door. She considered climbing back into bed while the cabin warmed up, then scolded herself. What was the quote, "Begin as you mean to go on"?

There was plenty to do, including splitting more firewood and cataloging the photos she'd taken over the past several days. She was behind on making notes about each shot and didn't want to lose her impressions or any other information.

Yellowstone was in its annual baby boom and there was nothing like seeing a bison calf kicking up its heels with the pure joy of youth or a pair of pronghorn antelope babies taking their first steps. Life exploded in the park each year and it was a delight to watch. Over the past two months, she'd shot thousands of photos—bison, coyote pups, elk, even Calliope hummingbirds.

Digital photography was amazing. She could see her work immediately and evaluate where she needed to modify her settings to get a different effect.

Unfortunately people weren't so easy to figure out.

Alaina opened the stove and fed more firewood into the crackling flames. She glanced around the cabin, envisioning it decked in Christmas decorations. Though modernized, the rough wood beams overhead had been left. They'd be perfect for evergreen swags and strings of lights.

She loved Christmas and the snow falling outside had automatically made her think about the holiday. She'd brought a few decorations with her, but would have to get more. If Montana was anything like most places, she should be able to start buying them by the end of summer.

Her family was upset that she wasn't planning to come home this year for Thanksgiving or Christmas, but she didn't want to lose a minute of her time on the Double Branch. Anyway, she was tired of them urging her to start dating again, to find someone and *get on* with her life.

They meant well, and she'd gone out a few

times with an old high school friend to sat-
isfy their concerns, but enough was enough.
She was quite content on her own.

GIDEON TRIED NOT to smile as he recalled
how Alaina had looked when she opened the
cabin door. Still beautiful, but her silky hair
had been mussed and her shapely form concealed by thick layers of clothing beneath her
jacket—clothes she appeared to have slept in.

It was reassuring. Even though she claimed
to have been camping the past few weeks,
if she was this uncomfortable during a June
snowstorm, she was unlikely to head out
when the weather was a more serious risk.
He'd needed to adjust to the weather himself
on the Double Branch. The ranch was at a
higher elevation than where he'd grown up,
so it was colder, snowier and winter usually
arrived earlier and hung on longer.

In the horse barn, he cleaned the stalls
and filled the feed and water troughs. The
cowhands kept their mounts in another barn
closer to the bunkhouse, but these were the
horses Gideon had bred himself or were left
from his great-grandfather's day. Four of the
mares had been bred to Brushfire and would
deliver next year.

"How are you doing, Griz?" he said to the horse in the last stall.

Grizzly snorted and turned his gaze away. He was a fine stock horse, but he hadn't been the same since Colby Westcott's death. Some people didn't think horses grieved, but Gideon knew differently. Despite his great-grandfather's advanced age, he'd spent hours each day sitting in the barn or by the paddock with Griz, communing with nature and each other. They'd shared a special connection.

For a while Gideon had worried the horse would just fade away without Colby, but he'd finally begun eating again. He could even be ridden, though he wasn't interested in bonding with anyone else.

Outside the snow was still falling in a steady curtain, but it was the string of white lights on the roofline of the cabin porch that made Gideon stop and stare.

Christmas lights.

Alaina had brought Christmas lights with her, and had braved the snowstorm to hang them.

In June.

Heaven help him.

At the main house, he carefully brushed the wet snow from his hair and clothing before stepping inside. His mother insisted she was in charge of the housekeeping while she was there and he didn't want to cause her more work.

"How is Alaina doing?" Helene asked.

"Fine. She's hung Christmas lights on the cabin porch."

"Really?" His mother hurried to the window to look out at Alaina's efforts. "Goodness, isn't that pretty?"

"It's June, not December."

"They're just white lights, son. A lot of people keep them up all year. Businesses, too."

Gideon shook his head. He believed in practicality and strings of twinkling lights were decidedly *im*practical. Alaina belonged in a photography studio doing portraits, or taking pictures of animals from behind tall sturdy fences.

"Maybe we should invite her to lunch," his mother said as she turned around.

"Mom, you're welcome to be friends with her, but she isn't a guest. She's a tenant. Besides, I don't think she likes me."

"Nonsense. You just need to loosen up so she can see how nice you are."

Gideon hung his coat on a hook. "I'm not interested in loosening up. Or interested, period."

"You needn't get your feathers ruffled. She isn't interested in you, either."

He swung around, shocked. "You've talked about it?"

Helene smiled serenely. "Not directly, but when I mentioned your single ranch hands, she said that she isn't interested in romance. I get it. Her husband was the love of her life. She had a wonderful marriage and feels nothing can compete with it. So you don't need to worry about her hoping to find someone while she's here. She's focused on her career."

"Right, she's going to be the next Ansel Adams, Alfred Stieglitz or Diane Arbus."

"Imagine one of my down-to-earth sons knowing enough about art to quote the names of famous photographers," Helene teased. "But I don't think Alaina wants to emulate someone else's work. She hopes to be recognized on her own merits."

"Fine. By the way, what did Libby say when she called earlier?" Gideon asked to change the subject. "She sounded edgy, but wouldn't tell me what was wrong, just wanted to talk to you. Has her trip been delayed by the weather?"

Helene's expression went from teasing to serious. "Dr. Barstow canceled her internship. Out of the blue, he called and said she wouldn't be going tomorrow, after all."

Gideon scowled. "I don't understand. Her grades are always great and she was paying her own way. What possible reason can he have? He was getting free skilled labor."

"She's trying to find out," his mother said. "It's so frustrating. Libby has done everything that Dr. Barstow asked and even turned down other opportunities because he'd offered her the internship."

"I'll get the truth out of him. Snow or not, I'm leaving for Bozeman right now."

"No, you aren't. Libby was worried you'd do something rash, which is why she told me about it first. We have to trust her to handle this."

"It isn't a question of trust," he protested, "but when something isn't fair, you have to—"

"No." Helene gave him a hug. "You're a good brother, but she's a woman now. We need to respect her wishes."

Still bothered, Gideon went to the kitchen to get a cup of coffee. The day his mother and stepfather had brought Libby home from the hospital he'd sworn he would take care of her. For the first time *he* was going to be a big brother and taking care of her was his job. Now he was being told hands off.

It crossed his mind that Alaina Wright would probably think he was archaic for wanting to protect his sister, but he didn't care. Libby was bright and talented—a go-getter who was going to take the archeology world by storm. It wasn't right that she was being disadvantaged.

"Chin up, Gideon," his mother said, re-filling her own cup. "Libby will let us know what she learns. Nothing can be done until then, and she'll have to be the one to take action, unless she asks for help."

"And when was the last time she wanted my help?" Gideon asked, his tone laced with irony. "She didn't even ask when she moved from her dorm room into an apartment. I could have brought my guys down and had everything done in an hour, instead she hired a group of fellow students. It was the same with putting all her stuff into storage the other day."

Helene smiled faintly. "Exerting your independence with big brothers around isn't easy. Attending college in Montana was a compromise, you know. Her first choice was the University of New Mexico. Maybe she'll get her post-graduate degree down there."

Gideon winced. New Mexico was a long way away.

"Knowing when to let go is something every parent has to figure out," his mother continued. "You'll understand if you ever have a family."

"That isn't going to happen unless I find them under a cabbage leaf."

Helene sighed. "I wish you wouldn't let Celeste have so much influence over your future. Ranching is hard enough without having someone to share it with. You weren't even married to her that long."

Gideon's jaw tightened at the reminder of his ex-wife. He'd met Celeste when she'd taken a job teaching in his hometown of Shelton. It wasn't until after the wedding that he'd discovered she hated small towns and didn't even *like* kids, much less want one of her own.

Apparently Celeste had thought a Montana ranching community sounded deliciously romantic until she was actually living there. When he'd taken over as foreman at the Double Branch for his great-grandfather, she'd announced she was returning to Chicago, because there was no way she was going to live on such an isolated ranch. Divorce papers had arrived a short time later. The settlement she'd wanted, though hardly justified, had emptied his savings at the time, but he hadn't fought it. Writing a check had been an easy escape from a big mistake.

From now on he was going it alone. The only thing he regretted about staying single was missing out on a family.

"Who could that be?" his mother mused as a vehicle drove by the house and parked.

Gideon went out to the porch and saw a Bannister County sheriff's SUV.

"Hey, Deke," Gideon said as the deputy got out. He and Deke Hewitt were close to the same age and had become good friends over the past several years. "Coffee?"

"I won't turn it down. Especially if your mom made it."

"My coffee isn't that bad."

"Not if you enjoy drinking diesel fuel. How ya' doing, Danger?" Deke said to the German shepherd who was dancing around his feet. He leaned down and rubbed the dog's neck before giving the calmer Cookie a pat. "Is this a new herder?" he asked.

"A Labrador retriever?" Gideon laughed. "Not the usual breed for working cattle. Cookie is my sister's dog. We're keeping him here for the summer."

As they came inside, the dogs went to

their respective beds in front of the fireplace. Cookie immediately began chewing the snow from between his toes, but Danger simply turned his feet and belly to the warmth and yawned. He still had his thick winter coat and was well insulated from the cold.

"Good morning, Deke," greeted his mother. "Would you like some breakfast?" she asked. "I started eggs, just in case."

"That would be a treat. We had a couple of tourists who got lost and went off the road in the snow last night. No injuries, and luckily they stayed in their vehicle, or else the situation might be worse. I've been directing traffic for the tow truck."

In the kitchen Gideon poured a mug of coffee for his friend and Deke drank it down, quickly followed by a second. He was dressed for cold weather, but a chill could creep in, regardless.

"I understand someone new is staying on the Double Branch," Deke said. "In the foreman's house."

No privacy in Bannister County, Gideon thought ruefully. "That's right. It's a budding wildlife photographer. She moved in yesterday afternoon."

"She?"

"Yup. She's trying to get her career off the ground. I've rented the cabin to her for a year."

His mother put a plate of scrambled eggs, bacon and toast in front of Deke. "She's a lovely woman. Her name is Alaina Wright and she's also interested in Bannister County history. I'm going to call your uncle this morning and arrange for her to photograph my great-great grandfather's journals at the museum, along with the Theodore Roosevelt letters."

"Don't set it up for today," Deke said hastily. "The roads are slick and I'd hate to clean up after another accident."

"I won't. A weekday would be best, anyhow."

DEKE NODDED. HE scooped huckleberry jam onto a slice of toast and bit into it. Nobody made better jam than Helene Cranston and her huckleberry was the best of all. Last year she'd paid his nephew's scouting troop to pick five gallons of hucks.

"What else do you know about Mrs. Wright?" he asked casually.

Aside from tourists, they didn't get many newcomers to Bannister, so he liked to learn as much as possible about them. It was how his friendship with Gideon had started. Even though Gideon had been Colby Westcott's great-grandson and a frequent visitor to the Double Branch, keeping an eye on the situation here had seemed warranted. Everything had turned out well and Deke was convinced the elderly rancher had lived longer due to his great-grandson's presence.

"Alaina is a widow," Helene explained. "She's awfully sweet and quite capable."

"Never mind that, she wants to take pictures of wolves," Gideon said in a dire voice.

Deke frowned. Wolves were a touchy subject in Bannister County. "Let's keep that under our hats," he suggested.

"I've already told my ranch hands not to talk about her, or what she's doing. She hadn't even been here a full day before asking if they'd seen any."

Phew.

Deke had been a boy when the authorities began reintroducing wolves to Yellowstone, but he remembered how upset it had made people. Some of the older ranchers were still unhappy about the decision, though none had experienced a serious loss in their herds because of it. Their resistance probably harked back to a time when wolves were an archetypal enemy, deeply distrusted, though they rarely attacked human beings.

"Maybe she won't find any," he said after swallowing a bite of the scrambled eggs. "They're shy. I've lived here my whole life and never seen one."

"Maybe. Mrs. Wright knows they don't range far when they have pups to protect, and it's hard to believe she'll go out in deep snow."

Helene gave her son a stern look. "Don't underestimate Alaina. She's very determined."

"We'll have to wait and see," Deke said. In her own way Gideon's mother was just as stubborn as her son, and he didn't want to land in the middle of a debate between the two of them.

He finished his breakfast and thanked Helene for the meal. Ranchers in Bannister had their quirks, but they were a hospitable lot. He just hoped they would know better than to be rude to the newcomer because she wanted to photograph an unpopular predator. Actually, no predator was popular, but there was something about wolves that some folks couldn't tolerate.

GIDEON CONSIDERED BRINGING Danger with him when he rode out later, then decided the dog was better off at home, snoozing in front of the fire with Cookie. Danger had other ideas, following him to the barn and eagerly wagging his tail. He was a working dog, and no matter what the weather conditions might be, he wanted to be part of the action.

Snow could distort visibility and Gideon was cautious as he rode out. He may have gone overboard when warning Alaina about the dangers of a bear attack, but it wasn't something to take for granted, even this close to the ranch buildings. Grizzlies presented a greater risk to his herds than a pack of wolves.

He'd never lost a cow to a wolf, but he had to bears.

A weak ray of sunlight peeked between the clouds as he rode. Though it quickly disappeared, he knew the snow would melt just as rapidly once the storm front had passed.

He inhaled a deep breath of the crisp air. Ranching in the mountains was different from back home in Shelton County, but he loved it here.

Suddenly he reined in Brushfire, his jaw dropping as he saw Alaina prone on the ground, taking pictures of a yellow glacier lily crusted with snow.

"What are you doing?" he demanded.

She looked up as she accepted Danger's enthusiastic greeting with pets and neck rubs. "It's a remarkable invention called photography. You should check it out sometime."

"Give me a break. You're lying in wet snow."

She shrugged. "So I am."

"You have to be more careful. Getting wet can lead to hypothermia on days like this. Not only that, I could have been a wild animal creeping up to attack you."

Alaina laughed. "Not a chance. I've been watching you ride toward me from the moment you came around the trees and hillock that blocks the view of the main house and barns. Danger barked and scared the bluebirds I was photographing, so I focused on something that wouldn't be frightened by a dog or a big cloppy horse and its rider." She gestured to the glacier lilies.

"Brushfire isn't cloppy."

"Ooh, sorry, I didn't mean to insult him."

"And I don't believe you saw me coming," Gideon added, his protest sounding feeble, even to himself.

"I have proof." Alaina got up, pressed some buttons and turned the camera around for him to see. Sure enough, she'd photographed him riding across the valley. "Want to see more?"

"No. Why are you out here already? It's snowing and you just got to the Double Branch."

"Because I was restless and snow makes for interesting pictures. I'll be going out during the winter, so a small June blizzard isn't a big deal. By the way, when did you notice *me*?"

"In plenty of time," he said, refusing to admit that he'd failed to see Alaina until he was practically on top of her.

Anyway, one of the ways to avoid bears was making noise so you didn't surprise them, which meant he didn't try to be silent when he rode. That was also one of the advantages of having Danger with him. Unless you'd told him to be quiet, Danger barked at everything.

Alaina, on the other hand, had kept a low quiet profile to take her photographs.

He supposed she'd have to stay in a location for hours, waiting for her subjects to appear. While he could offer suggestions about wildlife trails to observe, she might get annoyed again. Besides, why help her find spots that presented a greater risk? In particular he was thinking about the wolf pack ranging on an upper section of his ranch for the past two years. He rarely saw them and only knew the general location of their den, but telling others was a bad idea. He doubted that even his ranch hands had guessed a pack lived there. It seemed best, because this way he didn't have to deal with unhappy neighbors who were afraid that wolves would start killing their cattle.

"I can give you a ride back to the ranch," he offered.

It was either that, or worry about Alaina being caught flat if the weather changed again. She had a small backpack, but it didn't look loaded enough to contain much survival equipment.

From the way Alaina eyed Brushfire, he suspected she wasn't fond of horses. "Thanks, but I'm fine. I was getting ready to return on my own and would rather walk."

"Suit yourself."

Gideon rode on, then after a few minutes, drew in the reins and glanced back. He was relieved to see Alaina heading toward the ranch center.

Brushfire snorted and stamped a foot on the ground. He wanted to go, not just stand around. Danger scampered about, letting out loud yips in agreement.

"All right, you two," Gideon said, patting Brushfire's neck.

The new growing season was here, snow notwithstanding, and they had a lot of miles ahead of them.

CHAPTER THREE

IT WASN'T NICE of her, but Alaina wanted to laugh at the memory of Gideon's expression when he'd seen one of the pictures she had taken of him. He believed she was ill-equipped to live on the edge of a wilderness, much less take forays *into* that wilderness. But she wasn't a fool—life had dangers wherever you went.

Exhilaration zinged in her veins.

She was finally in Montana after all her planning and training. Mason's sister was the only one who'd understood why she wanted to challenge herself so completely. Janet had offered her legal services, carefully drafting the agreement with Gideon Carmichael to make sure he couldn't wiggle out after a month or two and try to keep all of the money. Janet was a sweetheart, but she had a dim view of human nature, probably from dealing with so many corporate sharks.

Alaina hadn't been sure a legal contract was necessary; now she realized it was for the best. It wasn't that she thought Gideon would deliberately cheat her, but he already seemed to regret his decision to let her live on the Double Branch.

He was a difficult man to figure out. Though the ranch seemed prosperous, ranching had more than its fair share of ups and downs. Everything from the weather to market prices for beef could affect annual profits, which was why she'd thought he would welcome the income from renting his foreman's home.

Back at the cabin she spent several hours examining photos on her large 4K monitor and making notes on each series of shots. She was especially pleased with the ones she'd taken of bison in Yellowstone's Lamar Valley. A band of mist clung to a distant layer of hill and trees, and the colors of sunrise suffused the scattered clouds with peach, gray and silver, breaking the intense blues and greens. Amid it all were the buffalo with their massive shoulder humps, gorging on the grass.

Alaina had hoped to see wolves, but aside from a lingering howl drifting across the valley, she hadn't gotten lucky. It might have been different if Mason had been there; he'd had a gift for finding them.

She pushed the thought away.

The sound of a vehicle arriving caught her attention and she got up to look out the window.

It was the same model SUV that Alaina owned, and the driver parked in front of the main house. The front door flew open and Helene came rushing out to throw her arms around the newcomer. Cookie raced in circles around the two women, barking excitedly until the young woman crouched to give him some affection.

Could it be the daughter Helene had mentioned?

Alaina wondered if she should go over and say hello. It felt odd not to, and even odder when Helene gestured toward the cabin and shook her head. Alaina went to the kitchen and made a cup of tea, still trying to decide what the proper social response should be in the situation. After all, Gideon treated her like an annoying blip to his daily schedule, while Helene seemed eager to become friends. It made things awkward.

Twenty minutes later a knock on the door ended Alaina's internal debate. She answered to find Helene and the new arrival on the porch.

"I hope you don't mind," Helene apologized, "but I want to introduce my daughter. Libby's plans have changed and she'll be staying at the Double Branch this summer."

"No problem, I was in the middle of a break," Alaina assured her. Yet she winced, thinking Libby may have hoped to stay in the foreman's cabin, only to discover someone else was in residence. "Please come in."

"It's nice to meet you," Libby said. "Mom tells me you're a professional photographer."

"Trying to be. So far I've sold only a few pieces, though my agent is confident she can get contracts for my work this year. Won't you have a seat?"

Libby's expression turned glum as she sank onto a chair with Cookie at her knee. "You're doing better than I am. I was offered a summer internship by a well-known archeologist, but it fell through. I was supposed to—"

"Her boyfriend sabotaged her," Helene broke in indignantly. "He actually thought she'd move in with him if she didn't go, so he called and told the excavation leader that she'd changed her mind and didn't want to admit it. She was cut from the team without even being asked. Can you believe that? They just started dating a few weeks ago."

"*MOM*." LIBBY GAVE her mother an incredulous look. She hadn't wanted to disturb her brother's new tenant in the first place, and now personal details were being revealed that she'd never intended to go outside the family.

"You must be disappointed in the archeologist for allowing that to happen," Alaina said quietly.

A measure of the tightness in Libby's chest eased.

It helped that *somebody* understood the part that hurt the most. She wasn't in love with Raymond and had been hoping for a graceful way to end the short-lived relationship. But she'd looked up to Dr. Barstow. He was a best-selling author and had worked on nearly every continent doing archeological digs. His finds were extraordinary.

"He obviously isn't as admirable as I thought," she said flatly. "So maybe I'm better off this way."

"Are you looking for another dig to join?"

"I've made inquiries, but haven't heard anything yet. Most of my free time outside of class and studying went to helping get everything set up for the dig in New Mexico. It's a completely untouched site. Dr. Barstow thinks it could be a whole new cultural group or unique off-shoot of the Anasazi."

"Which means you've also lost out on a rare opportunity."

The sympathy in Alaina's eyes was almost too much and Libby gulped. She didn't want her mother to know how bad she felt about losing the internship. She missed her father terribly, but it was worse for Helene, so they were all trying not to upset her about anything. Libby had hated telling her about losing the internship, but she'd hoped asking her to keep Gideon from charging down to confront Dr. Barstow would provide a sense of purpose.

Sometimes it seemed as if nothing would ever be right again. How could Dad be gone?

All of her grandparents were still healthy and active. Dad's folks had conceded that Montana winters were more than they wanted to handle and had moved to Florida. But the reason her maternal grandfather had retired was because he'd decided it was time for his eldest grandson to take charge of the family ranch, not because of his age. Even Grandpa Colby had lived into his late nineties. He'd been a great old guy, gruff and hard on the outside, and pure marshmallow under the skin.

"Darling, are you all right?" Helene's anxious question brought Libby back to the moment and she squelched a sigh.

Spending the summer at the Double Branch was the last thing she'd expected to do. It wasn't a question of money; her inheritance from Grandpa Colby ensured she could choose whatever career she wanted without worrying about practicality. But she hadn't wanted to remain in Bozeman and fend off Raymond's abject apologies, who'd belatedly realized that he had not only crossed a forbidden line, he'd leaped miles over it.

What an idiot to believe she wouldn't find out what he had done.

Cookie whined and pressed his jaw harder on her knee, sensing her mood. He was the one good thing about her internship falling through. She'd hated the thought of being separated from her loyal pal for several months.

"I'm fine, Mom, but maybe I should have asked Gideon before coming up here. I could stay in Shelton. At the house, maybe."

Her childhood home, just outside the Shelton town limits, had been unoccupied since the funeral. Her oldest brother, Flynn, was taking care of the horses, along with checking on the buildings, but that wasn't the same as someone living there. It would be hard because of all the memories, but she'd have to face it sooner or later.

"No," Helene said adamantly. "Just this morning Gideon was complaining that you don't let him do anything for you. He'll be ecstatic that you're here for the summer."

Hmm. Big brothers were nice, but they could also be a headache of major proportions when they had old-fashioned protective instincts.

"Oh, and, Alaina," Helene continued, "I've contacted the museum board about you photographing Jonah Westcott's journals and the letters from Mr. Roosevelt. The letters span more than three decades, including a good number after he became president. Nels is going to be in and out of town on business for a while, but he'll call to set up a time when his schedule calms down."

"That's great. I'm looking forward to seeing them."

"I've never had a chance to read the journals or letters," Libby said. "How about letting me be your photographic assistant? Free labor is hard to come by—at least that's what I kept telling Dr. Barstow when he canceled my internship. He unctuously said it didn't matter if Raymond hadn't told the truth because I obviously needed to get my personal life in order."

The crumb, she added silently.

Alaina smiled. "You're welcome to come along. I don't have lighting equipment, so an extra pair of hands could be useful."

"I'm a fast learner."

Libby liked Alaina. She seemed reserved, but her mom had explained she was a widow, so that might be the reason. Or maybe it was Gideon's fault. He had his demons and an attractive, sophisticated woman like Alaina must remind him of Celeste. Ugh, what a disaster *that* marriage had been. Not that Alaina was sophisticated exactly, but she seemed self-assured and quietly certain of what she wanted.

"Alaina, I hope it's okay," Helene said, "but Nels asked if you'd be willing to take photos for a new museum brochure. The old one is dreadfully dated. The thing is, their budget is entirely committed to getting the brochures printed. But he can give you credit as the photographer."

"I'll be happy to help out. I'd want to take pictures of the museum, regardless."

"That's kind of you." Helene stood up. "We won't keep you any longer, but will you join us for dinner?"

An undefined emotion flickered in Alaina's eyes. "Thanks, but you need time as a family, and I should spend the evening working. I hope to send a package to my agent in a few days."

Libby rose more reluctantly than her mother. Though she hadn't wanted to disturb Gideon's tenant, the visit had turned out to be a welcome break from the emotional turmoil tearing her summer plans apart. And having Alaina instinctively understand the core issues was another plus.

ALAINA WATCHED HER two visitors and their sweet Cookie cross the slushy ground and go into the main house. Even if Libby had hoped to stay in the foreman's cabin for the summer, she hadn't shown resentment over it not being available.

It was sad that she'd encountered betrayal so young.

Well, they couldn't be separated by more than eight or nine years, but Alaina felt older than twenty-nine. She'd been married and worked with her husband in a rewarding life, and lost him horribly. She had also been betrayed, the way Libby had been betrayed, but her other experiences put it in perspective. Compared to Mason's death, having someone try to steal a collection of photographs was hardly the end of the world.

Coming to Montana and starting her new career was a reminder that her life hadn't ended with the accident. Mason hadn't wanted her to lose herself in grief. It was what he'd made her promise in their last few minutes together, to live fully, to follow old dreams and find new ones.

Alaina went back to the room she'd turned into a studio. She needed more surface work space, but she could get folding tables down in Bozeman, along with a snow shovel so she'd be prepared for next winter.

She gazed through the large window, trying to clear her mind of everything except her plans for the next year. The cabin was on the far end of the large ranch and it looked across the valley. She couldn't see much except when someone rode past.

Like Gideon Carmichael.

She wrinkled her nose at the way he'd intruded on her thoughts, then shrugged philosophically. Gideon might be a pain in the posterior, but at least their encounters were stimulating.

OVER THE NEXT few days, Gideon remained around the ranch more than usual to keep an eye on his sister. She didn't *seem* brokenhearted, but she was good at keeping her feelings to herself. He still remembered the time she'd fractured her wrist as a kid—no tears or fuss, just a stoic trip to see the doctor.

Her ex-boyfriend had been incessantly calling her cell phone. When she didn't answer after two days, he'd switched to the ranch number. It was an irritant since the small phone company that serviced Bannister County lacked the equipment or programming to provide caller ID. All they offered was a no-frills service. When Gideon had finally gotten to the telephone ahead of his mother and Libby, he'd told Raymond in no uncertain terms to leave his sister alone or face the consequences.

Libby had been furious, saying it was her business and he shouldn't interfere, but Gideon didn't care. The creep had ruined something special for her and he didn't deserve courtesy.

They'd finally agreed to let callers leave messages on the machine and to return any calls that weren't from her slimy ex-boyfriend.

It was sad to realize his sister had inherited his lousy luck with the opposite sex.

On Tuesday Robert Pritchett arrived with

the additional firewood Alaina had ordered.
He winked at Gideon as he got out of his
truck. The truck had a hydraulic system that
raised the front of the cargo bed, and some
of the wood crashed out into a broad pile before he moved the vehicle again, then again,
to deposit the rest.

"I'll take care of stacking that for ya', Mrs.
Wright," he said to Alaina.

Gideon automatically stepped forward to
lend a hand, then saw Alaina shake her head.

"Thanks, I'm fine. Remember, I didn't pay
the extra amount to have it stacked, and I
don't want to keep you from other deliver-
ies."

The handyman's face grew pained as she
began carrying armloads to the racks at the
side of the cabin. Gideon was in similar
agony. His instincts as a gentleman were at
war with his need to keep things on a busi-
nesslike basis with Alaina. The easier everything was for her, the more likely it was that
she'd stay. Not that he had any intention of
keeping the full amount she'd paid, no matter what their agreement stated. He would
prorate any time she spent on the ranch and
return the balance.

Two of his cowhands rode up and got off
their horses. They looked at Gideon. He

made a gesture to indicate, *Go ahead*, but their help was refused, as well.

Now there were four of them watching. They exchanged awkward glances with each other.

"Mrs. Wright doesn't need this much wood," Robert said. "I told her the cabin had a good layer of insulation, but she said it was better to be safe than sorry."

Despite the absurdity of the situation, Gideon appreciated hearing that Alaina was being cautious. True, winter on the Double Branch was nothing like the heart of Yellowstone, but even though the main house had a central heating system, Gideon cut eight to ten cords of wood each year to use. Electricity wasn't always reliable so far out in the country, and he enjoyed a crackling fire after a long day of work in the cold.

Robert kicked a clod of dirt. "It ain't right. Four of us standing around, watching someone else toil away."

Gideon agreed, he just didn't think Alaina would back down. He suspected she had a temper and a will of iron. And he admired her independence.

So what should they do?

Leave her with a task the four of them could have already finished? It didn't sit well with him, and judging by the reluctance of the others to go about their business, they felt the same. Him and his big mouth. The right time to establish boundaries would have been after Alaina settled into the cabin and after he'd learned whether there was any need for those boundaries. As it turned out, her boundaries were more rigid than his own.

Another vehicle drove in and Gideon groaned. It was Deke Hewitt.

Deke joined the group, eyebrows raised. "What's up?"

"She won't let us help," Robert said glumly.

Deke looked nonplussed. "So you decided to just stand here and watch?"

It was a good point. Too good. The situation was getting more ridiculous by the second.

The sound of a door slamming could be heard across the ranch, followed by the crunch of approaching footsteps. It was Libby. She eyed them up and down and let out a disgusted sniff.

"Pathetic," she muttered before marching over and collecting an armful of wood.

"That's all right, Libby, I can manage," Alaina protested.

"I know, but I just found out Dr. Barstow's

dig team is now *entirely* male. I need to work off my frustration or explode."

"He bumped the other women from the group, too?"

"That's right. Assuming the new site turns out to be worthwhile, this will look fabulous on the male interns' résumés. He's giving them a boost in their careers and leaving the women out cold. Maybe I should have gone into paleontology or some other 'ology instead."

"Can't the university do anything?" Alaina asked as she filled her arms with another load.

"They're looking into it, but Dr. Barstow isn't connected to the school. While he's taught at various private colleges, he's now a full-time researcher and author. We met at a seminar he conducted off campus. I could scream when I think of the hours I spent working on permit applications and other prep. I'm even starting to question whether the discoveries described in his books are more fiction than fact, except that sort of thing is hard to fake."

"My sister-in-law is an attorney. She mostly works in corporate law, but I could ask her opinion about a lawsuit. Even if you can't nail him on discrimination, he made promises he apparently didn't intend to keep."

"I'll think about it."

As they talked, the wood was being shifted with surprising speed. Gideon hoped he could quietly join them, but when he took a step forward, Alaina gave him a withering glance and shook her head again.

Darn it, anyhow.

The aggravating part was that he had only himself to blame. He'd made it all too clear that he expected her to be self-sufficient. Now Deke, Robert and his ranch hands were looking at him as if he were an ogre who didn't know how to behave as a respectable human being. Gideon believed in equal rights for everyone. But at the same time he was bigger, stronger and more experienced at certain tasks, which made it difficult not to jump in and handle those jobs.

Or maybe he'd learned the impulse from his stepdad.

Stewart Cranston had been like everyone's favorite uncle. Following a bad storm, he or his deputies had checked on every single outlying resident and asked folks in town to contact their neighbors to be sure they were all right. He'd replaced flat tires, jumped dead batteries and been the one who everyone—

man or woman, young or old—called if they had a problem. Surely that wasn't a flaw. It was just being someone who cared.

Gideon turned to his employees. They couldn't keep hanging around like stick figures while Alaina and Libby worked. "You'd best get going," he said.

"Right, boss." It was Nate.

Clearly reluctant, they remounted their horses and rode out, still shooting unhappy glances back at Alaina and Libby.

Now Gideon needed to get rid of Deke and Robert Pritchett.

"Robert, thanks for bringing the wood."

"Yeah, sure." Robert got into the cab of his truck, muttering again, "It just ain't right."

Gideon grabbed Deke's elbow, whose attention seemed to be lingering more on Libby than Alaina. While he and Deke were friends, he didn't want his sister to get involved with a guy in law enforcement, particularly when that guy was thirteen years her senior and she was recovering from a broken romance. It was hypocritical since Gideon's stepfather had been a sheriff, too, but the sheriff's office was a whole lot busier in Bannister County than it was in Shelton.

"Deke, do you want a cup of coffee?" he asked.

Deke seemed to have trouble tearing his gaze away. "Uh, sure. That sounds good."

"Then let's go."

ALAINA WAS GLAD when they no longer had an audience. She wasn't trying to be unreasonable, but she didn't need help with something as basic as stacking wood. And she hated giving up a shred of independence. She was even wondering if she'd let Mason handle too much, despite her efforts to be an equal partner in their marriage.

As for Gideon and the other guys?

Maybe the unwritten Code of the West said that men were obligated to rush in with assistance, whether it was needed or not. But she wasn't an orphan or poor widow on the frontier—she was a capable woman who didn't balk at hard work.

Besides, there couldn't be a fitness facility within fifty miles. Moving and splitting wood was one of the ways she planned to stay in shape for her trips into the high backcountry. Not that this latest load needed any splitting. To keep her muscles toned on days she wasn't hiking, she might have to fill her backpack and go up and down the loft staircase for exercise.

"I'm going to Bozeman tomorrow to shop

for a few things," she told Libby when they'd finished with the last chunks of wood. "Is there anything I can get for you or your mom?"

Libby brightened. "I'd love to go, too, if you wouldn't mind stopping at my storage unit. The clothes I have were picked for working at a New Mexico dig site, so I need more stuff."

"I wouldn't mind in the least," Alaina said, pleased.

Being able to return a favor was nice, particularly since she'd thoroughly enjoyed the look on Gideon's face while she and his sister took care of the firewood delivery.

She owed Libby extra for that.

CHAPTER FOUR

GIDEON CAME ACROSS from the barn the next morning as Alaina stood by her vehicle.

"Do you need something?" he asked.

She shook her head. "I'm waiting for Libby. We're driving down to Bozeman."

"Right, shopping."

For some reason the assumption irritated Alaina, though it was perfectly logical. People who lived in remote locations like Bannister County often had to shop in a larger community. She needed to be less sensitive.

"I want to get two or three tables for my equipment so I can spread out when I'm reviewing photos or cleaning my lenses," she explained. "I have a desktop computer and a large 4K monitor for final checks on photographs. They take a fair amount of space. I also prefer sturdy, uncluttered surfaces for storing everything."

He nodded. "Camping must have been tough."

"I didn't set up the desktop except when

I was staying in a place like the Old Faithful Inn, but I managed all right in the campground. My biggest adventure was when a young moose wandered through and stuck his nose in the back of my SUV. I'm not sure why he was interested, but he left tooth marks on one of my camera straps. It was a tug of war between the two of us."

"How do you know it was a he?"

"Female moose lack antlers and other obvious evidence of being male."

Gideon cleared his throat and Alaina saw a flicker of discomfort in his eyes. Honestly, he was a rancher. The facts of life couldn't be a mystery to him, while she'd spent over six years in close proximity to a group of wolf biologists who were entirely down-to-earth. But maybe Gideon didn't think they knew each other well enough for a frank discussion, or he could be in big-brother mode, afraid his baby sister might overhear.

"I have three older brothers who act as if I'm still wearing ponytails and carrying a Hello Kitty book bag," she said, deciding Libby must be the reason. "I'm not, but that doesn't stop them from treating me like a child. If Libby—"

"I know my sister is an adult," he interrupted, embarrassment growing in his face.

"But that doesn't make her punctual. Dad used to say…" He stopped. "Uh, never mind. You'll be waiting awhile. Libby is notoriously late for everything."

"That's what you think," Libby said as she walked up to them. "I'm a responsible adult now. Alaina and I agreed to meet at 7:00 a.m. and it's seven on the dot."

"That's right," Alaina agreed, wondering what Gideon's father *used to say* and why he'd grown somber all at once.

Oh, yeah, she thought with regret. His stepfather had recently passed away.

Gideon's fondness for his stepfather was the nicest thing she knew about him. Well, he also seemed devoted to his mother and sister. He might not know the best way to show his devotion, but neither did the men in her own family.

For the most part, Gideon had shown himself to be ill-tempered and inflexible, with hard edges she was still discovering. Maybe he was built that way, or maybe his ex-wife was to blame. But there was one thing Alaina was certain about—he either didn't think she belonged in Montana, or he was being difficult because he hoped she'd leave. She had news for him—the harder he pushed, the more she was determined to stay.

"Shall we go?" Libby asked brightly.

"You bet."

As Alaina drove away from the ranch, her passenger sighed. "I heard what Gideon was saying. Dad would tease and claim I'd be late for my own funeral. Then he'd hug me and laugh. He didn't get uptight about stuff. He just enjoyed life."

"I love being around people like that."

"Yeah. I miss him so much." Libby's voice wobbled. "It's hard. We don't tell stories about him any longer, not even the funny ones that would make us laugh. I guess we're afraid of reminding each other that he's gone. Especially Mom."

"My family was the same way about my husband," Alaina said. "It can take a while to get past the awkwardness. You could ask Helene if it's painful to talk or hear about your father. It might not be an issue. She's already mentioned him to me a couple of times."

Libby brightened. "Really? I mean, when one of us starts to say something, we usually stop or change the subject, as if we might have said something we shouldn't have. But Dad was fun and cheerful and he loved us so much. It's stupid to pretend we don't think about him."

"You can tell me all you want about your

father," Alaina said. It had been the same after the accident. Her friends and family had walked on eggshells around her until she'd told them to quit it. Mason had been a beautiful part of her life, and while she would miss him forever, she also remembered their time together with joy. Having no one willing to talk about him had made the loss seem even worse.

"You may be sorry after a while and tell me to stop."

Alaina glanced at Libby and saw her face was filled with an uncertain vulnerability. Losing a parent at any time was awful, but each age had its special issues. Libby's mental landscape of the future had just gotten torn apart—a landscape that probably included things like her father being there to celebrate her college graduation and walking with her down a wedding aisle.

"I won't be sorry," Alaina promised. "Helene told me that your interest in archeology comes from your dad."

"He had a gazillion books in his home office—practically everything ever published about the Anasazi. He also had a special interest in Montana history and the use of high-altitude locations by ancient humans."

Alaina nodded, staying focused on the narrow, twisty road that led to a more heavily traveled state route.

Libby adjusted the shoulder strap of her seat belt. "I just wish I'd inherited Dad's intuition about people. I should have known something wasn't right about Dr. Barstow the moment he introduced his wife."

"Oh?"

"Yup. He's fifty-six, and she's my age."

"Are they happy together?" Alaina asked, trying to keep her expression neutral.

Libby made a face. "I guess."

Alaina turned onto the state highway and tried to think of something to change the subject. "You mentioned mountain use by prehistoric groups. I've been fascinated by the story of Ötzi, the ice mummy found in the Ötztal Alps."

"That was an incredible find. But great things are also being discovered in the United States." Libby went on talking about ancient villages uncovered in Wyoming at altitudes few archeologists had ever expected to locate anything.

Alaina relaxed.

She knew better than to be sensitive about the age difference between her and Mason. When they'd fallen in love, she'd decided if other people had problems with it that was their issue, not hers. Convincing Mason had taken longer, but he'd come to accept it, as well.

AFTER ALAINA AND his sister had driven away, Gideon hurried to finish his usual morning tasks. He wanted to go into Bannister to help paint the sheriff's office, a community project the local radio station had been promoting for the past two weeks. Deke had also mentioned it. Off-duty deputies weren't required to participate but as Sheriff Hewitt's son, Deke was in a special category. Remembering the wry acceptance on his friend's face made Gideon grin.

"Is something funny, son?" asked Helene as she walked over from the house.

"Nothing important. I'm just getting things done so I can go help with that community project."

"That's why I came out. I baked cookies for the volunteers, along with two huckleberry coffee cakes. They're in your truck."

"Don't you want to come with me?" Gideon's concern was growing again. His mom seemed better than before, but she was remaining on the ranch most of the time, rarely going anywhere.

Helene shook her head. "I have things to do here. If you don't mind, I'm going to start sorting out the attic."

"No problem, but that's a big job. I'll stay and help."

"Absolutely not. I'm looking for the old Westcott family recipes, the ones my great-grandmother used, and that could take days with all the odds and ends up there. I'll see you later."

Gideon was disappointed, but maybe things would improve with Libby's unanticipated stay at the ranch.

In Bannister he found the volunteers were in the middle of a break. They were drinking coffee from a battered coffee maker that he recognized from ranch association meetings.

"Hey, everyone," he called, "I brought cookies and coffee cake from my mom."

The volunteers eagerly collected the various treats Helene had provided.

"You'd think they'd never eaten before," Deke murmured.

Gideon rolled up his sleeves and opened a can of paint. "I don't see you holding back."

His friend brushed the crumbs from his fingers. "I was just taste-testing. You can reassure your mother it was great."

"I'll do that."

Deke's uncle was there as well and as Gideon painted a window frame, he looked at Nels speculatively. This was the first time he'd seen Nels since his mother had said he was her childhood sweetheart. She would have been much better off with him than Gideon's biological father. Nelson Hewitt was a solid guy, if a bit stodgy. He owned the hardware store in town, having opted to go into business rather than law enforcement like his brother.

"Watch it," Deke yelped, ducking as Gideon nearly slapped his head with a dripping paint-brush. "Where's your brain, pal?"

"Sorry. I was thinking about something my mother told me a few days ago. Did you know that she and your uncle used to date when they were kids?"

"Uncle Nels has talked about it. I think he still carries a torch for her. He has a framed picture of them in the mountains when they were hiking and another of her and their friends swimming. I have to say, your mom was a real stunner. Still is, for that matter."

"Now it's your turn to watch it," Gideon warned.

Deke chuckled. "Just making sure you're paying attention. I'm not a fan of scrubbing paint from my ear."

Gideon returned to work, making an effort to stay more focused. The volunteers were getting the job done, but they were also enjoying the company. Community projects were important in Bannister. With the majority of the county population living outside town on ranches or small farms, something was needed to pull people together periodically.

Shortly after the crew had eaten a lunch donated by the Made Right Pizza Parlor, Gideon heard a swooshing, clicking noise. He looked up and saw Alaina taking pictures of the work in progress. He went over to her.

"I thought you were in Bozeman."

"We only had a few errands and it doesn't take all day to drive down and back up again. Libby called her mom and Helene mentioned the painting party here in Bannister. Since I wouldn't have time to do much work anyway, I suggested we come by."

"And take pictures Maybe you should consider being a photojournalist rather than wildlife photographer."

"Not a chance."

Gideon was startled when Alaina lifted her camera and took a picture of him. "Why did you do that?" he asked.

"Because you're the closest thing to a

grouchy grizzly that I'm going to see today and I want to practice my wild bear picture-taking skills."

"I don't think that's funny."

"I didn't think you would."

He gritted his teeth. If anything, Alaina was practicing her bear*baiting* skills and she already excelled at that. How did a woman who looked so sweet manage to be so aggravating?

"You—" Gideon stopped, abruptly noticing that his sister was chatting with Deke.

Flirting, actually. And Deke was flirting right back with the "aw, shucks, ma'am" way he had of talking with a woman he found attractive. It was effective, too. Deke was popular with the opposite sex.

"They're a nice-looking couple," Alaina said quietly.

"They barely know each other," Gideon felt compelled to say. "And Libby is really young. Deke had a degree in criminal science and was already a deputy sheriff when she was playing volleyball in middle school."

Sadness seemed to briefly darken Alaina's unique eyes. "She seems old enough to know what she wants."

"I just don't want her getting hurt."

Alaina's expression was gentle, even kind.

"I know, but you're reading a whole lot into a single moment. They're talking. That's all. And whatever happens is up to them."

A peculiar sensation crept through Gideon. He wasn't superstitious, yet he knew that single moments were important. But how did you know which moments were going to change your life? Like the one when he'd seen his ex-wife and decided that he had fallen for her at first sight? A fateful moment, to be sure, just not one he would care to repeat.

He shook himself. "Sorry, I shouldn't have gotten so personal. I'll try to keep my mom and sister from disturbing you too much. Since they're used to having more people around, the ranch may feel lonely to them for a while."

"That's all right, I can look after myself."

"You keep saying that, it's just hard to believe."

"Because of the way I look?" she asked, sticking her chin in the air. How many people had she frustrated with her obstinate nature over the years? It must have been quite a few.

"Realistically, someone shouldn't carry more than 20 percent of their body weight while backpacking," he said carefully. "I'm too smart to guess how much you weigh, but 20 percent of your body weight can't be nearly enough equipment and food to safely hike and camp."

A twinkle crept into Alaina's eyes. "Too smart to guess my weight, huh?"

"It's in the basic training about being a guy. Don't say anything about a girl's weight. Always be polite to her father, be sure to compliment her mother and never *ever* say something like, I hope you won't look like her in thirty years."

Alaina pulled a smartphone from the pocket of her jeans. "I took this of my mom on my last trip home. There's no creative photography involved, so looking like her wouldn't bother me."

She handed him the phone and he could see her point. The woman on the screen looked twenty-five and, in her own way, was as beautiful as Alaina.

"You have her eyes," he said, returning the phone, "but not her hair or skin tone. Is that from your dad?"

"No. It's probably from a generation or two back, though I can't say for sure. Both my folks were orphaned young and grew up in foster homes. Mom talks about doing genealogy research, but she's a doctor and doesn't have much spare time. I've always envied people with lots of relatives—you know, grandparents and aunts and uncles and cousins. Libby tells me it's like that for you."

Gideon had rarely given it much thought. Yeah, he came from a big family, particularly if you counted his stepdad's branch of the family tree, which he did. On top of that, a fair percentage of Bannister County's population could trace their ancestry back to Jonah Westcott and his brothers.

"We add a good number to Montana's population," he admitted. "But large families mean there are a lot more people who feel justified about getting into your personal business. And by the way, you haven't made me forget my point about how much you can carry in a backpack. It's a valid concern."

"I told you before, I'm planning to cache supplies once I establish observation points. And I won't carry a tent during warmer weather. I'll get by."

I'll get by.

Her blithe words made him even more uncomfortable. He was rapidly coming to the conclusion he should never have agreed to let Alaina stay at the Double Branch. At the very least he should have taken his overdeveloped sense of responsibility into account before signing the agreement. It didn't matter that their contract said she would take care of herself—he still *felt* responsible.

Gideon looked at her curiously.

Wildlife photography was a very solitary career unless you were part of a film crew. Alaina didn't give the impression of being someone who avoided people, so she couldn't be a hermit or anything like that.

"What made you decide to become a photographer?" he asked.

She brightened. "Cameras have fascinated me since a teacher in junior high school talked about photography in the Civil War and how much pictures from the battlefields affected people."

"I can see how glamorous that must have made it sound," Gideon said in a dry tone.

She laughed and shook her head. "Not glamorous. But it had an impact on people and how they saw war. Photographers such as Alexander Gardner and Timothy O'Sullivan were right there, seeing battles and the aftermath, and through their eyes and skill, the world saw it, too."

"Too bad their pictures didn't put an end to all war, everywhere."

Alaina's face sobered. "True. But I'm still fascinated by the concept of capturing an instant in time and preserving it forever. I love our wild spaces, and with people spreading to every corner of the globe, photographs may be all we have left of them someday."

Gideon shuddered. "That's a horrible thought."

"Oh? I thought ranchers wanted to tame the wilderness."

"My great-grandfather saw nature that way, but I try to coexist."

"In that case, there may be hope for you yet."

She sauntered away, leaving him to consider what her cryptic half smile might have meant.

CHAPTER FIVE

ALAINA STOPPED TO adjust the straps on her backpack, then continued up the slope of a hill.

The sun was bright and warm and the scent of ponderosa pines rose, filling her senses. An eagle cried and she tipped her head back to watch it soar across the sky. A hawk followed and they rose in unison on a current of air before the eagle beat its more powerful wings and drew away.

It was so beautiful that her breath caught.

This part of the world had always spoken to her, ever since her family had visited Yellowstone on a family vacation. For months she'd dreamed about the beauty of the geysers in the park, the power and mystery of the bears she'd seen, and when she couldn't sleep, she'd replayed in her mind the grunting sound that buffalo made while grazing. The memory of those low rumbles had been more soothing than a lullaby.

After another hour she stopped and checked

her GPS unit to see how much progress she'd made. While she couldn't hike quickly with a full pack, she wasn't doing badly. The important part was to stay alert to her surroundings and be prepared. A great picture could be missed simply because she wasn't ready to take it.

Something at the corner of Alaina's eye made her instinctively reach for her camera, but a better look revealed it was a horse and rider in the distance. She had to expect to see range riders on her outings. She continued climbing, keeping watch for any movement in the landscape.

The sound of hoof beats gradually sank into her consciousness. As they became louder, Alaina frowned. She looked around again, and this time she could tell the rider was Gideon Carmichael.

Though they'd had a relatively pleasant conversation the previous week in Bannister, she'd seen little of him since.

She pinned a pleasant expression on her face as he rode closer, Danger trotting alongside. "Fancy meeting you out here."

He didn't say anything for a long minute. "Good afternoon. I didn't realize you were going for a hike today."

Alaina blinked. "I've gone hiking almost every day since I moved in."

Gideon dismounted and came closer, leading his horse. "Yes, but from the look of your pack, you expect to be gone overnight."

"For more than one night," she said. What was he leading up to? Her activities were none of his business.

"About that, I've been thinking it would be helpful if you told us when you plan to be away. Mostly for extended absences, of course. Also which direction you're going."

Alaina cocked her head. "Our agreement doesn't require me to check in and out with you."

"Except it's reasonable to let someone know where you'll be and how long you expect to be gone."

She settled her feet more firmly on the rocky slope. "When you returned the agreement to my sister-in-law, you included a terse letter emphasizing that you couldn't allow your ranching operations to be impacted by my presence. I presumed that included things like notifying you about my movements as if I were a child who needed supervision. And you wrote that letter, despite the agreement stating the very same thing."

Gideon's face darkened. "Why do you turn everything I say into something negative?"

"Maybe it's your delivery." She swung her backpack off her shoulders and put it on the ground before reaching down to pet Danger. "To be honest, I didn't expect to have this many conversations with you."

His jaw tightened visibly. "I admit to a lack of diplomacy since you arrived, but I had no intention of creating a situation that puts you in jeopardy."

Alaina shrugged. She knew there were risks to wilderness hiking and camping, and those risks increased when someone was alone, but she didn't want to wake up in forty years and wonder where her life had gone while she was doing something else. If she'd learned anything from Mason's death, it was that you couldn't put things off for a future that might not exist.

"Let's cancel the agreement," Gideon urged. "I'll return every penny of the money you gave me. In a certified check. There must be other *better* places for you to work. I'll ask around. I know guys who work for the forest service. They may have an unused fire lookout cabin available."

She shook her head. "Not a chance. A deal is a deal and you can't back out of it. But I'll leave a note on my door if that makes you happy. Doing more could be interpreted as interfering with your ranch operations. Think about it… How annoying to have someone continually telling you what her plans are. And what if I change them? I'd have to call and tell you what I'm doing and where I'll be, all over again. That would almost be like having a wife, which isn't a good idea since I've heard how you feel about the wedded state."

If looks could kill, she'd be dead on the spot.

Maybe her last comment had been uncalled for, but Alaina was becoming annoyed. Teasing Gideon had been fun in the beginning, but he was still acting as if she didn't have a shred of common sense. At the very least he was treating her like an overbearing big brother and she had enough of *them* back home.

"Truly, you don't need to worry about me," she said, relenting. Even if Gideon was being difficult, he seemed honestly concerned for her safety. On top of that, it didn't appear that he was trying to chase her away from the Double Branch and still keep the money she'd paid him. "I'm texting information on my hikes to my sister-in-law and have regular check-in times so Janet will know if there's a problem. She also has an application that tracks my satellite phone, so I'm covered."

Gideon felt like an idiot.

Things had been so quiet the past few days that he'd begun hoping it would remain that way. He and Alaina had even successfully avoided close contact with each other, though he'd spotted her several times within a mile or two of the main house, taking pictures.

Then this morning his mother had casually mentioned seeing her leave at dawn with a heavily loaded backpack. "She was headed west, but she could have gone anywhere once she was out of sight," Helene had said, sounding so unconcerned that he'd nearly choked on his toast.

"She needs to let someone know where she's going to be," he'd snapped.

Libby had rolled her eyes. "Alaina knows what she's doing. She has loads of backpacking equipment in the cabin, along with snowshoes and a sled for winter travel. You have to give her a chance."

Helene had added her agreement, saying Alaina was very levelheaded.

Then Libby had leaned forward, a wicked twinkle in her eyes. "I'm curious, is there more to your objections than worrying about the ranch's liability in case something happens to her?"

"Absolutely not."

Gideon had stomped out to the barn without another word, wishing again that he'd never taken Alaina's money. She was an East Coast tenderfoot who didn't belong on the Double Branch. He wasn't concerned about liability—according to his lawyer, the liability release she'd signed was ironclad. But for some reason, that made the whole thing more worrisome.

Several possibilities kept occurring to him, the top being that Alaina was either dangerously naive or else she didn't care if something happened to her. He didn't like either thought. So after trying to focus on clearing the bushes encroaching on the paddock for a few hours, he'd saddled Brushfire and ridden out to find where she'd gone.

Still, perhaps Libby had guessed right and there was more to his feelings toward Alaina than simple concern. She was a beautiful, intriguing woman who cared about animals and was radically remaking her life after the loss of her husband. He admired what she was doing, even though it was frustrating to worry about a greenhorn's safety.

"Look, Alaina, I'm sorry," Gideon said. His behavior since her arrival had been inexcusable. "I should have realized you'd made arrangements. It was wrong to assume you weren't prepared."

Surprise flickered in her blue-green eyes. "Okay," she said cautiously.

"But I'd like to suggest a compromise."

The surprise in her face turned to suspicion. "What sort of compromise?"

"I know every inch of the Double Branch and the mountains around it. There was only one person who knew these mountains as well as I do, and that was my great-grandfather."

"And?"

"And I want to propose taking you on tours of the ranch and upper backcountry by horseback. I can keep an eye on my herds at the same time. That way I'll feel more confident you won't get lost or have another problem. We can take day trips to start, say a week apart, and then go on a few overnight excursions, higher up in the mountains. Don't worry, I'll pick a calm horse and saddle it for you. I can also give you riding lessons."

"I know how to ride."

"Great, then lessons won't be needed."

ALAINA'S THOUGHTS RACED.

She was torn between irritation and recognition that the tours Gideon was suggesting would give her a huge head start in finding the best locations to do her photography. She wasn't worried about getting lost with a map and GPS tracker, but it wasn't the same as seeing the countryside with someone who possessed an intimate knowledge of the area.

She'd considered hiring a professional guide, but had decided she might just see the places where they took everyone else. Another alternative had been consulting with other professional wildlife photographers in the region, but she was wary after such a bad experience with her so-called mentor.

"What do you think?" Gideon prompted.

Alaina hesitated another moment before nodding. "All right, but we'll have to amend the paperwork and decide on a fee for your guide services."

Exasperation shot across his face. "I don't want to be paid. Consider it a peace offering, something to compensate for making assumptions that I shouldn't have made."

"I won't do it without revised paperwork and for a fee," she said patiently.

"You're already paying me."

"For use of the foreman's cabin, not for your personal services as a guide. Does five thousand sound right?" Alaina had no clue if it was a ridiculously high sum or totally inadequate, but she had to begin somewhere.

"I'll be watching my herds at the same time. You'd be paying me to do something I have to do anyway."

"I'd also be riding one of your horses."

"They need to be ridden to stay in good condition," he countered. "I have horses for my men to ride, but not the ones in the main barn. So this would benefit my animals."

"I'm still paying you."

They dickered back and forth until he reluctantly agreed to three thousand dollars. But Alaina refused to start the tours until Janet had revised the paperwork, they'd both signed and he'd cashed the check. She wanted the situation to be clear—Gideon wasn't doing her a favor. He would be a guide, paid for the service.

"At least have her email the agreement. It would speed things up if I can print it out here," he argued. "We could also do an electronic signature."

"That isn't how she does things," Alaina said firmly, not wanting to explain her sister-in-law used a custom paper with a unique watermark to limit the possibility of alterations or forgeries. Since there were same-day courier services in Manhattan, where most of Janet's clients lived and worked, it usually wasn't an issue. Janet also remained leery of electronic signatures and was watching to see how they fared in court over a period of time.

"I would never have guessed you were so stubborn," Gideon said finally. "At least not on the first day you visited the Double Branch. You've been proving it to me ever since."

She sighed. "It's just that I spent my childhood being treated like a fragile china doll that needed protection, so now I get overly defensive about my independence. But it isn't your problem and I'm not trying to *make* it your problem."

"Why were you treated like that?"

"Trust me, it's a boring story."

"That's okay, until haying starts, I'll be spending most of my time watching cattle graze, repairing fences and digging out invasive plants when I find them. Compared to that, anything would be interesting."

Alaina doubted it. The tasks he'd listed included staying alert to the presence of predators and riding in the most beautiful country in the world. If ranchers found the activity overly boring, they wouldn't do it for long. Libby had even said range riding was the favored assignment for the cowhands, and that she respected her brother for not giving all the duller maintenance tasks to his employees. Instead he did many of them himself, bending over backward to be a decent boss.

The unconscious admiration in her voice had told Alaina a good deal about their relationship. Libby might get annoyed with her brother, but she loved and thought well of him at the same time.

"Alaina?" Gideon prompted. "Is the china doll story a deep dark secret?"

"Hardly. My mother fell down a flight of stairs when she was pregnant with me. I was born early and spent six weeks in a preemie unit. From then on, the whole family saw me as delicate. That may have been true when I was a baby, but I grew into a healthy child who was always trying to get into trouble. It never occurred to them that I might not have tried so hard if they hadn't put so many restrictions on my activities."

"*That* I can believe. I also believe you found ways around those restrictions."

"More times than you can imagine. I was a wild child, but my parents never knew it. Instead, I appeared to be the dutiful preacher's daughter, doing whatever was expected."

Alaina's pulse jumped at the smile she saw in Gideon's eyes. She was suddenly very aware of him as a man.

"So, who else knew you were an undercover wild child?" he asked.

"My best friend and a few other kids. We never got caught, which means that most everyone back home thinks I still have my halo and angel wings. That's how preacher's kids are seen a lot of the time, either super angelic or out of control."

Gideon turned his head to one side and gazed at her as if looking for something. Then the corners of his eyes crinkled with humor. "I can almost see where the halo used to be attached. But seriously, it must have been tough growing up that way."

Alaina hadn't anticipated he would understand, though just because they disagreed on various issues, it didn't mean he was insensitive.

"A little. Don't get me wrong, I had a good

childhood. But it might be easier on my parents if they'd seen the real me when I was younger because my choices now wouldn't seem so out of character to them."

"Parents worry no matter what, and then at some point we start worrying more about them. The cycle of life, I suppose. Though sometimes that cycle stinks."

Alaina saw pain in his eyes and knew he must be thinking about his stepfather. She wished she could say something to help, but hearts healed at their own pace.

The sorrow in Gideon's face vanished as quickly as it had appeared. "How about your brothers?" he asked. "Were they angels or hellions?"

"A little of both. After college they found jobs near Port Coopersmith, so my parents started to expect that all of their kids would live close by. Then I married Mason and it upended their image of the future."

"When your husband died, they must have hoped—" He stopped. "Sorry, that's too personal."

"It's all right. My family *did* think I'd move back after the accident. They even told me I could have my old room at the house. And that no one would mind if I wanted to start teaching my old Sunday preschool class again."

"Ouch."

She shrugged. "They meant well. They'll figure it out sooner or later, though I might have to get really frank with them first. What I want is a middle ground between the wandering life I had with Mason and being the dutiful child who returns home and does what everyone expects." She grinned. "Of course, it might be different if Connecticut were next door to Yellowstone."

"Of course." Gideon smiled back and rubbed Brushfire's nose. "Are you sure you won't start the tours with me before the paperwork gets done? You'll lose valuable time."

Alaina picked up her pack and eased it onto her shoulders. "I won't be losing time. I'll call Janet tonight and tell her we need a revised agreement. In the meantime, I'm continuing my hike. I'll be back in a few days."

"I thought you might wait for overnight trips until after I've shown you around."

Aha.

That was why he was so eager to be her tour guide; he'd hoped to delay the times she was out alone. But while Alaina felt trepidation about camping by herself, it wasn't going to stop her. She had to get used to being on her own in the mountains or other wilderness areas if she wanted to pursue wildlife photography. If she backed off from her plans today, it would take longer to summon the nerve again.

"Don't worry," she said. "I'll set up camp at least two hundred feet away from a water source, not on a game trail, away from dead trees that could drop a limb on me and I'll find a site well before sundown."

Danger whined, looking back and forth between them, obviously sensing the increased tension in Gideon.

"Then take Danger with you."

Alaina laughed. "He's a terrific dog, but he's noisy. I'd never get any wildlife photos with him around."

"If you tell him to be quiet, he won't make a peep unless there's a threat. And if you keep an eye out for where he's focused, you might see something you wouldn't otherwise. Give him a chance. I'll make it up to you if he spoils any of your pictures."

Alaina didn't know how Gideon could make it up to her if she lost a great photograph, or how she would prove it in the first place. On the other hand, it might be nice to have Danger's company. He and one of the barn cats had gotten into the habit of coming over in the evening for a love fest. Obviously the German shepherd's first devotion was to Gideon, but he seemed to like her well enough. And the cat was a complete charmer, with a purr that practically rattled the windows.

"Don't you need Danger to help with the cattle?" she asked.

"We aren't in the middle of working them for any special reason, so it's no problem."

"I don't have anything to feed him," she said, still stalling.

"No problem." Gideon went to his horse and removed a fluorescent orange contraption from one of the saddlebags. "This is a dog backpack with a two-day supply of water and kibble in bear bags, along with other items that might be useful. I usually don't put it on him except when we're involved in a search-and-rescue operation. But since that can crop up at any time, I stay prepared."

He called Danger over and fastened the straps around him. The German shepherd's tail wagged furiously. He obviously saw the pack as part of a great game.

"Uh, all right," Alaina said, aware she was being railroaded into having the dog's company, along with a two-night limit put on her outing because she'd never let him go hungry. Still, Danger was a nice animal and probably knew the ranch as well as Gideon. Maybe better.

The important thing she needed to accomplish wasn't even taking pictures, it was getting used to camping by herself. It was one thing to stay in a crowded campground, another to be high in the mountains all alone. Surely accepting Danger's company didn't mean she wasn't being as independent as she wanted to be.

GIDEON WASN'T HAPPY as he watched Alaina continue climbing, but at least Danger was at her heels. He'd given Danger the Guard command, though it wasn't necessary. The German shepherd had been schooled as a working dog by the finest trainer in Bannister County. Danger understood that since Alaina lived on the ranch, she was now a member of his pack. And you protected the pack, it was as simple as that for him.

Grandpa Colby hadn't been able to do ranch work in his last years, but he'd continued training dogs for ranchers around the area. Gideon suspected that Colby Westcott had wanted to leave an animal he'd specially trained to his great-grandson, so had picked

Danger from a neighbor's litter of puppies and encouraged them to be friends.

Few people outside the family had understood Colby. To the world he'd been an aged taciturn man who possessed an uncanny skill with horses, cattle and dogs. His family had known someone entirely different.

With a sigh, Gideon finally turned Brushfire and headed toward his herds on the upper range of the ranch. He didn't want Alaina to think he was following her, so he rode east a mile, before turning again to continue climbing the mountain slopes. As a rule, his cattle ranged to an elevation just above where whitebark pine started growing and he automatically assessed the health of the trees as he rode. Cold winters were necessary to control pine beetle infestations and he was hoping this next winter would be especially chilly.

Movement to the east caught his attention and he lifted his binoculars. It was a mother grizzly bear and her cubs. She was digging in the ground, probably for glacier lily bulbs or cow parsnips, while her babies played. He watched for a moment, relieved they weren't close to the route Alaina had appeared to be taking, or near any of his herds.

As the summer progressed, bears often

climbed higher, following the snow melt for easier forage, but sometimes they tried for easier pickings from his cattle.

An echo of something Alaina had said came back to Gideon…about masses of people spreading across the planet, and the chance that photographs might be all that was left of the wild spaces someday.

His jaw hardened.

He refused to let that happen to the Double Branch. There might be easier ways to raise cattle and *much* easier ways to make a living, but this life was in his blood and he wasn't going to give it up.

CHAPTER SIX

THAT NIGHT ALAINA lay in her sleeping bag, listening to the sounds coming from all directions, both familiar and unfamiliar.

Okay, she was nervous.

It was dark except for a shimmer of starlight and she was miles from other human beings. Every rustle in the brush or clatter of rocks from the nearby slope seemed magnified.

This is what you wanted, her conscience reminded her.

She lifted her head to look at Danger, who was lying nearby. He rose to his feet and padded over.

"Good boy," she murmured, combing her fingers through his thick fur.

Alaina put her head down again and gazed skyward, thinking about the flash of awareness she'd felt when she and Gideon were talking on the trail. And all because of a smile in his eyes that hadn't even reached his mouth.

She'd enjoyed going out with her old high school buddy while on visits to Port Coopersmith, despite just doing it to make her parents stop worrying. Scott had kissed her good-night each time, but they'd finally agreed there weren't any sparks between them.

Scott had a terrific smile, so why hadn't she responded to him instead of Gideon?

A sudden noise made Alaina bolt upright. Danger was focused on the dark perimeter of the campsite, but he didn't show any signs of being alarmed. She tried to slow her rapid heartbeat and watch without panicking. After a minute, a large porcupine crossed in and then out of view.

She rolled her eyes and lay down again. *Fine.*

Maybe Gideon had a valid point about her inexperience with solo backpacking and camping, not that she'd ever admit it to him. But at the very least she could admit it to herself and be grateful he'd maneuvered her into taking Danger along. There were limits to what survival and other courses could teach.

Touring the backcountry with Gideon would help her get acquainted with the area and become more at ease. And since she was paying him, she could look at the tours the way she'd see any training class.

Except with a class, her pride wouldn't be on the line as much.

Danger rested his muzzle on her shoulder while Alaina's thoughts kept circling around his owner. There wasn't any harm in acknowledging Gideon's appeal, though she'd be wise to remember his more annoying qualities.

Like the assumption she couldn't saddle a horse.

She couldn't, but how would he know that? However silly, she wanted to prove him wrong. There must be videos on the internet that could teach her the basics, and after she returned to the Double Branch, she could ask Libby to help her practice. Preferably when no one else could see them.

Alaina yawned and wiggled to get more comfortable.

Danger made a small snuffling sound, but didn't stir. Surely if he was relaxed, she had little to be concerned about. Besides, thousands of people went backpacking each year. Rarely did anything happen to them.

It was that reassuring thought that finally followed her into sleep.

JUST AS ALAINA had hoped, Libby was delighted to help her learn to saddle a horse.

"Let's go to the barn right now," she said when Alaina finished explaining. "Gideon and the cowhands are gone for the day. I told him I'd start putting the horses in the paddock and cleaning the stalls, so I need to go over, regardless."

It was the first time Alaina had been inside one of the Double Branch barns and she looked around curiously. There was a big difference between *this* building and the stable where her parents had taken her as a child. It was to be expected; Gideon's barns supported a working ranch, while that one had been a professional riding school.

Libby opened one of the stall doors and led out a tan horse with a white blaze on its face. "This is Nikko. Gideon mentioned he'd be showing you around and that he thought Nikko would be the best horse for you to ride. He's a gelding and very easygoing."

Nikko nudged Alaina's shoulder and she froze, instantly on edge.

"He just wants you to rub his nose," Libby explained.

Alaina cautiously stroked Nikko and he nickered. The other horses stretched their heads over the stall doors, tossing them as if to say, *I want some of that*. All except one. At the end of the barn there was a dark brown horse who seemed totally disinterested. Alaina had noticed him before. While the other horses clearly enjoyed each other's company in the paddock, he kept apart from them. Apparently Gideon had even built a special covered area where he could drowse on hot days, because he refused to join his paddock mates in the shade of the trees.

"Stay with Nikko while I take the others outside and put hay in their feed trough," Libby said, tying the end of Nikko's lead rope to a post.

Nikko didn't strain on his halter when the other animals walked out past him. He seemed nice…as nice as the horse that had thrown her when she was a kid.

Ironically she hadn't gotten hurt because of something the animal had done. Rather, the saddle band had been too loose and the saddle had slid to his underbelly, taking her with it. After months of begging her parents to arrange riding lessons, a freak accident had put an end to them on the very first day.

But as she'd told Gideon, she'd found ways to exert her independence, ones that might have turned her mother and father prematurely old if they'd known.

"You're grinning, what's so funny?" Libby asked when she returned.

"Nothing important. The last horse you took out seems sad. Do horses get moody?"

Libby sighed. "That's Grizzly. We think Griz is still grieving for my great-grandfather. You're welcome to try making friends with him. Carrots are his favorite treat. Gideon buys them in bulk for the horses. There's a supply over by the shelf."

Alaina promised to think about it.

She wanted to get more comfortable around the large animals, and the process might be easier with one who wasn't as sociable as the others. It was one thing when a cat demanded attention, another when a thousand-pound horse did it.

The funny thing was, she hadn't been bothered when the moose tried to stick its head in her SUV, and he'd been even bigger than Nikko. The only thing she'd worried about was getting down on the ground where he could step on her foot.

Alaina wiggled her toes inside her boots; she liked them the way they were. Getting them crunched would put a serious damper on her plans to hike all over the area, whether a moose *or* a horse was responsible.

"Um, should I get different boots for riding?" she asked.

"Riding boots are best." Libby came over and measured her feet against Alaina's. "You know, I have several pairs over at the house from when I used to stay with Grandpa Colby every summer. They're too small for me now, so they might fit. You're welcome to them."

Alaina was touched. "That's nice of you."

Libby smiled. "No problem. Let Gideon think they're yours. He'll assume you have loads of riding experience."

"Okay," Alaina agreed, though she wasn't sure how wise it was to keep *too* many secrets from Gideon. He was smart enough to know when he was being misled.

"This is the tack room," Libby explained, taking her into a separate area at one end of the barn. "Most of the riding gear is stored in here."

Alaina blinked. There were quite a number of saddles sitting on racks. Curious, she went over and looked at the embossed leather on several of them. Best All Around Cowboy was tooled on the leather flaps, followed by Shelton Rodeo and a year.

"Did Gideon win all of these?" she asked.

"Yup. Our hometown holds an annual

rodeo and Gideon usually won top honors before moving down here. And he won at other Montana rodeos, too."

"They seem like nice saddles."

Libby nodded. "The ranch association donates them up in Shelton. The rodeo used to be pretty small, then a rodeo champion married one of my cousins two years ago. He bought a ranch in Shelton County and runs a rodeo training school there, so the rodeo has turned into a big deal. It's good for the town, but I liked it better before."

"I'd feel the same way. But who needs this many saddles? They can't wear out that often."

Libby chuckled. "Not if you take care of them, which Gideon does, but he uses a different saddle for each horse. That one is for Nikko." She gestured to a rack along the wall.

"That makes sense. I've been watching an internet video on how to saddle horses, so is it okay if I try on my own? Then you can tell me how I did and what to fix."

"Good idea."

LIBBY WATCHED AS Alaina put a saddle blanket on Nikko, smoothed it carefully, then lifted the saddle over his back. She was intensely focused and seemed to be counting to herself. Each step was completed meticulously.

She finally turned around. "How is that? Did I get the girth tight enough?"

Libby checked everything and smiled her approval. "You did great. You just need practice to get faster. Mom and I are going to the farmers' market in Bannister this morning, but we can work on it later after I've cleaned the stalls. You understand horses, which is a big help."

"I'm not a horse person," Alaina said, shaking her head.

"I don't know about that. You kept talking to Nikko and you adjusted the cinches properly."

Alaina made a face. "Since you said this was his saddle, I looked for wear marks on the leather straps to figure out where they're usually buckled."

"Smart."

Though the open barn door, Libby saw Deke drive in and park near the house. It was the second time he'd been there since they'd talked in town.

"We have company," she told Alaina. "Deputy Hewitt. I'll go out and distract him."

"Uh, okay. I'll unsaddle Nikko and put his tack away."

"Thanks." Libby walked out to the deputy sheriff vehicle. "Hey, Deke."

His smile widened. "Good morning. Was that Mrs. Wright I saw in the barn?"

"I was trying to talk Alaina into riding with me, then I remembered the farmers' market this morning," Libby said, hooking his elbow in hers and drawing him toward the porch steps. "She offered to unsaddle my horse when you got here."

"I don't want to disrupt your day. Or hers."

Or hers?

"If you'd prefer, I could ask her to come out and take care of Nikko myself," Libby suggested, trying not to feel miffed. She didn't suffer from a lack of confidence about her appearance, but she was honest enough to know that Alaina had her beat when it came to sheer looks. Worse, Alaina didn't even seem aware of her otherworldly beauty. It would be irritating, but how could you resent someone who was so nice?

"No need. I presume everything is turning out okay with Mrs. Wright's stay at the Double Branch."

"Mom and I have to keep telling Gideon to give her a chance, but other than that, it's fine."

Deke hiked an eyebrow. "Give her a chance?"

Libby shrugged, guiltily pleased that he hadn't shown any interest in seeing Alaina.

"Gideon is a worrywart. He's fussed about whether she can cope on her own and that sooner or later he'll have to send a rescue party out for her," Libby explained. "But Alaina returned last night from a two-day camping trip and didn't mention having any trouble. I'm sure he'll be more relaxed about it after he's shown her around the area."

DEKE NODDED.

On his last visit to the Double Branch, Gideon had explained about the upcoming tours he'd be conducting, though not how they had come about. With another friend Deke might have teased that he was making moves on Alaina by offering to be her guide, but teasing Gideon about women wasn't a good idea.

"Maybe he has a good reason to be concerned," Deke suggested, though he didn't want to discuss a virtual stranger. While Alaina Wright seemed nice enough, it was Libby that he wanted to know better. "We've teamed up several times to search for missing day hikers and backpackers."

She shook her head. "I think it's something

else, but you never know with Gideon. He changed after moving to Bannister."

"It was probably his divorce. But he's a private guy and I doubt he'd appreciate being talked about."

Libby gave him a long considering look and Deke wished he understood what was going on behind her sparkling blue eyes. The women he usually found attractive didn't have Libby's intensity. Whether that was good or bad, he hadn't figured out.

"So, why are you here?" she asked, tipping her head in challenge.

Deke thought fast. "In my official capacity. I wanted to find out if your former boyfriend is still bothering you."

Irritation flew across her face. "Raymond is my problem and I'll take care of it. Besides, he's harmless."

Deke had heard that before, but anyone could be dangerous given the right circumstances. "Okay, then what about Dr. Barstow? You're going to sue him, right?"

"Again, my business. I'll deal with Dr. Barstow in my own way."

Deke's frustration grew as Libby walked up the porch steps. She was about to go inside when she turned and caught him watching her.

"Are you coming in for coffee or not?" she asked. "Mom usually starts a fresh pot when she hears someone arrive."

"Coffee," he said, hiding his delight. He was trying to cut down on his caffeine consumption, but if Libby was offering an invitation, he was accepting.

Period.

ALAINA COULDN'T KEEP from smiling as she watched the interplay between Libby and Deke from inside the barn. They were too far away to hear, but body language was universal. It was easy to see why Gideon had suspected the deputy sheriff was interested in Libby, but less easy to understand why it might be a concern.

Surely he wouldn't be friends with Deke if he didn't think he was an honorable person.

"Do you want to go into the paddock?" Alaina asked Nikko after she'd put his saddle and blanket back into the tack room.

The horse tossed his head and she could swear he understood. She led him to the paddock and opened the gate. He trotted in and she carefully latched it back, not wanting to be accused of letting the horses escape.

Griz had moved to the far side of the enclosure and she rested her arms on the fence to watch him. She understood grief. It could eat at your soul until you felt empty inside. Somehow, knowing horses could feel the same emotion made them seem less intimidating.

Alaina waited until Grizzly was looking in her direction before putting a carrot on one of the posts, then she walked to her cabin. Her instincts said it would be best to go slowly with him, making no demands, just small overtures. As a kid she'd tamed more than one feral cat that way.

The carrot was still there when she came outside with her laptop, but Griz had come a few steps closer. She'd noticed he often seemed to be standing in that same location by the fence, even though the grass was more lush on the far end. On the outside of the paddock fence was a weathered chair, identical to the Adirondack rocking chair that Alaina enjoyed sitting in the most. Maybe Colby Westcott had used it when visiting his horse pal and nobody could bear to take it away.

She pulled her chair to the side of the porch where she could easily look across the valley, but also see the rest of the ranch, then took out her phone and dialed her sister-in-law's private office number.

"Hi, sweetie," Janet answered.

"Hey, Janet," Alaina said. "I just wanted to find out when the revised paperwork might be coming."

"I sent the contract addendum by the fastest means possible, which might not be that fast."

"What do you mean?"

Janet chuckled. "You're living on a ranch, in a remote corner of the world. I had trouble finding a courier service that offered two-day delivery, much less overnight."

Alaina laughed, as well. "That's one of the costs of living where there's fresh air and wildflowers outside your window."

Her sister-in-law groaned. "Don't make me envious. It's warm and muggy here, more than usual for this time of year. I'd love to chuck my suits for a pair of jeans and a T-shirt."

"I thought you were a confirmed city gal."

"You're inspiring me to think about different choices. I'm proud of you, Alaina. It takes guts to do what you're doing, but please don't say that makes me sound like your mother."

"Not *my* mom. She sends a steady stream of emails, asking if I've finally come to my senses. More than one, *every single day*. I'm tempted to put her address in my spam filter, along with the rest of the family."

"That's a parent for you. Will you be disappointed in me if I say that having guided tours is a great idea?"

"Of course not," Alaina said fondly. "Will you be disappointed if I suggest selling your law firm and getting licensed in Montana?"

"It's an intriguing thought. The snow must be cleaner there than in the city."

"Practically a guarantee." Alaina thought about the Christmas lights she'd put up after it snowed on her first day in the cabin. They'd given the place a lovely cozy feel. "It wouldn't cost as much to live here, either. You might even meet a big bad handsome cowboy and decide to get married again."

"Not happening. One divorce was enough. Let me know when the addendum arrives and you've sent it back. Oh, and Mr. Carmichael called in time for me to incorporate the changes he requested."

"Changes?" Alarmed, Alaina squirmed upright, not an easy task in an Adirondack rocking chair. "What changes?"

"About giving permission for you to take pictures of ranch activities, etc. Essentially, you'll have access to all of his operations, without penalty or restriction. He said he'd discussed it with you."

Alaina thought about her conversations with Gideon and his suggestion that she concentrate on photographing something other than wolves. Obviously he was still hoping she'd pursue subjects that required less hiking and camping alone.

"Alaina?" Janet prompted. "The alterations are to your advantage, which is why I didn't confirm with you after he called. Does this mean you didn't talk about it?"

"Let's call it creative truth telling. We didn't discuss it as changes to the agreement, but Gid...Mr. Carmichael is trying to persuade me to shift the focus of my work. He's protective in his gruff, unsmiling way. I think he must be channeling my family."

A chuckle sounded through the phone. "He's way off base if he thinks he can change *your* mind. But now I'm curious. Email a picture of your cowboy when you get a chance."

"He isn't my anything, unless it's a pain in the posterior."

"It's just that..." Janet hesitated. "You know I'd be okay with you finding someone else, right? My parents should never have said what they did."

"They apologized."

"That doesn't make up for it. And I don't want what they said to influence any possibilities for the future. You deserve to be happy and that's what Mason would have wanted. He never would forgive Mom and Dad for the way they acted."

Janet had been furious with her parents at Mason's funeral when they'd bitterly declared that his death was nothing to Alaina, she would just go find someone new and the least she could have done was give them a grandchild.

It had been out of character for the Wrights. Though they weren't warm people, they were decent. A letter had arrived a month later with an awkward apology, but even at the time, Alaina had understood— they'd lost their son and grief made people lose all sense of perspective.

"Don't worry," Alaina said. "I *am* happy. I miss what Mason and I had together, but you don't find that kind of magic very often."

Yet despite her assertion, Alaina had spent an inordinate amount of time the past two days thinking about Gideon. Having his dog along had been a reminder of him, but that didn't entirely explain why he kept popping into her thoughts on a regular basis.

"Sometimes you never find magic," Janet said, an edge in her tone. Her ex-husband, a renowned heart surgeon, had turned cheating into an art form. The irony was that he'd loved Janet. He simply didn't seem capable of being faithful.

Alaina turned her head and waved at Helene and Libby as they came out of the main house to leave for the farmers' market in Bannister. Deke had already left.

"I wish you could be with someone you deserve," she murmured to Janet, whose marriage had ended shortly after hers had started with Mason. Alaina had spent hours commiserating with her new sister-in-law, cementing their friendship.

"It's the luck of the draw and I'm not looking. By the way, I sent two packets, one addressed to you and one to Mr. Carmichael. There's a certified check in your envelope. I thought it would save time if you had it ready. Oh, gotta go. My next appointment is here."

Alaina thanked her for the help and leaned back in her chair, rocking gently. But it was hard to focus with so many other thoughts circling in her mind.

Saddling Nikko had been easier than expected, and it was even easier to reverse the process because she hadn't needed to worry about disturbing his hair in the opposite direction it was growing. The video she'd watched had made a point of that—ruffling a horse's hair beneath the saddle could cause discomfort, so never *ever* do it.

Surely all the steps became second nature once you'd saddled enough horses.

She looked over to see if Griz had come closer to the carrot she'd left for him. He was just a few inches away and made a grab for the treat as she watched.

Alaina's heart ached to think about the horse, grieving his days away. Would it help or hurt if she went and spent time in that chair? After all, she could work on her laptop there, as well as on the porch. The 4K monitor wasn't necessary to do the initial sort and note-taking on her photographs.

She was about to go over when a horse came into view from the valley. It wasn't noon yet and she knew the ranch hands riding the range were normally gone all day. She lifted her camera and looked through the telephoto lens.

Gideon.

He was shirtless, carrying a calf in his arms and leading Brushfire, who was limping. Danger was staying close to both of them, but he didn't appear injured. Neither did Gideon, for that matter. She focused on Brushfire's leg and saw it was wrapped with something.

Gideon was the embodiment of a robust cowboy and Alaina couldn't resist taking several pictures before hurrying out to meet them. Danger raced forward to greet her, then ran back to his post at Gideon's side.

Gideon frowned as she approached. "Why are you out here without a day pack?"

"Because I'm not *out* here. I was sitting on the cabin porch and saw you coming. Let me carry the calf," she said.

He shook his head and adjusted the baby against his chest, who was voicing displeasure with the world in loud bawling cries. "This little girl might be a newborn, but she must weigh sixty pounds. You can lead Brushfire."

"All right."

With just a brief hesitation, she took the horse's reins and stroked his nose.

"What happened to his leg?" she asked as they walked.

"Rock came down a scree slope and hit him. It's my fault. I was trying to hurry because of the calf. I don't think the leg is badly hurt, but I didn't want him to carry any additional weight. I soaked bandages in cold water as a compress and wrapped my shirt around it to help keep the swelling down."

Alaina widened her eyes. How many miles

had Gideon walked, carrying the calf and leading Brushfire to spare his horse's injured leg? He didn't even seem to be breathing that heavily.

"Did the baby's mother die?"

GIDEON SHOT A look at Alaina.

Orphaned calves were a fact of life to ranchers, but most people turned into sentimental mush when confronted with the nitty-gritty of life on a cattle ranch.

"I'm not sure," he said. "We don't move cows to summer pasture that haven't dropped their calves, so I have a mystery on my hands. As for her being alone, the mother may have rejected it or they were accidentally separated. Calves need colostrum as soon as possible for both nutrition and antibodies, so I didn't hang around looking for longer than necessary."

He hadn't seen any evidence that the mother had died, such as birds circling in the sky, but it was still possible. That was his reality. He hated to lose a cow as much as any rancher, but it wasn't something he could always prevent.

"I haven't studied wild herd animals in depth, though I know orphaned bison survival rate isn't good, even when being raised as livestock," Alaina said.

Gideon nodded. "Cows *can* be raised by hand, but it isn't ideal since they aren't getting natural antibodies from their mother's milk. This late in the season is a problem, too. They need to gain around a hundred pounds a month to do their best over winter."

"A hundred pounds a month? That's even more than a baby bison gains on average."

Alaina used her free hand to pat the calf's head, but it continued complaining. *I'm honnnngry,* she bellowed. The world she'd entered had disappointed her mightily and she wanted everybody to know.

Gideon needed to get nutrition into her quickly, but he also had to get another cold pack on Brushfire's leg and decide if the veterinarian should be called.

"Could you ask my sister or mom to come out here?" he asked as they approached the barn. They were both experienced with helping orphaned calves.

"Libby and Helene already left for the farmers' market, but I can do whatever is needed."

"All right." He gave her instructions on where the frozen colostrum—the first form of milk produced by a mother cow—was stored in the calving barn and how to thaw it in a five-gallon bucket of warm water. "Use the small packages so it will melt quickly. Also keep a close eye on the thermometer. Water over a hundred and forty degrees degrades the natural antibodies," he explained.

"Got it. I'll be back as soon as possible." She fastened Brushfire's lead to a post and took off at a run.

Gideon put the calf on a mound of hay. Danger immediately began licking the baby, the way he had licked her when first located, simulating the bath she would have gotten from her mother. The calf quieted a little, though she still looked sorry for herself.

Gideon unwrapped his shirt from Brushfire's leg and removed the compress, then ran his fingers over the injury. The area was warm, marginally swollen and there was a small abrasion that was producing serum.

Better safe than sorry, Gideon thought, getting out his phone to ring the veterinarian. Dr. Wardell was on the far side of the county on a case, but promised to be there as soon as possible. Gideon disconnected and put a fresh compress on before removing Brushfire's saddle.

Before long Alaina had returned with a nursing bottle.

"You said the calf would need over a quart,

so I have more bags thawing," she said. "I thought she could drink this in the meantime. How is Brushfire?"

"The injury doesn't seem serious, but the vet is coming to check him." Gideon took the bottle, crouched and eased a finger in the calf's mouth. She began sucking and he slid the long nipple on the bottle alongside, then removed his finger. Some calves took several tries to figure out bottle-feeding, but this little girl got the idea immediately.

Alaina knelt on the other side and offered to hold the bottle.

"Okay, but it's going to be messy. You can see she's already slobbery and she may headbutt you, the way she'd butt her mama's udder to try to make the milk come faster."

Alaina shrugged. "Conveniently, you have a washer and dryer in the cabin. I'll survive."

While she was feeding the new baby, he went down to the calving barn to get the remaining colostrum that Alaina had left to thaw.

He appreciated her willingness to offer a hand. Brushfire probably would have been all right waiting until the calf had gotten some food, but now he didn't have to. Gideon just didn't like feeling indebted.

Plainly Alaina felt the same, which was

why she was insisting on paying him for the tours and making sure everything was signed and legal. Around Bannister a verbal agreement was usually all you needed.

He sighed.

The one trait he and Alaina seemed to have in common was a mulish determination, so the next twelve months were going to be interesting, to say the least.

CHAPTER SEVEN

THE MORNING AFTER finding the orphan calf, Gideon headed down to the calving barn, certain he'd find both Libby and Alaina there with the new baby.

That calf was still a mystery to him.

He timed his cow's pregnancies so they delivered during the early spring months, not early summer. It made calving a hectic period since a fair percentage of the cows needed some type of assistance, especially the first-time mothers.

Laughter came from inside the building and Gideon stood in the main door, watching Alaina and his sister fuss over the new arrival. Along with other chores, Libby had insisted on taking over the orphan calf feedings, and though his tenant had a camera hanging from around her neck, she was helping.

"Look at Rita bat her eyelashes," Alaina said, holding a nearly empty nursing bottle for the calf to suckle. She rubbed its knobby head. "A day old and already a flirt."

"Rita?" he asked.

Both women jumped.

"In honor of Rita Hayworth," Alaina explained, a defensive look growing on her face. "And I'm helping, not interfering."

"You assisted with her first feeding, so you're entitled to be here. Besides, I told your lawyer you could have all the access to ranch operations that you wanted."

"Janet mentioned that." Alaina's tone was dry. "Has the paperwork come, by any chance?"

"It arrived an hour ago. Envelopes for each of us. I heard you were going into town to photograph Jonah Westcott's journals at the museum, so I thought we'd drive together and have the addendum notarized. The Bannister Credit Union has a notary public on staff."

"You don't want to hang around while I'm taking pictures. I'll go in my SUV and meet you there." Alaina set the empty bottle aside and used a towel to wipe the calf's muzzle.

Gideon shrugged. "It's a waste of gasoline to bring two vehicles. While you're working at the museum, I'll get a load of boards from the lumberyard and buy supplies at the hardware store."

"Oh. Well, I'll need to change my jeans first. As you've pointed out, calves get slobbery. Libby is going, too. She offered to assist at the museum."

"That's what Mom told me."

"And I still have to sanitize the bottles," Libby said after Alaina had left. She put the new calf in her enclosure. "But I've already given the older calves their milk replacer and put out starter feed."

"I saw the calves in the pasture. Go ahead and change your clothes, I'll finish."

"But I want to save you work," his sister protested. "You didn't expect to have someone else at the ranch this summer."

"I've told you a dozen times, I love having you here," Gideon said, wishing she didn't feel the need to repay him. As far as he was concerned, the Double Branch was his siblings' home, too. The same with his mother and grandparents. The ranch belonged to him legally, but it was part of a long Westcott family heritage and they were always welcome. "Go on, I've got it handled."

"All right. Come, Cookie."

Cookie padded after his mistress. He was a fine dog, not suited to working cattle but devoted to Libby.

Gideon swiftly sanitized the bottles and

nipples his sister had used for the calves. Except for the new orphan, the others required only two bottle feedings each day and would soon be weaned. The Double Branch had a decent success rate at saving orphaned calves and he would do his best to ensure Rita was one of the lucky ones.

Rita?

He shook his head at the mental slip. Naming orphan calves wasn't a good idea. When you turned at-risk animals into pets and became attached to them, it was even tougher when they didn't survive. And he already took things hard enough when he lost one. A dead calf meant he'd failed.

Gideon checked on the new calf in her pen. She was lying in the hay, asleep after the hard work of filling her tummy. One of the barn cats was curled up against her. Suki's primary job was pest control, but she was also a natural-born nanny. More than the other cats, she kept the orphans company, sleeping with them, kneading their shoulders and giving them baths.

He rubbed his jaw, wishing he knew where the newborn had come from. Another rancher's cow could have roamed onto his rangeland, but what had happened to her after giving birth?

Two of his hands were up there today, checking brands and otherwise investigating.

Gideon put the last bottle on a rack to drain and then walked up the slope to find Alaina already waiting by the truck. He gestured to the large carrying case at her feet. "That's a lot of equipment."

"I just hope it's enough. With any luck I'll get decent pictures, but I've never worked on something like this before."

"I doubt you need luck."

ALAINA BLINKED AT the sideways compliment. While she was confident of her abilities, photographing old documents was new to her. She didn't know what condition they might be in or if the paper had darkened, making them hard to read. Scanning might be a better option, but she wouldn't dare press an old journal onto a screen and risk damaging the spine.

"I'll do my best," she murmured.

Gideon rubbed the back of his neck and seemed uncomfortable. "About the calf. I should have warned you that orphans have a rough time, particularly newborns. We do what we can to help them survive, but calves are better off when they have their mothers and are out on grazing land."

"Libby told me the same thing. But I'm well aware that life isn't always fair and it doesn't offer guarantees."

"You're talking about your husband's accident."

Alaina shook her head. Oddly she *hadn't* been thinking about Mason, though his death had taught her more about cold, hard reality than she'd ever needed to learn. "When you're on a field study, you don't interfere with nature. I'm passionate about wolves. At the same time, I love the animals that unfortunately become their prey. I had to accept the balance of nature or break my heart over everything that happened."

"Still, naming a calf makes it harder if you lose them. You forget they're livestock and they become more like a family pet."

Alaina smiled faintly. "Surely a motherless calf needs to know someone cares about her. Love has a healing quality of its own."

Gideon didn't look convinced. "My great-grandmother would have agreed, but Grandpa Colby was upset when she got involved with the hopeless cases, saying he didn't want to watch her break her heart."

"How many times did she save the hopeless cases?"

"More often than he expected," Gideon

admitted. "But it's also a question of resources. I can't spend days taking care of an individual calf. I try, but work on a ranch never ends and you can't neglect the rest of the herd."

Brave talk, Alaina thought.

Especially when he must have walked miles to spare Brushfire's injured leg while carrying a calf in his arms. She'd lifted Rita a couple of times and, newborn or not, that baby was *heavy*. Toting sixty-some pounds of wriggling, wet, complaining calf couldn't have been easy, even for such a strong man.

"Sorry to keep you waiting," Libby exclaimed as she came down the porch steps, toting a large cooler bag. "Honest, it wasn't my fault. Mom wanted to send lunch with us and she was still getting everything together."

"Lunch is hours away," Gideon objected. "We could have gotten a meal in town if it was needed."

"You know how she is. Food is the answer to most of life's problems. She suggested a picnic in the park so we could show Alaina where the Founders Day celebration will be in August. Don't read anything into it," Libby added hastily. "She just wants you to relax before haying season becomes too frantic."

With a frown he took the bag and put it inside a cargo container in the back of his truck. Alaina almost felt sorry for the guy. After all, he was trying to get errands done efficiently and Helene wanted to turn the day into a social outing. Nonetheless, it probably wasn't a case of matchmaking. His mother seemed to accept that her son wasn't likely to get married again.

Over Libby's objections, Alaina got into the back seat with her equipment bag, so brother and sister could sit in front. It wasn't too cramped, though the space had probably been designed for children. A pang went through her. While she and Mason had talked about having a family, it hadn't been feasible to take a baby on field studies. *Someday*, they'd said. But someday had never come.

Alaina shook her head. There wasn't any point to thinking about might-have-beens.

She fastened her seat belt and leaned forward as Gideon headed toward the main road. "Libby, I forgot to ask, how was the farmers' market?"

"They had the usual stuff for this time of year. Jerky, honey and a few salad greens for sale, plus flowers and plants. It didn't matter. I was mostly trying to get Mom out of the house."

From her position behind Libby, Alaina could see Gideon's strong profile. A muscle in his jaw pulsed. "I thought being at the Double Branch would help. Now I'm not so sure. That's one of the few times she's left the ranch since she got here."

"She *is* better," Libby insisted. "It's just easier for me to see because I haven't been around as much. When she stayed at my apartment, she just sat and read during the day, except she almost never turned a page. She insisted on cooking, but then she wouldn't eat, and I'd find her mopping the kitchen floor and ironing my clothes in the middle of the night."

"At least she's eating and sleeping more now."

"That's right."

Alaina settled back again, aware she was hearing a discussion Gideon would probably have preferred to keep within the family. She couldn't make herself invisible, so to give them a sense of privacy while they talked, she opened the envelope Janet had sent her and took out the addendum to the contract.

The language, while sprinkled with legal terms, was straightforward. It amended the clause that said Alaina would do nothing to impact ranch operations, and added the agreement about Gideon giving her a series of tours. As promised, there was also a certified check made out to Gideon, along with a receipt form for him to sign. Janet's note said that it should be all right for Alaina to hand the check over once she had the notarized addendum in hand.

Alaina was surprised that Gideon hadn't wanted his own lawyer to review the language first, but he might have done a phone consult.

She looked up as they were passing the roadside tavern outside town, then quickly refocused on the addendum. She tried not to dwell on unpleasant memories, but seeing a bar or tavern could raise a boatload. The truck responsible for killing Mason had been carrying liquor for a similar business. Several cases had gotten smashed in the accident and the odor had permeated the air. The smell of scotch still turned her stomach. But even worse was knowing the deliveryman had lost control because he'd been drinking himself.

Libby's voice broke into her grim thoughts. "Alaina, you must be a million miles away. We're here."

Alaina blinked, realizing they were in a parking lot with the credit union on one side and the post office on the other.

"Sorry. I was reading the paperwork."

No customers were waiting inside the small credit union and they were able to have the agreement signed and notarized with minimum fuss. As soon as Alaina had her copies, she gave Gideon the certified check and had him sign the receipt.

"Why don't you cash or deposit it now?" she suggested.

His jaw tightened, but he went over and handed it to the teller.

Alaina waited long enough to be certain he'd follow through before telling Libby that she would meet her at the museum. "I want to mail my lawyer's copy to her," she explained. "The museum isn't far from here, right?"

"It's just down the street, next to the hardware store." Libby pointed east. "Don't worry about your equipment bag. I'll take care of it."

At the post office, Alaina wrote the address on a priority envelope and enclosed the receipt and her sister-in-law's file copy of the agreement. Another customer, an older man, came in as she turned to leave. She gave him a smile, thinking he had the pinched expression of someone perpetually displeased with the world.

"Do I know you?" he demanded abruptly, blocking the exit.

"I don't think so. I just moved here."

He thrust his face close to hers. "You look real familiar."

"Maybe you've met my doppelgänger," she suggested, refusing to be intimidated or take a step backward.

"Your doppa-*what*?"

"Yancy, come over here and leave that lady alone. What do you need?" called the postal clerk.

"What do you think? I gotta get my mail, the same as always." Yancy stomped to the front desk.

Alaina left in a hurry. At the museum she found Libby on a bench by the door, the camera bag tucked behind her feet.

"Mr. Hewitt told me he'd be here at nine thirty," Alaina said, checking her watch. "Gideon must be running his errands."

"He's at the lumberyard."

Alaina got a camera from her bag and took pictures of the museum sign and building while they waited.

A few minutes later a man came over from

the hardware store, introducing himself as Nelson Hewitt. "I've met Libby a number of times, but she may not remember me."

Libby smiled. "Of course I remember you, Mr. Hewitt. You're the judge for the races at the Founders Day celebration."

"I'll be doing that forever. But please, call me Nels. Both of you," he urged. "Alaina, I took the letters and journals from the display cases this morning and put them in our meeting room, where the lighting is better." He unlocked the museum and turned off the security system.

"Have they been photographed or scanned before?" Alaina asked, wondering if she was simply duplicating someone else's efforts. At the same time, she was determined to get photos herself, if only for the opportunity to touch something that Theodore Roosevelt had handled.

"I hate to admit we don't even have transcripts," Nels confessed. "It's a relief to know they'll finally be documented. I'll leave you to work, just keep the front door locked. We don't have any docents coming in today."

Alaina nodded. She enjoyed small-town museums, but they were often run by volunteers with little time for things that a larger facility would do automatically.

A large skylight illuminated the meeting room and she decided to wait until the sun had climbed higher before working in there. Meanwhile, she visited the various sections of the museum, taking pictures for their new brochure.

The natural history room was the only location where she didn't linger. It was too eerie and heartbreaking, with wolves, bears and mountain lions dominating the taxidermy displays. A number bore a discreet placard saying Donated by G. Carmichael, in memory of Colby Westcott.

Ugh.

She'd gone back and forth, speculating about Gideon's attitude toward predator species in Montana, but this was *not* a good sign.

In the museum's meeting room, Alaina took a few artistic shots, using the play of light and shadow across the journal pages and letters. They both put on the cotton document gloves Nels had left, then she rigged her tripod to keep the camera steady and centered. The letters were the easiest and she took photos of each page and the envelopes, before starting on the journals. Libby patiently turned each leaf of the leather-bound books, allowing Alaina to concentrate on her equipment.

The temptation to read the entries was overwhelming, but she resisted, knowing Gideon could return at any minute.

It was irritating. *He* was the one who'd insisted they drive in together, so she shouldn't feel the need to hurry. In any case, she was documenting an important part of his family history, something most people would be glad to have done.

Still, maybe she was assuming more about the situation than was warranted. Gideon might be okay with having an excuse not to rush back to the Double Branch.

She was so intent on her task that a knock on the outer door made her jump.

"I'll see who it is," Libby said and hurried out.

The distinctive timber of Gideon's voice rose from the other room and renewed awareness crept through Alaina. While she hadn't totally changed her mind about men or romance, he was making her think more about it. She couldn't deny missing the physical closeness in marriage, but it was the unspoken communication and shared understanding that she missed the most.

The memory of a shirtless Gideon carrying the calf intruded into Alaina's mind again and she pressed her lips together. Okay, maybe she missed the various aspects of marriage equally. But that didn't change anything. She'd already had the best and didn't expect to find it again. Accepting anything less was unthinkable.

"How is it going?" Gideon asked as he came into the room. She looked up, silently conceding that he was just as attractive in his jeans and work shirt as he'd been bare-chested.

She swallowed and pushed the thought from her mind. "I'm making good progress. Libby has been a big help."

Libby returned and they went back to work. Alaina kept reminding herself not to get too excited. Letters and journals were often about everyday activities, which might be interesting but not historically significant.

Still, she was awed by the chance to read letters from Theodore Roosevelt. They'd been written by a man responsible for preserving huge amounts of land for the future. A president, who'd met countless people as famous as himself. An adventurer, whose exploits were still the stuff of legend. How could they be dull?

She was so focused on her task she didn't immediately realize Gideon was peering over her shoulder.

"Do you need something?" she asked, inhaling sharply.

"No. But my great-grandfather loaned everything to the museum when we were kids, so I've mostly seen this stuff in display cases."

He put on a pair of document gloves and picked up one of the Roosevelt letters, staring at it intently. Alaina wondered if he felt the same excitement as she did at handling something so intimately connected with history. Maybe it was an even bigger thrill for him since the missives had been written to one of his ancestors.

Libby turned another page of the journal.

On it was a date and in large shaky script, *After all these years, I finally begin to understand Theodore.* Alaina took a picture, her curiosity rising to an even greater height.

"I wonder what he meant," Gideon mused. "What else did he write?"

"I don't know." Alaina turned the remaining pages in the book. They were all blank. "Apparently he stopped journaling after this. Is the date significant?"

"Not that I recall. But Jonah didn't live much longer, so he could have been talking about old age. Maybe it's something he and Roosevelt discussed in their letters."

That seemed possible. Theodore Roosevelt had died at a relatively young age in modern terms, but his body had paid a toll for his many adventures, particularly on his ill-fated expedition down the River of Doubt. At sixty, the former president must have felt closer to ninety.

"Hello," called a voice. It was Nels Hewitt. "I came to see if you were done."

Alaina smiled at him and began packing equipment in her bag. "I just took the last photo. Naturally, copies will go to the family, but with their permission, I can give the museum a set."

"Excellent. I'll return everything to the display. Colby Westcott paid for climate-controlled cases and it's best if the exhibits aren't out for too long. Not that any of us have had curator training, but he researched the subject before loaning us the material."

"Thank you for giving me access."

"You're welcome."

Gideon seemed reluctant to stop looking at the letters and journals, but he didn't object, taking off the gloves he'd donned and putting them with the rest.

"Come on, big brother," Libby said, pushing him toward the door. "I knew Alaina was nearly done, so I called Deke when you got here. He's meeting us for lunch."

GIDEON LIFTED AN EYEBROW. "Isn't Deke on duty today?"

Libby shrugged. "He's entitled to a lunch break and Mom always makes a ton of food. You know she'll be upset if we don't eat it all."

Gideon cast a look at his tenant as they got into the truck and saw her blue-green eyes glinting with laughter. At least someone thought the whole thing was funny.

"Alaina, how about doing our first tour on Thursday?" he asked to change the subject. "I'd suggest tomorrow, but I have a ranch association meeting in the evening."

"Thursday is fine."

"I thought we'd do the lower elevations of the ranch first. The terrain will be easier for someone who hasn't ridden in a while. We can go higher in later outings."

Her mouth opened and closed. He suspected she wanted to protest, saying she didn't need something easier, then had thought better of it.

He drove to the park on the edge of Bannister. Deke was already waiting for them.

Libby waved and hopped from the truck, rushing over to where he was sitting.

"This is nice," Alaina said as she got out.

Gideon retrieved the cooler bag before gesturing to the brass plaque on a stone monolith. "This is the Mary Westcott Park. My great-great-something uncle gave the land in honor of his fiftieth wedding anniversary. Altogether he and his wife were married for seventy-six years."

"That must be a record."

"It is for Bannister County, at least."

Alaina traced the names and then looked up. "I see the town added a second plaque after they were both gone, honoring him, as well. *Seventy-six years.* That's a whole lifetime."

Gideon recognized the shadowed regret in her eyes. "I didn't mean to make you sad."

She shook her head. "Don't apologize. It's nice to hear stories about long happy marriages. They *were* happy, right? I'd hate to think they stayed together being miserable."

He smiled faintly. "Very happy, by all accounts. And they went peacefully within hours of each other. Do you—"

"Hurry up," Libby called from over at the picnic area, interrupting him. "We're hungry and Deke has to get back on duty."

DEKE NUDGED LIBBY. "My lunch break isn't *that* short. Maybe they were talking about something important."

"Arguing is more likely. So, when are you asking me to dinner? You keep showing up at the ranch with the weakest of excuses. I'm guessing it has something to do with little ole me being there. Correct me if I'm wrong."

A choked laugh came from Deke's throat. Libby was the most straightforward person he knew. He liked her, and he liked the way she didn't hide how she felt. At the same time, he knew Gideon had doubts about his sister getting involved with a man who was so much older than her.

Truth be told, Deke had doubts about it himself.

He was at a point in his life that marriage and children sounded appealing. He'd enjoyed casual flirting and dating, but he didn't want to be an old man by the time he raised a family. Libby, on the other hand, had another year of college, a post-graduate degree to earn and a career to establish that meant a great deal to her. She probably wouldn't be ready to have kids—if she wanted them in the first place—for at least ten years. By then, he'd be in his midforties.

"Ooh, I've shocked you into silence,"

Libby said merrily. "I keep forgetting that things are more old-fashioned in Bannister than at college. Am I supposed to be demure and pretend I don't like you until you say something first?"

"I'm not shocked, I'm flattered. How about Friday at the Made Right Pizza Parlor?" he asked against his better judgment. After all, they were just getting acquainted. It was too early to start worrying about the future.

"Sounds good. I'll meet you there at six."

"All right, but I'm paying."

"Then I'll buy the beer," she said in a soft voice that her brother couldn't overhear.

Deke looked at her sharply, unsure if she was even *old* enough to buy alcohol. The question alone underscored the differences between them.

He sighed. "We'll talk about it."

CHAPTER EIGHT

ON THURSDAY GIDEON was surprised when Alaina came to the barn earlier than the time they'd agreed to and saddled Nikko herself, saying Libby had shown her which tack to use.

It was an even greater surprise when Griz trotted across the paddock to eat the carrot Alaina put on a fence post, and then nickered at her. There couldn't be two more different people than his great-grandfather and Alaina Wright, so why would Griz have responded to her in the first place?

"Do the trees still produce fruit?" Alaina asked as they rode past the ranch's orchard and old vegetable garden, fallow since his great-grandmother's day.

"There's a decent crop of apples and plums each year," Gideon said. "I keep a few crates of apples for the horses, but my mom and grandmother pick and preserve the rest. I don't do much aside from watering and maintaining the fences to discourage deer."

"You don't spray any pesticides?"

"I wouldn't dare, or my great-grandmother's ghost would rise up to haunt me. She read Rachel Carson's *Silent Spring* when it came out and told Grandpa Colby that she'd divorce him if he ever used pesticides again. He didn't argue the point."

Alaina grinned. "I understand Colby Westcott was a strong individual. Your great-grandmother must have been just as strong."

"She was, though I doubt a dispute over pesticides would have ended their marriage. Grandma Vivian found natural ways to help control pests, but I don't have time to use them. I'm afraid the trees are on their own."

"Libby said the old vegetable garden almost covered an acre. Was the ranch ever self-sustaining with so much homegrown fruit and produce?"

"Close to it. In the early years, the family mostly bought cloth, coffee, flour, sugar, salt and cornmeal. Times were simpler then."

Gideon tried to assess Alaina's posture on Nikko without being too obvious. She wasn't as relaxed as someone who rode often, but at least she didn't bounce up and down in the saddle like some of the greenhorns he'd seen. And her slim figure showed to advantage on a horse.

He was irritated with himself for noticing. It wasn't that he was oblivious to Alaina's beauty...but that was the problem. He was *too* aware of it. She was also interesting and softhearted, which made it difficult to just dismiss her from his thoughts. What had possessed him to get into a personal discussion about her childhood that day on the trail?

He could easily envision the determined little girl she'd once been, frustrated by the well-meaning constraints from her family. An impish smile must have concealed whatever secret plans she had for rebellion.

But the last thing he needed was to complicate his life, so his best bet was to simply treat Alaina like a client.

Keeping that in mind, Gideon gestured to the fields in front of them. He was a tour guide today, nothing more. "We winter most of the cattle on this part of the ranch."

"Is that why you have more fences and windbreaks here?"

He shrugged. Alaina probably didn't appreciate fences as a wildlife photographer. "Windbreaks help protect the cattle during storms, and fences are part of containing the herds for winter feeding. We also keep the bulls separate until the females are ready to breed again. Small temporary pens are used when we're branding and vaccinating calves."

"Libby mentioned you do freeze branding. That's when cold is used to freeze the hair follicles, right?"

"Yes. I think it's less stressful for them."

"Do your fellow ranchers agree?"

"Let's just say it hasn't caught on." Gideon's decision to switch to freeze branding had caused controversy at the ranch association meetings. Folks in Bannister County clung to tradition the way lichen clung to a rock. "It was one of my first decisions after becoming foreman. My great-grandfather wanted to go back to the old way, but changed his mind after watching me use the method."

"HE MUST HAVE recognized it was easier on the calves," Alaina said, intrigued by the play of emotion on Gideon's face. Now she saw a crooked smile growing.

"Calves are noisy, no matter what. We have to temporarily separate them from their mothers, so that's when the fun starts. But Grandpa Colby saw that sometimes they barely notice a freeze brand being applied. He wasn't unreasonable. He just felt at his age, he already knew the best way to get things done."

Alaina heard fond respect in Gideon's voice, rather than frustration or triumph. It was nice. He could have resented his great-grandfather for trying to keep running things and having to fight him on points where they disagreed; instead he seemed to cherish Colby Westcott's memory.

So far her stay at the Double Branch wasn't turning out the way she had expected. She'd wanted to immerse herself in the wilderness, to fill every cell and pore of her being with the mountains and its wild creatures, envisioning days or weeks when she didn't see or speak to anyone.

Instead she was taking pictures at a museum and photographing orphan calves being bottle fed. Then helping to feed them. She was watching Libby Cranston and Deke Hewitt sidestep through the first stages of either friendship or romance, unsure of what they wanted from each other, but convinced there was something. She'd spent hours learning to saddle and unsaddle a horse and how to groom it properly. And she was leaving carrots for Grizzly on every possible occasion, hoping to coax him into becoming less isolated.

Then there was Gideon. The enigma, who was making an effort to be chatty today.

In a way they were alike, each wanting to be alone, and yet forced together by circumstance. He was doing it over a misplaced concern over her safety. While for her part, she'd agreed to the tours as a chance to locate the best wildlife observation points in the shortest period of time—which was why she would have preferred to just head for the high country. The closer she got to the Yellowstone wilderness area, the better chance she'd have to see wolves.

Still, if she were going to be honest with herself, that wasn't the only reason for riding with Gideon. She had a growing curiosity about ranching…and about ranchers. Once upon a time she would have said she was immune to the "strong, silent type," but Gideon was getting to her in his own subtle way.

"How does freeze branding mark your cows?" Alaina asked, determined to think about something else.

"The hair is shaved and grows back white, which stands out, maybe even better than a traditional brand. Most of our cattle are black, but if a calf has white hair in the brand location, we leave the brand on longer, which keeps the hair from regrowing altogether. Either way, ownership is marked, so a buyer can tell if a cow has been stolen."

Alaina blinked. "Is cattle rustling still a thing?"

Gideon let out a disgusted sound. "You bet. I'd hate to tell you how much a single cow can be worth. And in today's world of ATVs and GPS units, it's almost easier to steal cattle than rob a convenience store."

"I wouldn't do either one."

He gave her a lopsided smile. "Me, either." The humor on his face faded. "I take the well-being of my herds seriously. Fortunately, most of my summer grazing land is a fair distance from any access roads. It's still possible, but for the easiest approach, a thief would have to come close to the ranch center, which puts them at greater risk of being caught."

"So you don't have as much trouble as some ranchers?"

"No losses to date, except to predators."

Alaina looked away, remembering the taxidermy exhibits Gideon had donated to the museum. Even now he was carrying two rifles in scabbards on his horse's saddle, and she was sure he was prepared to use them.

They rode in silence for a while. Her camera hung on a strap around her neck and the valley was lushly green, but she wasn't confident enough to split her attention between riding and taking pictures.

"Do you get any elk migrating out of the Yellowstone ecosystem?" she asked finally. "I know some of the northern herds cross to feeding grounds in Montana and compete with cattle for food."

"The Double Branch gets a small number. They winter up the valley from the house. We try to prevent them from eating the hay and protein cake put down for the herds, but I wouldn't be surprised if they got some of it."

It was a piece of information Gideon hadn't volunteered before and Alaina wondered what it would be like to photograph wild elk from the cabin's loft window. Living in such close proximity would be amazing.

There were herds of cattle beyond the pastures Gideon had mentioned that were used for haying and Alaina saw him assessing them as they passed. Twice he stopped, got down and tightened the wire on a fence. The second time she shot several pictures, hoping Nikko wouldn't bolt when she wasn't in full control of his reins.

It was impossible not to be fascinated by the fluid way Gideon's muscles bunched and pulled, his shirt strained taut against them.

He was strong from heavy physical labor and it showed.

"I meant to ask, did you find out what happened to Rita's mother?" she said as Gideon mounted Blackbird again, one of the horses he was using while Brushfire's leg healed.

"Jeremy located a cow that had recently given birth," Gideon explained. "From the brand, we know she belongs to a neighbor, Victor Reese, who's going to ride over and collect her. When he gets a chance, that is. Victor doesn't know how she got there, but one of his heifers went missing last autumn, so it could be her."

Alaina's stomach fell. She was glad the mother was alive, but what did that mean for Rita?

"Victor said to keep the calf," Gideon added, answering the question without being asked. "She would have died if we hadn't found her, and still could, so if we're willing to put the effort in, he thinks the Double Branch should benefit."

"That's generous."

"Yes and no," Gideon said wryly. "Victor's kids used to raise his orphaned calves, but now that they're grown and living elsewhere, he doesn't like to bother. Regardless, this isn't the first time that some of his

cows have found their way to the Double
Branch. He probably won't fetch her for several months, hoping she'll get fat on my grass
instead of his."

"That's cynical."

"It's realistic. He runs too many cattle, so
his rangeland is overgrazed. Most ranchers
aren't like that. One of these days I'm hoping he'll sell his ranch to me."

"Glad to hear it," she said.

Obviously ranching was more complicated
than she'd thought, with villainy and greed
coming into play. *And decency*, she acknowledged. However difficult Gideon might be,
he seemed honest. She also didn't think he'd
stay in the business if there were too many
unsavory apples in the barrel, so to speak.

A short time later Gideon suggested they
stop and eat the food Helene had sent. They
picnicked in the shade by a creek, with Danger splashing in the water and chasing silver flashes of fish. Alaina was tempted to
remove her borrowed boots and roll up her
jeans for a wade herself. Or even to go swimming in the deeper parts. Her muscles ached
from the morning ride, but she was determined not to show any weakness.

So after eating she took pictures of Danger
having fun, then started getting shots of the

wildflowers along the meandering waterway. A while later she made her way back to the picnic site and saw Gideon lying on his back with his hat over his face.

Well, why shouldn't he sleep?

He seemed to work eighteen hours a day, seven days a week. If she'd ever had the idea that ranching was easy, her stay at the Double Branch would have proven her wrong.

Curious, Alaina examined the cowboy hat that Gideon had insisted she wear. It looked new, making her think he'd purchased it in Bannister while she was working at the museum. After all, the town had a boot and leather shop and he was annoyed about the additional three thousand dollars she'd insisted on paying him.

The hat was made from quality cream suede leather, soft enough to be comfortable, yet not so much it would lose its shape. She couldn't imagine a down-to-earth rancher or cowhand wearing such a pale color, *or* wanting the narrow blue-green braided leather band at the base of the crown.

Feminine, without being too obvious.

Alaina wrinkled her nose and set the hat aside as she lay on her stomach to photograph water striders in the creek. The insects skittered across the surface like comic ice-skaters.

She was so intent on getting the best pictures of the agile bugs she didn't realize Danger was next to her until he stuck his wet nose into her neck.

Alaina rolled over, laughing softly. Danger's tongue was hanging from one side of his mouth and he wore an expression of silly joy. Though a working dog, he enjoyed his playtime, too.

"Good boy," she murmured. "I didn't mean to make you feel ignored. Are you anxious to get going?"

The German shepherd cocked his head to one side, but didn't utter a peep. As promised, he was obedient when given the command to be quiet.

FROM UNDER THE brim of his hat, Gideon watched Alaina talk to Danger and rub his neck.

She seemed to have a gift with animals, horses included.

He yawned and plucked a long strand of grass, automatically assessing its condition. Forage grew fast and furiously after winter. The trick was cutting it for hay when it had the greatest nutritional value, while also taking the weather into account. With clear skies predicted, three days ago he'd assigned Jeremy, Chad and Nate to begin cutting the east fields with the ranch's swathers. Soon they'd all be in a frantic push to mow, bale and store the Double Branch's hay.

Winter would return all too soon.

It had been rash to insist on doing tours for Alaina at the start of such a busy period on the ranch. Still, someone had to keep an eye on the herds, and he would only be taking her out once a week. He didn't need to plan any overnight outings until later.

Suddenly restless, Gideon sat up. "Are you done?" he called to Alaina.

"I'll never be done taking pictures, but we can continue whenever you like."

She stood and collected the hat he'd given her. Though he saw few signs she was suffering any ill-effects of their long morning ride, he thought it might be wise to cut things short. Alaina was so stubborn she probably wouldn't tell him if she was uncomfortable. Or even in acute pain.

"Do you mind if we head back?" he asked once they were both mounted. "That way I'd have time to check on how the mowing is progressing. Maybe even do some work myself."

Alaina shook her head. "It's fine. Oh, before I forget, I'm meeting with Nels on Monday. Is there a problem with giving him a copy of the photographs I took of the letters and journals?"

"I've talked to everyone in the family. We all agree it's okay. The rights to the content belong to us, my great-grandfather made sure of that."

"Colby Westcott must have been really sharp."

Gideon smiled. "He was remarkable, and not just as a rancher. He was also a real-estate whiz, investing across Montana and surrounding states. Some ranches have to get by with ancient mowers, balers and other equipment, but not Grandpa Colby. He was old-school when it came to raising cattle, but he got the best haying equipment that money could buy and built barns to store it."

"That must have left you in a better position when you inherited the ranch."

"I was fortunate."

Gideon didn't want to discuss his inheritance or how the rest of the family had shared in Colby's estate. Few people had known the true extent of his great-grandfather's financial worth. But it was only on paper that Gideon looked wealthy; it would only be true if he sold the Double Branch, something he'd never do. He had to watch his expenditures and losses the same as any other rancher. And with only one real payday each year when he sold cattle in October, he needed as much financial cushion as possible, which was why Alaina's offer to rent the foreman's cabin had sounded so attractive.

"You obviously work long hours," Alaina said after a few minutes, "but days like this must be one of the rewards. I mean…it's so beautiful and peaceful out here in the sun, I feel like a sleepy, contented cat."

"It *is* a good day," he agreed, tempted to tease and ask if she wanted her neck scratched the way his barn cats enjoyed. "So I'll try not to say anything that ruffles your fur."

She grinned. "Wow. In the beginning I didn't think you had a sense of humor, yet you keep surprising me."

"That isn't my fault. Whenever Danger steals my funny bone it takes forever to find where it's buried."

Danger yipped at hearing his name and Alaina laughed. "Oh, right, blame everything on the dog."

Gideon couldn't recall the last time he'd had this kind of fun, almost flirtatious exchange with a woman. It was his own fault—he was usually worried they'd get the wrong idea. Except that wasn't an issue with Alaina. If anything, he should be concerned about developing feelings for a woman who was devoted to the memory of her husband.

"I take it a sense of humor is important to you," he said.

"Only the way breathing is important," Alaina returned without missing a beat. "Laughter is seductive."

"A lot of things are seductive. But I admit to being out of practice in that particular area."

"Me, too. Maybe it's like riding a bike and you never forget how." She stopped and wrinkled her nose at him. "Do you have the feeling this conversation has gone out of control?"

"Yeah, but I'm blaming the sunshine. And Danger."

Danger yipped again.

Alaina leaned over and patted Nikko's neck. "It's a good thing neither one of us is driving and that the horses know the route home." She straightened. "So to blatantly change the subject, tell me why you're a rancher. Is it more than family tradition?"

Gideon shrugged. "I don't know what to

say except that I've never wanted to be anything else. My stepdad was a sheriff and I respected him, but ranching is in my blood, however trite that sounds."

"It isn't trite. I feel the same way about photography, and apparently archeology is in Libby's blood."

"Yeah. Dad used to take us out to look for artifacts and even as a kid, Libby amazed us with her patience."

The discussion stayed impersonal and since he was taking a direct route back, it wasn't too long before they reached the ranch. Alaina handed him the cowboy hat he'd given her, a challenging expression in her blue-green eyes.

"Keep it for the next time," he suggested. "Or for when you're out taking pictures."

"Libby has been trying to talk Helene into riding with her, so one of them may need it. Remember, you promised not to ruffle my fur," Alaina reminded him lightly.

Gideon let out a breath, both exasperated and amused. Did *everything* have to be a debate?

"Fine. No fur ruffling." He took the hat and tossed it into the tack room. When he came back outside, Deke had driven in and was getting out of his personal truck, wearing civilian clothes.

Deke's schedule changed regularly and he was on the midnight shift this week, giving him afternoons free. He worked hard and everyone knew it. He'd probably be elected sheriff when his father retired, continuing a long Bannister County tradition of having Hewitts in the office.

"Hey, Deke," Gideon called to his friend, "I'm going to check on the mowing. Do you want to ride along with me? We've been out riding, so Nikko is already saddled."

Curiously, his friend glanced at Alaina, who was still standing by the paddock fence with Nikko. Gideon belatedly realized he'd been headed in her direction instead of toward the ranch house.

"Sure," Deke said. "Let's go."

ALAINA WAŚ RELIEVED as she watched the two men ride away. She was even more sore now than she'd been at lunch and hadn't looked forward to Gideon being amused by her stiff gait. Nonetheless, she'd been prepared to groom Nikko the way any good horsewoman would do.

Now she didn't have to.

"Where's Deke?" Libby asked as she walked across the compound.

"Gideon invited him to ride with him to check on the mowing."

Libby scrunched her nose. "My big brother did that deliberately. He keeps hinting Deke is too old for me."

"What do *you* think?" Alaina asked carefully.

"It didn't even occur to me until Gideon started fussing," Libby said. "Mostly I was flattered Deke was interested. But I enjoy his company and he isn't *that* much older."

"Maybe your brother is concerned because you haven't finished college," Alaina suggested, trying to keep a neutral expression on her face. While she'd be a hypocrite to believe the age difference was an insurmountable issue, a lot depended on the people involved.

"Maybe, but it's my life." Libby's face brightened. "I'm going to saddle one of the horses and follow them. Want to come with me?"

Alaina restrained a groan. She wasn't sure when she'd be prepared to get on a horse again. *If ever.*

"Sorry, I need to work."

Alaina got a carrot for Grizzly and put it

on the usual fence post, then headed for the cabin and took a warm shower to soothe her tired muscles. With all the hiking she'd been doing, who would have thought that riding a horse would have so much impact?

She debated going out on foot with her camera, then decided to take her computer over to the rocking chair by the paddock.

Now would be a good time to give Griz some company.

If ALAINA HAD thought she was stiff and sore immediately after her ride with Gideon, it was nothing to how she felt the next morning.

Her thighs, her hips, her back…muscles she hadn't even known existed were protesting.

"Ohmigosh," she groaned, easing her legs over the edge of the mattress. This could have been Gideon's grand plan all along, to ensure she wouldn't wander off on any hikes on her own. It took her over twenty minutes to get dressed. Then, thinking it was unwise to walk downstairs on such wobbly legs, she sat at the top of the stairs and went down each step on her bottom.

Alaina felt triumphant when she reached the main floor. This wasn't any different from the first time she'd gone on a marathon bike ride. Of course, she'd been fourteen then, not twenty-nine. So perhaps she needed to go light on activity, exercising parts of her body that *weren't* hurting.

Surely log splitting used different muscles than riding a horse. After breakfast she went out to assess the remaining logs from the first load. Robert Pritchett had warned her to be careful with any chunks that had knots because they were harder to split. He was right. They were the only pieces she had left.

Alaina lifted the ax.

It hurt.

She tried whacking a piece of wood.

It hurt even more.

She dropped the ax and sat on the chopping block, watching as Gideon, Jeremy and Nate conferred near one of the ranch trucks. Gideon looked over at her and she waved cheerily. It looked as if he frowned, then they all got into the truck and drove out, presumably headed for the fields being mowed.

Alaina was glad he hadn't come over to ask how she was doing, or she might have used language that would scald his ears. No doubt he knew how she felt and thought the whole thing was extremely funny.

Or was she being fair?

Their ride the day before had shaken her view of Gideon. Beneath his solemn exterior she'd glimpsed a thoroughly enjoyable trace of whimsy.

After a slow walk to the other side of the valley and back, Alaina carried her computer to the paddock and sank into the weathered rocking chair. She suspected Grizzly would respond more readily if she pretended not to be interested, so she opened the laptop and began reviewing her photos from the museum. A while later soft hoof clops approached and from the corner of her eye, she saw Grizzly standing on the other side of the fence.

She held a carrot in the air without looking at him. After a moment there was a gentle tug as he accepted a treat from her hand for the first time.

Despite her aches and pains, Alaina smiled. *Success.*

CHAPTER NINE

"I WASN'T SURE what sort of images you wanted for the museum brochure, so I took a variety," Alaina explained to Nels as he looked through the photos she'd taken.

"These are amazing, better than I even imagined they could be. Our old brochure is embarrassing."

"I don't agree," she protested, examining the tri-folded copy he'd given her. It had been designed for low-cost reproduction on a photocopier, but that didn't mean it was embarrassing. "The information is interesting and the artwork is attractive," she added.

Nels beamed. "Deke's mother—my sister-in-law—did the art. She's a sculptor now. It's amazing what she creates by welding metal scraps together. The grizzly bear next to the Welcome to Bannister sign is her work."

The interconnected family relations in Bannister reminded Alaina of her hometown. Apparently the Hewitt family had been protecting Bannister County with a sheriff's badge since the early days. Nels was the rare exception, having gone into commerce rather than law enforcement.

"Tell her I love the sculpture," Alaina said.

Nels nodded. "About the brochure, as I told Helene, we'll give you photo credit. I just wish we could pay something."

"It's a fair exchange for being able to work with the letters and journals. Your museum is impressive. The, uh, natural history section is especially well-supplied." Alaina almost choked getting the words out, but it was true; it was unusual to see such a fine collection in a small museum.

"Gideon Carmichael is responsible. After Colby died, Gideon donated the Westcott family's hunting displays and animal skins. He didn't want to be thanked—says he won't keep that kind of thing in the house—but we still acknowledged his donation on the displays."

Score one for Gideon.

Alaina shut down the computer and gave Nels a portable hard drive with the files.

"Thanks," he said. "We hope to have the brochures distributed by Founders Day."

"Good luck."

Alaina shook his hand and headed for her SUV. She felt better after a few days of rest and gentle exercise. Surely it wouldn't be as bad the next time she went riding with Gideon, and eventually she wouldn't even notice a difference. It was just a question of building muscles that weren't accustomed to being used that way.

"Alaina," called a voice.

She looked up and saw Deke waving as he crossed the street. He was in uniform, so presumably he was on duty. "Hi, Deke."

"I was hoping we could talk before you returned to the ranch."

"Oh?"

He looked uneasy and Alaina hoped he wasn't going to ask her out. Not that he seemed like one of those guys who thought he could simultaneously date women who knew each other and get away with it, but you never knew.

"You may have heard that I had dinner with Libby on Friday. I tried to discuss the business about Dr. Barstow with her, but she cut me off again."

"Again?"

Deke shifted his feet. "I brought it up another time when I asked about that former boyfriend who was harassing her."

"I'm not sure how much of a problem the

ex-boyfriend still is, but why did Libby cut you off on Friday?"

"I have no idea, but Dr. Barstow shouldn't be allowed to get away with discrimination. We have female deputies in this county. They're great at the job, yet they still face resistance because they're women. It's wrong."

Alaina was charmed. Libby had told her that Deke expected to run for office when his father retired. When the time came, he'd probably make a good candidate for sheriff.

"Anyhow," Deke continued, "I hate seeing Libby lose out on something important, so I ordered a background check on Dr. Barstow. While I didn't find anything specific, something seems dodgy about the guy."

"And?" Alaina prompted.

"A while back I heard you suggest Libby file a lawsuit against him. You also mentioned that your sister-in-law is an attorney. Is there any chance you could speak to her and get an opinion on Libby's legal options? She's going through so much with her father's death and everything else, I just want to help. I'd be happy to pay for a consultation."

"Taking legal action is up to Libby," Alaina said gently. "I know you mean well, but you don't want her to think you're going behind her back."

He looked dismayed. "That isn't what I intended."

"Tell you what, I'll bring it up again with her and see how she feels."

"Thanks." The radio on Deke's belt suddenly spewed a series of beeps and code words, catching his attention. "Sorry, I've got to go." He waved his hand and returned to his vehicle. A moment later he zoomed up the street, lights flashing.

Alaina drove back to the Double Branch, thinking about Deke's request. She understood how he felt. Libby's reluctance to do anything about Dr. Barstow confused her, as well. Yet she must have her reasons.

Cut grass was drying in long windrows on both sides of the road leading to the ranch house. When leaving for town, Alaina had waved at whoever was driving the swather around the field, equipment that she'd learned both cut the hay and laid it in a row to catch the wind and dry. They'd now finished this section and moved farther away.

At the cabin she got out of her SUV and stretched. It was a gorgeous day and she decided to stock her backpack for another overnight camping trip. But before she could go inside, the door of the main house flew open and Libby dashed toward her.

"Do you want to take a ride?" she asked eagerly.

Alaina suspected Libby was bored. "Uh, I don't know if that's a good—"

"Just a short one," Libby said. "It'll help you be in better shape for the next time you go out with Gideon."

Alaina agreed and changed into her borrowed riding boots. In the barn she saddled Nikko, though when she swung her leg over his back, she hesitated a moment. Steeling herself, she settled into the saddle. While a slight ache crept through her thighs, it wasn't too bad.

Libby was already outside. "This is Firefly," she said, leaning over to pat her horse's neck. "Gideon mated her with Brushfire this spring. He doesn't do as much horse breeding as he'd like, though he has several pregnant mares right now."

From what Alaina had seen, she was amazed Gideon ever got any sleep, much less have time for side pursuits. On the other hand, could horse breeding be considered a side pursuit when the animals were so necessary to running the ranch?

They rode toward the pastures being mowed

and after a while she cleared her throat. "Libby, I ran into Deke earlier. He knows the decision is up to you, but he's concerned that you don't want to take any action against Dr. Barstow. He feels strongly about it because he sees the challenges female deputies still encounter around Bannister."

Libby sighed. "It's sweet that he cares, but I don't want anyone interfering."

"Don't you think action is justified?"

"Of course I do, but what if a lawsuit backfires? Dr. Barstow is respected and successful. If I sue him for discrimination and lose, he could blacklist me as a troublemaker with his colleagues and in academic circles. He could even do it if I win, and winning the battle doesn't count for much if you end up losing the war."

Alaina nodded. It was a valid point. Academic and professional politics were inescapable. Even on field studies through the university, which should have been pure research, Alaina had seen rivalries and disputes. Mason had done what he could to keep it under control on his team, but people were people.

A mile south of the ranch road, they found Gideon and one of the ranch hands had started baling hay. A third of the vast field was already studded with large round bales.

"They just started cutting a few days ago and the hay is already dry enough to be baled?" Alaina asked.

"The swather also crimps and crushes the grass," Libby explained. "It's called conditioning, which helps the hay dry quickly, provided the weather cooperates. Did you know I offered to run one of the swathers and my dear brother refused?"

Uh-oh.

Now Alaina knew why Libby had wanted to go out to watch the haying operations. She was already feeding the orphan calves and cleaning their pens, along with shoveling out the horse stalls in the main horse barn, but she wanted to do more. Alaina understood. Even though she was a paying tenant, she felt a tug to get involved with all the tasks that needed doing at the Double Branch, despite having her *own* work to do.

"I used to run the swather at my grandparents' ranch before I left for college," Libby grumbled.

Alaina didn't know anything about ranch equipment or how safe it was to operate, so it wasn't a subject she could discuss. The most likely reason for Gideon's refusal was his protective instincts, but the terrain might be hillier and rockier on the Double Branch, making it harder to operate heavy machinery.

She rolled her eyes, annoyed with herself. Did she *really* need to come up with possible justifications for his behavior? It would be easier to keep her guard up if she didn't see his side of things.

"I also know how to run the balers," Libby continued. "Gideon has more equipment than he and his men can operate at one time. But will he let me help? *No.* On a ranch, everyone has to join in. That's standard. Why can't he get it? Sure, I'm doing some things around here, but I could be doing more."

On a ranch, everyone has to join in.

Alaina tucked that bit of information away for future reference. She wasn't sure how it might be helpful, but you never knew, particularly when dealing with a guy like Gideon.

WHEN GIDEON SAW his sister and Alaina appear on the edge of the field, he stopped the baler and got out of the cab. Ever since losing his stepfather, a concern kept lurking about the rest of the family. It was to be expected; he'd gotten the worst call of his life when Flynn had phoned about Stewart. So while it was unlikely that Libby would ride out with Alaina to give him bad news, Gideon felt an instinctive thump of worry at seeing them.

"I'll take over, boss," Nate said, hustling up to him from where he'd been working on the irrigation ditch. After the hay bales were moved, they expected to start watering again. A second mowing was possible if the weather cooperated.

"Thanks, I'm just going to touch base with Libby."

"Gotcha." Nate swung into the driver's seat and continued down the windrow of dry grass. Nobody wasted time during haying season; you never knew when the weather might change or something else could happen.

Gideon wiped the dirt and sweat from his face as he strode toward the horses, automatically evaluating Alaina's posture on Nikko. He was glad she seemed less stiff and sore.

He'd experienced the same deep muscle pain after being sidelined by a broken collarbone. After finally getting back on a horse, his body had felt as if the entire football team and their opponents had tackled him together. The original injuries had given him discomfort, but nothing like the rest. Yet Alaina kept pretending she wasn't going through the same adjustment.

Under other circumstances, he might have suggested a massage with liniment, but it was the sort of thing that could get him into deep, *deep* trouble.

"Libby, what's up?" he asked when he was within earshot.

"If something was up, I would have called."

"I can't hear my cell ring while running the baler," he said, annoyed. "Even inside the cab. You know that."

His sister gave him an innocent look. "How would I know? You think li'l ole me is incapable of running a baler, so I must be ignorant of how much noise and vibration they make."

"I didn't say you were incapable."

"You didn't have to."

Gideon couldn't stop himself from glancing at Alaina, but whatever she thought about the situation was well hidden.

"I want you to have this summer to enjoy yourself," he said finally. "Is that a crime?"

"Running big powerful equipment is fun. And besides, you need help. If I pitch in with mowing or baling, you'll get the haying done that much faster. Hopefully before we get any rain."

It was a valid point and Libby was qualified to operate both the swather and baler. Grandpa Joe wouldn't have allowed her to run either at the Carmichael ranch in Shelton without proper training.

Gideon nodded.

"All right, you can help. But if you hit something, do *not* start the equipment back up again until one of us has thoroughly checked it. I'm talking about me or one of the ranch hands inspecting it. We know this equipment inside and out and you don't."

Libby made a face. "I know what I'm doing."

"My ranch, my rules. I also want to watch you run the baler for a while, to make sure you haven't forgotten anything."

Libby promptly dismounted and handed him Firefly's reins. "Fine. I'll let Nate know I'm taking over."

"I didn't mean today," Gideon exclaimed, but she was already dashing across the field, waving her arms at Nate.

Alaina dismounted, too. "This could take a while."

"You don't have to wait for her. It's okay if you ride Nikko home." Gideon noted the camera hanging from around her neck. "Unless you're planning to take pictures."

"I'm considering a pictorial series called The Last Stand of Overly Protective Brothers."

He narrowed his eyes. "I'm not overly protective. I'm just the right amount of protective. Besides, after what happened to Libby's internship and with her boyfriend, I simply wanted her to have a relaxing break from school. What's wrong with that?"

"Nothing, but she expected to be working on an archeological dig and needs something to do. Or are you *trying* to give her more time to get acquainted with Deke Hewitt?"

Gideon glared. "That's none of your business."

"It isn't yours, either. Libby is an adult, in case you haven't noticed," Alaina retorted. "But there's something that confuses me. You're surrounded by examples of wonderful marriages in your family, yet you're opposed to it for yourself."

"You don't want to get married again, either."

"But not because I don't believe in marriage. I just can't imagine finding anyone else I'd love as much as Mason."

"You sound pretty sure of that."

Alaina's face softened. "He was a pretty special guy. I couldn't marry somebody without being completely and utterly in love with them. As for Libby, she's the only one who can decide if Deke is right for her."

"I'm also concerned about Deke," Gideon asserted. "Libby has plans for her life that don't include living in Bannister. He could get hurt, too. Maybe worse than my sister."

"That may be true. Love isn't easy."

Gideon had long held the opinion that love was impossible, at least for him. It wasn't just Celeste; his romantic track record stunk. There were nice women in his hometown, but he hadn't been interested in them, or them in him, which was how he'd ended up with Celeste.

Now he was being tempted by a woman whose heart was buried with her husband. *Not* a good idea—so he couldn't let it go beyond recognizing her appeal. It was best for a man to understand his weak points and move on. Since his judgment stunk when it came to the opposite sex, he was going to stick with something he understood, cattle ranching.

As long as he kept telling himself that, he'd be all right.

Alaina was looking around and he realized she was trying to find a place to tether Nikko.

"I'll tie him to the truck," Gideon said, taking the reins and securing both horses.

To save time, he and his men were driving to the fields. In the spare minutes between swathing and baling, they'd move the bales closer to where he wintered his herds.

His sister climbed into the cab of the baler and he watched it move forward again. She drove in a straight line, picking up the dry grass. At the end of the field, she correctly judged her turn and neatly started on the next windrow. Soon a bale was discharged out the back.

"I've been thinking about something," Alaina murmured.

Gideon nodded, his attention still focused on the baler's progress. "Yeah?"

"We should delay our next tour until the end of the Double Branch's haying season."

He looked at her sharply. "The contract addendum *you* insisted we sign—"

"Doesn't specify a time frame," Alaina interrupted. "You urged me to learn more about ranching, and one of the things I've learned is that you have a tight window to cut and bale your hay. It isn't reasonable to take time away when you're so busy."

It was almost as if she'd read his thoughts when they'd stopped for lunch the other day.

"I'll hire someone to cover for me when I'm gone," Gideon said, determined to do the tours as planned. "Nate can oversee everything when I'm not here."

"Then you won't come out ahead," Alaina objected.

"I didn't want to be paid in the first place," he reminded her. "But since you insisted I cash your check, it's my choice what to do with the money."

She crossed her arms over her stomach and glared. "Your ranch, your rules? You're still trying to keep me from hiking alone."

"I already know that's impossible," Gideon said wryly. "But showing you around remains a good idea. Once you've seen enough and decide on the right locations, we can begin delivering the supply caches you talked about."

"Fine. Whatever. I made the offer, so it's on your head."

Gideon restrained a smile at the frustration on Alaina's face. The smallest concession from her was a major victory.

LIBBY WONDERED WHAT her brother and Alaina were talking about so intently. At least Gideon wasn't still watching her drive the baler the way a hawk would watch a rabbit.

She wanted to be an archeologist, but that didn't mean she disliked ranching and the work that went with it. Haying was satisfying, and modern haying was a whole lot easier than when her ancestors had used horse-drawn sickles and rakes.

Maybe Deke and Alaina were right and she should file a lawsuit against Dr. Barstow. But he was famous and had more resources to fight a case than she had to win one.

Libby shook her head to clear it and turned the baler down another windrow.

Deke had suggested they have dinner again. She'd put him off, but maybe she should call him this evening and see when and where he'd like to meet. She was ashamed of quibbling about it. He was far more interesting than the guys she'd met in Bozeman, but it had shaken her when she learned that he'd gotten shot at a routine traffic stop and was still recovering.

Libby shivered, though it was warm in the baler's cab.

Losing her father had been the most awful thing she could imagine happening. It would be even worse to fall in love and expect to live your entire life with that person, only to have it tragically cut short.

Would her father want his daughter involved with someone in law enforcement like himself? Dad had often said that it took the right kind of person to deal with the risks one's spouse faced in the line of duty. Then he'd smile at Mom and everything felt right.

Now he was gone, the world was upside down and Libby wasn't quite sure if it would ever be right again.

CHAPTER TEN

AS THEY RODE out on Thursday, Alaina was thrilled when Gideon turned to go up the valley rather than heading for the lower level of the ranch again.

"Have you ever traced the elk migration route out of Yellowstone? I mean for the herd that winters on the Double Branch," she said, trying to sound casual rather than elated.

"Several times. As I told you, I know these mountains inside and out."

Alaina nodded.

They soon rode beyond the area she'd already explored on foot and she kept an eager watch on the ground and terrain around them.

"What are you going to do once your year on the Double Branch is up?" Gideon asked, breaking into her concentration.

"Eventually I'll probably buy a house in Montana or Wyoming. My husband and I kept a small apartment near the university where he was tenured as a researcher, but we were rarely there. To be honest, it never felt like home. More like a storage area for equipment."

"Was that your choice or his?"

"I married him knowing how we'd live, so it's fair to say we both chose it," she said evenly.

Alaina had gotten used to going from one field study to another with Mason, spending short intervals at the college for compilation of data. But being used to something wasn't necessarily the same as liking it. In the past she'd always pushed the thought away, thinking it seemed disloyal.

But it *wasn't* disloyal. It was simply a fact. Mason had known how she felt and they'd talked about a time when they wouldn't do as much field research.

"I enjoy having the cabin to come back to between my hikes," she added. "And someday I want to have a garden, even if I have to pay someone to tend it when I'm gone."

"You're welcome to plant a garden on the Double Branch."

"I'll keep that in mind." Alaina would enjoy taking Gideon up on the offer, but each week that passed was a reminder that she had less than a year left on the ranch. It was well into summer now, and fall would arrive all too quickly.

Silence fell until Gideon cleared his throat. "What other wildlife do you want to photograph? I don't mean just on the ranch, but what else are you hoping to see and do?"

She glanced at him and thought she saw genuine interest in his face. "The American West is my first love, but it would be wonderful to photograph Amur leopards and giant pandas in China, or the big cats and other wildlife in Africa. Then there's the possibility of underwater photography. And how about Antarctica and getting pictures of emperor penguins? That would be incredible."

GIDEON'S HANDS TIGHTENED on Brushfire's reins as Alaina's ideas continued to bubble out like champagne from a bottle suddenly uncorked. Clearly she'd sacrificed many of her dreams to take part in her husband's career, but now she was letting those dreams take flight.

"It sounds as if you have more ideas than time," he said finally, oddly dispirited. He'd rarely left Montana, but she wanted to explore the entire planet with her camera.

Yet he wasn't in love with Alaina, so her plans for the future shouldn't affect him. In fact he should be ashamed of trying to put roadblocks in her path, despite doing it out of a concern for her safety. She was amazing.

"True. And it may be wiser to become known for photographing animals in a specific ecosystem. I haven't decided that part yet."

"But wolves and bears are your first love."

Alaina nodded. "And in case you're wondering, I've loved them since I was a kid, along with the other animals in this area. Buffalo fascinate me almost as much as wolves. They're like ancient petroglyphs come to life."

"Bison are amazing creatures," Gideon agreed.

"So, what are your goals for the future?" Alaina asked lightly.

"Nothing too dramatic. I want to take care of the Double Branch and my family."

He gazed at the land rising beyond them, knowing he hadn't really answered her question. Alaina had enough goals and dreams for ten lifetimes, while he had a basic no-detour game plan.

"I've considered going organic, the way a cousin has done back in Shelton," he added, albeit lamely.

"Organic is good. And you shouldn't have

trouble getting certified if the ranch hasn't used pesticides since the 1960s."

"The drawback is that certification is a long, complicated process."

"It could still be worth doing." Alaina gave him a searching look. "Would Colby Westcott have viewed organic ranching as newfangled nonsense or as a profitable investment?"

"My great-grandmother would have approved, which is all that would have mattered to him."

"That's sweet."

"I'm not sure anyone ever called Grandpa Colby sweet, but I guess it is."

ALAINA LOOKED AWAY from Gideon's intense expression, reminding herself that she was supposed to be checking for signs of wolves or other animals.

She didn't know why she'd said so much about her hopes for the future. Maybe it was because he'd asked instead of making assumptions.

He was a good guide, stopping periodically to point out various landmarks, giving her time to enter the GPS coordinates on her map and make other notes. But when they rode up a side valley with a wide shallow river, she could barely contain her excitement. On the far bank she saw a broad scattering of bones. She reined in Nikko and lifted her camera to zoom in on the scene.

The open space was backed by brush and had a high concentration of tracks. Wolf tracks, most likely. A fair amount of scat was present, as well. She took one photo burst after another.

Alaina spared a quick glance at Gideon. He'd stopped, too, but was looking up the valley, so she swiftly entered the GPS coordinates in her notebook before shooting pictures of the surrounding area.

"I don't eat this well when I'm backpacking," Alaina said later when they were enjoying the lunch Helene had sent.

Gideon grinned wryly. "If my mom wasn't staying at the Double Branch, I would *never* eat this well. She tried to teach us kids how to cook, without much success. I love having her here, I just wish Dad…"

He looked so sad that Alaina put her hand on his arm. "I know it sounds like a cliché, but he'd want you to be happy."

"Not a cliché." Gideon touched an errant lock of hair curling over her shoulder. "This looks like liquid sunshine," he muttered.

Alaina pulled back, her pulse jumping.

"Cutting my hair short would be more practical, but I guess I'm not that practical."

"Practical isn't always best. So, what sort of things have you been writing down?" he asked in a more normal tone.

"Just GPS coordinates and stuff." She took out the notebook and showed it to him.

Gideon leafed through a few pages. "I can read the numbers, but the rest is like a picture language."

"It's my own version of shorthand. I have symbols for certain animals and landmarks, borrowed from maps or just invented." She pointed to an inverted *v* with squiggles across the middle. "That's a mountain with snow on the peak."

"And this must be a bear," he guessed, gesturing to another symbol.

"Yup."

Alaina was relieved when Gideon returned the notebook without further comment. She hadn't expected him to understand her annotations and didn't want him to speculate about the *PWRS* she'd scribbled next to a set of GPS coordinates. *Possible Wolf Rendezvous Site.*

If it was what she thought, it would be the first site she'd found entirely on her own and she wanted to keep it to herself for several reasons.

"You seem happy," Gideon said as they approached the ranch late in the afternoon.

"Oh?" Alaina tried to make her expression more neutral. "It was a good day. I hate to admit it, but you can see a lot on horseback, even if it isn't ideal for photography."

Gideon's eyebrows went up. "When you first arrived, I would have sworn you didn't even *like* horses."

"That isn't true. I even considered arranging for one to ride this year, then decided against it."

"You didn't have a problem getting pictures when Danger was with you, right?"

The German shepherd had darted ahead of them, but when he heard his name, he looked back and yipped.

Alaina smiled. "No, he's great."

"A good cattle dog is worth its weight in gold," Gideon said seriously. "I'm partial to German shepherds and border collies, but there are other breeds that do just as well with herds."

"Your ranch hands have a nice pack of Australian shepherds between them."

Gideon nodded. "Jeremy and Chad Singleton already had cattle dogs when I gave them jobs. Then Nate and the others decided to adopt their own. The animals are pets, but they also work, so I pay for food and veterinary needs."

"That's nice."

"It just makes sense. But that reminds me of a favor I wanted to ask."

"What sort of favor?" Alaina said cautiously, though she was amused by the way Gideon had dismissed her compliment. It *was* nice of him to cover expenses for the other dogs. And generous.

"It has to do with Danger," he replied. "My grandmother raises and trains border collies and she's giving me a couple. She and Grandpa Joe are bringing them to the Double Branch once the haying is done on their own ranch. The thing is, I don't want Danger to feel displaced while I'm getting to know the new dogs."

Alaina was still trying to sort out his family relations, but she knew that Helene's mother, Colby Westcott's daughter, had married a rancher in Shelton County. Grandpa Joe must be that rancher.

She cleared her throat. "What do you want me to do?"

"Will you take Danger on your hikes? That's why I asked if he'd been a problem the first time. It would help smooth the transition if he's already in the habit of going with you. And it would also keep him occupied while I'm busy with haying operations."

Alaina sent Gideon a long sideways glance. She was certain that he remained ambivalent about her hiking alone and would prefer her to have his dog along for protection. She was also certain he was concerned about the way Danger would react to the new border collies. The German shepherd was fine with Libby's dog and those belonging to the ranch hands, but he was accustomed to being Gideon's sole canine companion.

"All right, he can come with me," she said. Danger was a nice animal and no problem in the least. He'd also been a reassuring presence on her first overnight outing. "But I'll need his backpack and something to feed him."

"I'll bring it over later."

Gideon looked so pleased with himself that Alaina was annoyed. He should have the grace to be less smug about her going along with his ploy, especially since they both knew it wasn't entirely a case of her doing him a favor.

When they reached the barn, Alaina unsaddled Nikko and groomed him over Gideon's protests. The part she was the most uncertain about doing, lifting the gelding's feet to clean his hooves, went surprisingly well. He was an accommodating animal and she was grateful he didn't embarrass her by being difficult.

Gideon, who'd ridden Brushfire for the first time since the stallion was injured, wasn't as fortunate. It was plain the horse didn't appreciate *his* feet being touched, even by his beloved owner. She tried to keep a straight face as Brushfire snorted and half reared.

"Feeling your oats, huh? Stop being a knot-head and behave," Gideon scolded, though he didn't sound angry, more just keeping up a running chat to soothe the stallion. "Getting back at me for feeling neglected, right? Well, it won't work and you might as well cooperate."

Brushfire snorted again, stomped his fore-leg, then finally accepted the inevitable and stood quietly.

GIDEON KNEW HIS focus wasn't 100 percent and Brushfire sensed it. He was a fine stallion, though he could be rebellious on occasion.

He put Brushfire in the large paddock, then patted Danger, who seemed more energetic after a day on the open range than before they'd left.

Alaina might question his motives, but he was sincere about Danger needing a transition period. His cowhands wouldn't necessarily own cattle dogs in the future and it was only smart to have more that belonged to the ranch. Grandma Claire knew that better than anyone, and had taken matters into her own hands by training two for him.

Gideon was mostly concerned about taking the heart out of Danger. He wasn't old, but he also wasn't a pup any longer and might not adjust well.

Alaina had gone to her cabin, so Gideon retrieved Danger's backpack with its usual supplies and a large sack of dog food. He may as well bring it to her now.

"Oh, and there's news about Dr. Barstow," Janet said. She'd called to ask how the second tour with Gideon had gone and had already heard about Alaina's hopes that she'd spotted a wolf rendezvous site.

Excited and unable to sit still, Alaina looked out the front cabin window. "Oops, hold that thought. Gideon is headed this way. I'll call you back."

"Leave me on so I can hear the hunk's

voice. The pictures you sent of him were delicious. I'm anxious to find out if he sounds as good as he looks."

Alaina laughed. She didn't disconnect the call. Instead she slipped the phone into her shirt pocket. "Hi, Gideon," she said, opening the door.

He handed her Danger's backpack before swinging a sack of dog food off his shoulder and depositing it on the porch. "As promised. I appreciate you being willing to look after Danger. Do you want me to put his food in the pantry?"

"Thanks, but I can manage."

"Then I'll see you later. Let me know when you need another bag."

Alaina nodded, waiting until Gideon had turned around before dragging the sack into the cabin. She took the phone from her pocket after closing the door again.

"Still there, Janet?"

"You bet. I could sip my martini and listen to that deep voice all evening. Not that he said much."

"Gideon can be a man of few words. Now, what were you saying about Dr. Barstow?"

"Ah, yes. It bothered me, so I made inquiries. News is about to break that will seriously tarnish his reputation. So tell Ms.

Cranston that if she has friends on Barstow's current archeology team, they should get out right away. These things snowball and they won't want their names associated with him. Everything he's touched will likely come under suspicion."

Alaina winced. Janet had a passion for justice, which was great, but Libby was concerned about possible backlash.

"Uh, Janet—"

"Not to worry," her sister-in-law interrupted. "None of this will be connected to Libby Cranston. I can't even take credit, as much as I'd like to. A museum in Los Angeles recently purchased a gold Incan figurine that Barstow claimed he found in a wrecked Spanish galleon. The piece is genuine, but he wasn't the one who found it. Turns out, the figurine is actually from a private collection his grandfather bought at auction over sixty years ago."

"Wow. The museum must be unhappy."

"That's an understatement. The curator is trying to track the provenance prior to the auction, but it's murky after so much time. Before doing a press release, they're quietly warning other museums who've dealt with Barstow."

Alaina whistled. "How did he expect to get away with something like that?"

"He must have been doing it for years, but got careless or desperate. The real money is in his book sales, which meant he had to keep making fabulous finds to maintain the dashing archeologist Indiana Jones image. But nobody is that good or lucky. He was bound to be caught at some point."

"It was nice of you to check into him."

"You know how much I hate charlatans and cheats."

They chatted another few minutes before saying goodbye.

Alaina debated what to do, then sent Libby a text, asking her to come over for a visit after dinner.

If Dr. Barstow had kept Libby on the team, she would have been in New Mexico when the news broke. Student interns probably wouldn't be found guilty by association, but there were no guarantees. Libby might have seen her career end before it began.

So this was one thing that was coming out very right.

THREE AND A half weeks later, Alaina lay flat on her stomach in the rocky outcropping she'd found to watch the wolves. Her observation post overlooked a shallow river valley and provided enough seclusion for camping.

She rarely saw the wolves or their puppies during the midday hours since they had multiple rendezvous sites around the area. But mornings and evenings they sometimes came down to the water to relax and howl. They often showed up when the mountain breezes were strongest and it seemed to be a favorite time to howl, so she'd named the pack the Wind Singers.

Alaina looked over at Danger, who was lying on his stomach, head up, quietly alert. At first she'd wondered if he would become unruly at seeing or hearing his wild cousins, but while his eyes widened and his body tensed, he didn't move a muscle.

She peered again over the small ridge that helped keep the wolves from seeing her. Her location was ideal. The breezes were strongest off the slopes across the small valley, so her scent was carried away from them. And a quarter mile behind her, there was a bubbling spring where she could get water.

Danger moved slightly, catching Alaina's attention. He'd turned his head and the energy in his body had changed from watchful to eager. She followed the direction of his gaze and wrinkled her nose.

It was Gideon. Though still some distance away, she could tell he was riding Brushfire. *Drat*.

The Wind Singer pack wouldn't venture back into the open for days if he rode up the valley. What was he doing here, anyhow? The major push on haying was over, but the nearest herd was over a mile away.

Alaina did a quick visual check of the campsite, hoping Gideon wouldn't see *her* since she was above him in elevation. Aside from a solar unit recharging one of her camera batteries, everything was tucked out of sight in a rock crevice.

She flattened herself to the ground as much as possible. Following her lead, Danger did the same, though his ears were tipped forward and his gaze remained fixed on the horse and rider. This was their third consecutive day away from the ranch center, so he had to be missing Gideon.

Below the mouth of the spring, Gideon stopped and dismounted, tying Brushfire's reins to a tree limb. Then he climbed directly toward their location.

Alaina's mouth tightened. He was too darned observant.

"Surprised to see me?" he asked as he crouched to greet Danger, who was so excited he couldn't stop his tail from whipping back and forth.

Alaina shrugged. "This is your ranch."

Gideon sat next to her, staying low, and gestured to the camera and long attached lens she'd left in position. "See any wolves?"

"An otter family was splashing in the river earlier."

"That isn't what I asked. But to reassure you, I already know this area is the eastern edge of a wolf pack's territory. And for the record, the most I've done is fire my rifle to scare them away from a herd."

Alaina glared. "You could have told me about them when I first asked about wolves. I might have gotten pictures of the pups when they were even younger."

"Wasn't it more fun to discover them on your own?"

"That isn't why you didn't tell me."

"True. But I showed you this valley on our second tour, so I wasn't misdirecting you, either. I'm impressed. You even found the best place to observe the pack. I've been up here a couple times myself, though not this year."

"Lucky me." Alaina lay on her stomach again to watch the valley below.

Gideon followed suit, his warmth burning against her arm. It was infuriating to be so aware of him. She tried to clear her mind and stay focused on the area across the river where the pack usually appeared.

There were just five wolves in the group, not counting the pups. The alpha male was mostly black, while his mate's coat was the more typical tawny, with banded black, gold and white. One of the subordinates was white with black guard hairs, and the other two shared the female alpha's coloring.

Their intensity and beauty took her breath away.

From the corner of Alaina's eye, she saw Gideon using a pair of binoculars. He'd probably get bored before long. The pack didn't show up that often. A rancher was too busy to just sit and watch a river flow.

A silent hour passed and she sighed. Gideon was a distraction she didn't need. "Shouldn't you get back to the ranch before dark?"

"I have plenty of time. Besides, there's a full moon tonight and horses have excellent night vision."

"Hmm."

Another twenty minutes went by as the sun sank lower and there was a subtle shifting of day into summer evening. It was a time when golden light infused everything with a hint of magic…or at least it was magical to her.

Then it happened.

One by one, four wolves appeared from the underbrush. They were alert, noses high as they sniffed the eddies of air. After an endless moment the alpha nuzzled his mate as if signaling that all was well. Two of the subordinate members of the pack began playing, rolling on the ground in a mock battle. Alaina figured the third subordinate was still with the juveniles.

Her camera whirred as she took one burst of photos after another.

The fifth pack member now appeared with the puppies. There were four, around three months old and typically playful, stalking and pouncing on each other. They still had the awkward, charming look of babies, with feet and heads too big for their bodies and eyes only just turning from baby blue to an adult wolf's golden hue.

The play ended when the alpha male lifted his nose and let out a howl. The others followed suit, even the youngsters, and a chorus filled the valley, singing to music only they could hear.

GIDEON HAD NEVER heard the entire pack howling before; he'd mostly caught glimpses of the pack when he had a chance to come up this far. Now he held his breath, willing the haunting cries to continue.

When they finally faded, he saw Alaina was looking at him. "Incredible," he whispered. "No wonder you want to capture their wildness with your camera."

Her extraordinary eyes softened. "Their essence anyway. I call them the Wind Singer pack because they seem to howl the most when the breeze is blowing."

Wind Singer.

He wasn't a poetic sort of guy, yet it seemed a fitting name for a wolf pack.

They were so close together their breaths mingled. Gideon eased even closer. She didn't protest and he pressed his lips to hers, slowly deepening the kiss. He wasn't sure how long it lasted, but suddenly another long howl echoed through the air, rising and falling, piercing his awareness.

He jerked backward, disappointed with himself.

"I'd better go," he muttered.

Gideon descended to where Brushfire was tethered, unable to escape knowing he'd made a mistake, if for no other reason than he didn't want Alaina to think he'd changed his mind about a relationship. Yet at the same time, he *was* thinking about the possibilities, at least a little.

"Gideon, wait." Alaina's soft voice stopped him before he could mount Brushfire.

She put a hand on his arm, rose on her toes and kissed the side of his mouth, except it landed mostly on his lips and made him want more.

"There," Alaina said. "That gives you a better reason to be upset with me."

"I wasn't upset with you." He released a heavy breath. "I'm angry at myself. All right?"

"But nothing happened. Not really. Anyway, we're adults. It's silly to pretend we don't have normal feelings. Up there…it was magical. Golden light on the mountains, listening to wolves, the scent of evergreens and wildflowers. I wanted something, too."

"You want what you can't have, your old life back. That's what you're doing in Montana, isn't it? Recreating what you and your husband were doing together."

"Is that what you think?" Alaina asked, sounding incredulous. "Being a wildlife photographer is *nothing* like doing field research with a group of scientists more intent on a wolf pack's biometrics and behavioral characteristics than their beauty. My husband and I were lucky to get five minutes alone during the day, and I was usually asleep before he came to bed."

"But you're still studying wolves."

"I'm not studying them. I'm photographing wildlife, which includes wolves. What I learned from scientific fieldwork helps me find my subjects a little easier, that's all. The life I'm living now is what I dreamed of before I met Mason."

Gideon wasn't completely convinced, and it wasn't his business in the first place. The idea had mostly occurred to him because lately his mother was on a determined search for old Westcott family keepsakes, not just recipes. He didn't know if she was trying to remind herself of happier times or if something else was going on.

"Alaina, you're good with people, yet your childhood dream is to work in isolation from other human beings. I don't get it. The loner life fits me, not you."

She grinned. "You aren't a loner, either, though I'm sure that's what you want to believe. I've seen how much you enjoy spending time with Helene and Libby. You're friends with Deke. You attend ranch association meetings, and I've watched you chat with your employees for much longer than it takes to give them instructions for the day. That isn't being a loner."

"Are you trying to say we're alike?"

"More than you think. We enjoy people, but we also treasure our solitude. Besides, I'm not living in total isolation. I stay in touch with my family."

He reached down to rub behind Danger's ears. The German shepherd had followed Alaina from the observation post and kept sending worried looks back and forth between them. "It's okay, pal," Gideon murmured.

"Do you want to take him with you?" Alaina asked.

"*No.* Are we still going on another tour this week?"

"I'm looking forward to it. I'll be back at the cabin tomorrow."

"Thursday morning, then. Or I could meet you with the horses up here, if you'd prefer staying."

She smiled faintly. "That's all right. I'm hungry for fresh fruits and vegetables. I don't carry a lot of them when I'm backpacking."

"I suppose not." Gideon stroked Danger again before getting into the saddle and turning Brushfire toward the main ranch. When he looked back, Alaina was climbing back to her observation post, Danger at her heels.

She seemed to be thriving. And she kept a spotless campsite. He hadn't spotted a scrap of trash or food residue that might draw animals to her location. It had been reassuring to see.

His brain turned inevitably to the moment he'd kissed her...and to when she'd kissed him.

Maybe the magic of the moment was as good an explanation as any. Yet he knew it was more than that. He'd *wanted* to kiss her, no matter how much his good sense told him it was a bad idea. Alaina's motivation had probably been relief, since she must be thrilled that he wasn't bothered about the wolf pack. She'd tried to keep him from finding out about them, but he knew what was happening on his property.

Colby Westcott would be appalled at his great-grandson's tolerance toward predators, but maybe Colby had never heard wolves howl as a pack. Even the puppies had howled, noses up, crying right along with the adults, though one had stopped to scratch behind its ear, only to tumble backward. Just like any other puppy. Alaina's soft exclamation of delight had grabbed Gideon in the gut and refused to let go. His hands tightened on the reins.

He needed to get his head straight about her. It wasn't a good idea to think so much about a woman who was leaving in less than a year.

ALAINA GAZED DOWN at the river without really seeing it. The wolves had disappeared into the brush as if they'd never been there, leaving her with nothing to do except think about Gideon's kiss.

She touched the tip of her tongue to her lips. They were still tingling. From one perspective it was just a kiss. Well, *two* kisses, including the one she'd initiated. The trained biologist in her argued that kissing was merely an instinctive behavior, but it was also a pretty nice way of exploring whether something special was possible.

Gideon was radically different from Mason. The age disparity was just a small part of it; her husband had been a scientist first, while Gideon responded more from instinct.

The truth was, Mason wouldn't have kissed her at that particular moment. He would have been too busy writing down his observations. Later in the evening they might have found a moment for romance, but there was something to be said for spontaneity.

CHAPTER ELEVEN

"Please come with us," Helene urged a few weeks later in August. "Founders Day is so much fun. There's a parade and they have traditional games for both kids and adults. Also a barbecue lunch."

"But this is a family outing," Alaina protested. Gideon's grandparents, Claire and Joe Carmichael, had arrived late the previous day with the two border collies for Gideon, also hauling a horse trailer with Libby's horse, Ladybug. They'd timed their visit to coincide with the annual Founders Day celebration, something they rarely missed, according to Libby.

"You're part of the family," Helene declared. "Besides, Libby's college friends arrived late last night and they're going, too. They think you're marvelous for finding out about Dr. Barstow's shady dealings."

"I can't take credit. That was my sister-in-law," Alaina reminded her hastily.

"They're grateful to both of you. Please

come," Helene said again. "It wouldn't be the same if you don't. I can't bear to think of you alone, with the rest of us having fun. I wouldn't enjoy myself at all."

"Are you trying to make me feel guilty?" Alaina teased.

A dimple appeared in Helene's cheek. "Is it working?"

Alaina thought about how quickly the days were passing. She'd taken thousands of photographs, but each hour that she wasn't out there working meant she wasn't getting more. Animals didn't show up on cue, posing when you needed them, so a wildlife photographer could go days or weeks without getting a single great picture. And it seemed unlikely that Gideon would lease the cabin to her for a second year, especially considering his mixed feelings about her being there in the first place.

Still, the picnic sounded fun.

"All right, I'll go," she capitulated, despite her reservations. Those reservations weren't just about her work; she had concerns about spending any time with Gideon that wasn't completely necessary.

"That's wonderful. We're leaving at nine, which should get us there ahead of the parade. Come over and we'll sort out who goes in which vehicle. We bring as few cars as possible to take pressure off the parking areas."

A half hour later Alaina wasn't surprised when she ended up in Joe and Claire Carmichael's SUV rather than with Gideon. The tours were going well, but since the day they'd kissed, he'd erected an impersonal wall between them. The only exception was when he'd convinced her to give him access to the GPS tracker on her satellite phone, arguing that it wasn't any different from what he asked of anyone on the ranch. So she'd argued back that he should do the same and let her track him. Though he'd rolled his eyes, she could now check his location, as well. Not that she had bothered.

Perhaps it was easier this way, though she wouldn't have minded asking if the people around Bannister had a history of road rage—a week ago she'd encountered an aggressive driver, leaning on his horn and passing at a high speed, swerving so much she had nearly gone off the road to avoid being hit. She'd tried to get the vehicle's license number, but the plate was too splattered with mud. She didn't want to be paranoid, but it was hard not to wonder if alcohol was involved.

Alaina dismissed the troubling memory as Gideon's grandfather parked in town and they got out; it was too nice of a day to dwell on something unpleasant.

The group rendezvoused at a spot near the grandstand and soon brightly colored floats began passing by. Each of the marching bands did a routine for the judges, with the loudest applause coming for the local high school band, the Bannister Bulls. But the judges were impartial; a band from a neighboring county won the trophy.

"I used to be a drum majorette for the Bannister Bulls," Claire Carmichael told Alaina as they walked toward the park. "Whenever I see a band in a parade, it takes me right back to high school. I'd love to be that age again and know what I know now."

"But maybe if we knew how things were going to turn out ahead of time, we might never take a chance," Alaina murmured. "And how else would we grow?"

Claire nodded thoughtfully. She was a bright-eyed, vivacious woman who seemed younger than her seventy-odd years. "True. I hope my grandson is treating you well."

"Gideon has been very helpful," Alaina said. "I hope you don't mind me living in your family's original cabin."

"Not at all. I'm glad it's occupied. And I'm pleased my grandson is behaving himself," Claire said. "Since his divorce, he can be prickly around young women. I think he's trying to avoid falling in love again."

Gideon looked at them over his shoulder. "I heard that."

"I intended for you to hear me. You haven't said one word to Alaina the entire time we've been here. Where are your manners? Anyone would think you were raised by a pack of wolves."

GIDEON LOCKED GAZES with Alaina. He hadn't told his grandparents that she was the widow of a wolf biologist, or that she'd rather take pictures of wolves than do practically anything else in the world, with the possible exception of photographing a grizzly bear or emperor penguins in Antarctica.

"Better not insult wolves in front of Alaina," he said lightly. "She thinks they're beautiful."

"They *are* beautiful," Grandma Claire asserted. "To be honest, I never understood why Dad disliked them so much. Even so, that didn't stop him from inviting a group of scientists to stay at the Double Branch."

"I'd forgotten about that," Gideon said,

struck by the reminder. "They were evaluating the impact wolf reintroduction might have on ranches and native species."

"That's right. I was visiting part of that time and heard lively debates between Dad and the scientists. None of it was unfriendly, though. He was bitter the government went ahead with the project, but he didn't hold grudges against the people who supported it."

"I would have enjoyed meeting Colby," Alaina said. "He sounds fascinating."

"Dad would have liked you."

Gideon agreed. His great-grandfather *would* have appreciated Alaina. Not only was she an attractive woman, she was intelligent and kind. Yet the thing Colby would have liked most about her was how she'd coaxed Grizzly from his self-imposed isolation.

It was amazing.

Gideon had ridden home early one afternoon and seen Alaina sitting by the paddock in Grandpa Colby's old chair. Griz had playfully lifted her hat off, flipping it to the ground before stretching his neck over the fence to nuzzle her cheek. She'd reached up to stroke his nose, talking softly to him. It looked like a scene that had been repeated more than once, a private moment of play and affection.

Maybe there was something to the animal-whisperer thing he'd heard about. Gideon had tried and tried to coax Griz out of his funk, yet Alaina had done it in just a few weeks. Nikko, Danger and Rita were also devoted to her.

Gideon had stopped trying to keep everyone from calling the orphan calf by name. Rita was healthy and spirited and bossed the older calves around. A real character. She was a sweetheart about taking her bottle from Alaina, but sulking and difficult with anyone else. Not unlike Griz and Nikko.

His grandmother moved ahead to speak with Helene, leaving him alone with Alaina… which might have been her plan. His mom didn't seem intent on matchmaking, but the rest of the family might be willing to give it a shot.

"This looks like a popular event," Alaina said, breaking the silence between them.

"Founders Day is our largest community gathering. But we also have a holiday parade in December. Lighted tractors and that sort of thing. At the end they have a bonfire in the park where people drink hot cider and sing Christmas carols."

"I'll look forward to it. Christmas is my favorite holiday. Are there any descendants in Bannister County who still have the Westcott surname?"

"My great-grandfather was the last. For the past couple of generations, the sons had daughters, and the daughters had sons. At least the ones that survived long enough to have children. That happened on the Carmichael side of the family, too, which is why I use my mother's surname," Gideon added. He didn't want to explain that he'd refused to go by his biological father's name.

At the Mary Westcott Park, the scent of barbecuing steak and chicken filled the air, rising from giant barbecue units. Gideon had purchased a book of tickets ahead of time to avoid an argument about who would get to treat the group, so they joined the long line waiting for food.

Two of Libby's school friends immediately came forward to talk with Alaina.

"Hi, I'm Austin," one of them said, "and this is my brother, Nicholas. Libby told us about you. We were on Dr. Barstow's dig down in New Mexico. Thanks for getting the word out about him."

"That guy is a real creep," his brother

added. "We wouldn't have been there if we'd known what he'd done to Libby."

"My sister-in-law is the one you should be thanking," Alaina protested. "I just passed the message along."

"We still appreciate it."

"AUSTIN, NICHOLAS...GET back here with the rest of us," Libby ordered her friends. "You aren't allowed to jump the line."

"We were just thanking Mrs. Wright," Nicholas protested as they returned.

Libby winked at Alaina.

She was glad to have her college friends visiting, even though she'd felt out of place with them since her father's death. They didn't know how it felt to lose somebody close, so instead of talking about it, she just pretended that everything was fine.

At least she didn't have to pretend with Alaina.

Libby looked over and saw Deke speaking with a young family. She didn't have to pretend with him, either, but she was still uncertain about his job. He was handsome and confident in his uniform, keeping a watchful eye on the town. *That* side of his duties was fine. But there was a darker side, the one where he could get hurt or killed.

He headed toward her. "Hi, Libby. Enjoy the parade?"

"I always do."

She introduced him to her friends. Most of them were entering their final year in Bozeman except for Austin's brother, who was a sophomore. They all hoped to become field archeologists.

"I just got off duty," Deke explained after saying hello to the others. "I'd like to change my clothes at the office first, but I have an extra ticket to the barbecue. Will you eat with me?"

"Sure. I'm having lunch with Deke," she told her friends. "You guys go ahead."

Nicholas didn't look thrilled. The others were paired off, but his girlfriend hadn't gotten back to Bozeman yet. She had time, fall class registration didn't start for over a week, but the others had returned early at Libby's invitation. They loved the idea of searching for a Paleo-Indian site closer to school.

Libby hooked elbows with Deke as they walked toward the sheriff's office. "How about being my partner in the three-legged race?" she asked. "Fair warning, I race to win."

"That's no surprise."

The line of people waiting for food had shortened by the time they returned and they quickly got their meal—a sizzling steak, chili, a mound of potato salad and corn bread.

A HALF HOUR later Libby moaned and pushed her plate away. "I can't eat another bite if I hope to have room for ice cream. Do you want the rest?"

Deke forked the remains of her steak onto his plate. "I have a healthy appetite and this is better than my own cooking."

"It's *much* better than mine. Are you sure you want to keep dating me when I can't even make scrambled eggs in the morning?"

"I don't believe in the outdated notion that women are responsible for all meal prep."

"Sweet-talker. What does your mother say about that?"

Deke chuckled. "My mom is great," he said, "but domestic arts aren't her strong suit. I learned my way around the kitchen and a vacuum cleaner at an early age. Mom uses scrap metal to sculpt life-sized animal figures. Her work has sold as far away as Australia."

Libby's brow creased in thought. "I had a class where the prof did a segment on

Montana artists who use recycled materials. I think he talked about her. It was pretty cool."

Deke was proud of his mother's accomplishments, the same way he was proud of his dad for being a great sheriff.

"Gideon told me that you and your friends are going to look for sites to excavate on the Double Branch," he said casually. "What's that all about?"

Libby's eyes lit up. "Alaina said something that started me thinking. As far as I know, nobody has searched Bannister County for prehistoric settlements. When I mentioned it to Alaina, she remembered reading an entry in Jonah Westcott's journals that suggested *he* may have seen something. She's going over the journals again to look for clues."

"Why aren't you reading them yourself?"

Libby made a face. "I can't decipher Jonah's handwriting, while Alaina doesn't have any trouble. She says it's because she has years of experience reading scribbled scientific field notes. Anyway, she's doing a transcript and she'll also keep an eye out during her hikes."

"Supposing you find a dig site, will you bring your professors in from the college?"

Libby shook her head. "No, at least not right away. It isn't as if we don't have any training."

Knowing she was interested in doing fieldwork closer to home reassured Deke, but it didn't resolve everything. The age gap between them remained problematic, to him at least, and he still had no idea when or if she wanted a family. She hadn't said anything about liking kids and it seemed early in their relationship to just ask.

They were in different places in their lives and he didn't see how a relationship could work without major sacrifices.

Deke noticed his father was looking at them and smiling. It was interesting the way he'd arranged the deputy duty schedule, allowing his son to have time off in the afternoon for the Founders Day picnic. In the past few weeks, he'd frequently pointed out that the voting public preferred married candidates because it showed stability and maturity…and that Deke's interest in Libby Cranston had been duly noted.

Back off, Deke had finally told him. He wanted to run for sheriff when his dad retired, but he wouldn't get married just to increase his chance of winning an election.

GIDEON WAS CONTEMPLATING a lazy snooze under a shade tree when Libby came over with Deke.

"We're challenging you and Alaina in the three-legged race," she announced. "After so much food, we need to get up and move."

Gideon groaned. "I get up and move all the time, kiddo. This is the one day each summer that I can be lazy. Besides, the height difference between me and Alaina is ridiculous. The same with you and Deke."

"But Alaina will just spend the day taking pictures if we don't encourage her to join in. If you won't do it, I'll find another race partner for her."

He frowned. His baby sister understood enough about male psychology to guess he also didn't want to see Alaina racing with someone else. "Fine. If you can talk her into it, then I'll go along."

"I'll be right back."

She dashed to where Alaina was photographing a horseshoe game.

"This wasn't my idea," Deke said to Gideon in an aside.

"You don't need to tell me that."

They watched Libby talk to Alaina, who first shook her head before finally shrugging her shoulders. She took her camera off and handed it to Grandma Claire, then they returned to the spot Gideon had picked out for his afternoon nap.

"I guess we're racing," Alaina said wryly. "I hear you left the final no up to me."

"Sorry about that."

"Uh-huh."

Together they headed to where the various races were being conducted. They watched a hotly contested sack race being won by a lanky ranch hand. Then children in various age ranges competed in the three-legged races.

All of the adults competing in the three-legged race appeared to be married or courting couples and Gideon wished he'd been firmer with Libby. He no longer thought Alaina would get ideas, but his family was another matter. They'd never cared for Celeste, but they already seemed to think highly of Alaina.

"As usual, you get to tie yourselves together," Nels Hewitt announced, handing out colorful two-inch wide ribbons.

Without a hint of hesitation, Alaina stood hip to hip with Gideon and fastened the ribbon around her right thigh and his left. "We should do our best to win," she said, the light of competition in her eyes.

"Uh, sure."

While she wasn't quite as diminutive as he'd wanted to believe all summer, the top of her head still came barely to his shoulder. The size disparity was slightly less for Libby and Deke, but several couples in the race were close in stature.

"Let's coordinate how we move by counting off, one, two, one, two, with *one* meaning we move our free leg forward together, *two* being for our tied legs," Alaina suggested.

"Okay." Gideon was painfully aware of her pressed against him from hip to ankle.

And it was going to get worse.

"We're about to start," Nels called. "Remember, you have to race as a three-legged pair—you aren't allowed to lift a smaller partner and run two-legged."

Alaina put her right arm around his waist. Gideon sucked in a breath before putting his left around her shoulders.

He was right—it had gotten worse.

Nels held up his hand. "Ready, set, *go*."

The group lurched across the starting line, with several teams falling immediately.

"One, two, one, two," Alaina said as they stepped forward.

Gideon was impressed. She more than held

up her end of the race. Several times he took too long of a stride without thinking but she managed to hang on and step her free foot down to stay within the rules of the race. He would never have guessed she was such a fierce competitor.

It was only after they'd crossed the finish line that a misstep sent them tumbling to the ground. He twisted so Alaina landed on top of him rather than the other way around. The air whooshed from his lungs, mostly from the imprint of her soft curves; he got rougher knocks on the ranch every day. But it was the sound of her merry laughter that hit him the hardest. He couldn't recall the last time he'd heard someone so joyously happy and he would have kissed her if he hadn't been aware of everyone watching.

"Gideon Carmichael and Alaina Wright win first place," Nels announced.

A round of cheering and clapping sounded. Gideon looked over and saw his grandparents and mother had come over to watch. Heat crept up his neck, though there was no reason to be self-conscious. He remembered a Founders Day, not so long ago, when Mom and Stewart had run the three-legged race. They hadn't tried that hard to win, they'd just enjoyed being together.

Gideon smiled at the memory, his awkwardness forgotten. His stepdad really *had* been the best.

ALAINA INSTINCTIVELY TRIED to squirm away from Gideon, but her leg was still tied to his. They sorted out their tangled limbs and were sitting up when Nels came around with their first-place ribbon. And more importantly, he carried a pair of scissors.

Gideon cut the broad band confining their thighs and rolled to his feet. He put a hand out.

Alaina hesitated an instant.

Helping someone up was a common courtesy, but she hadn't let him assist with grooming and saddling Nikko, and she had faithfully done her share of the work on their overnight tours. Plainly it frustrated him, but she still wanted to prove she wasn't looking for someone to take care of her, even temporarily. Yet here, in the old-fashioned atmosphere of the park amid Bannister's patriotic salute to tradition, the small courtesy didn't seem like such a bad thing.

"Er, thanks." Alaina took his fingers and was lifted to her feet with astonishing speed.

She was brushing herself off when a male figure in the distance caught her attention.

She'd seen him several times today, looking between her and a sheaf of papers. Right now he was showing it to two other men. While he hadn't pointed at her, the weight of his gaze sent prickles across her shoulders.

Alaina shook the sensation away.

It was the old guy she'd seen at the post office back in June and he might still be trying to decide why she was familiar. She'd met strangers who reminded her of someone from the past and knew it could hover at the back of your mind until you figured out who and where and what. He might be the type who couldn't let anything go.

"Is something wrong?" Gideon asked, distracting her.

"No, of course not. I'm having fun."

He handed her the blue ribbon that Nels had awarded them. "Keep this as a memento."

"You don't want it?"

"I don't need a memento. I attend the parade and picnic every year, along with my mother and grandparents." Further proof that Gideon wasn't the loner rancher he pretended to be…and a reminder that he didn't expect her to be around next year. It was depressing, though she'd always known that living on the Double Branch was a temporary arrangement.

"Thanks," she said with a determined smile. "Winning a three-legged race is new for me."

"Don't they have a Founders Day in your hometown?"

"Port Coopersmith prefers Revolutionary War battle reenactments. They're a big tourist draw, even though the food they serve is traditional to what the army would have eaten."

"I'm almost afraid to ask what that might be."

"It isn't too bad. Basically it's boiled meat and beans, with bread and butter."

Gideon made a face.

"All right, it isn't that great, either," Alaina admitted. "But it's considered very authentic and visitors with a sweet tooth can always stop at the Day-and-Night Donut Hut."

He chuckled. "Your hometown has a donut shop that never closes?"

"Yup. It was the cool hangout when I was a kid. Probably still is. There aren't many choices in Port Coopersmith. It's just a tiny town on the Connecticut coast. No major landmarks, only a few revolutionary-era buildings."

"It sounds like it was a good place to grow up."

Alaina relaxed. She'd hoped participating in the race would get Gideon past any lingering discomfort over their kiss and it seemed to have worked. Now it was mostly her own heart she needed to worry about.

CHAPTER TWELVE

THE FOLLOWING THURSDAY afternoon was especially warm and Alaina fanned herself as they rode.

"Do you mind if we stop for a while?" Gideon asked. "The animals could use some shade. There's a stream ahead. The water comes down from a glacier, so it would be a good place to cool off."

"All right."

The heat was less oppressive under the trees and Alaina dismounted with a feeling of relief. Gideon tied the horses where they could get a drink and graze, and removed Danger's doggy backpack to give him water. Free of the orange vest, the German shepherd jumped into the current and rolled around happily. He was a water lover and rarely missed the chance to get wet when it was offered.

Alaina tucked her camera away and knelt upstream to splash her face. She yelped. "That's liquid ice."

Gideon grinned. "I told you it came off a glacier."

She scooped her hand in the water and sent a spray in his direction. He returned the favor and soon they were engaged in a mock battle. When it ended, they were both wet and laughing.

Alaina sat on the grass and wiped a drip from her chin. "That was fun."

"Yeah." He plopped next to her. "I can't remember the last time I did something so silly."

"What about the three-legged race and when you accused Danger of stealing your funny bone?"

"Except for that."

Alaina felt drunk with sunshine and pleasure as she put an arm around his neck. "Let's be extra silly."

Gideon didn't need more encouragement. He pulled her into a kiss filled with heat and passion. It was only when his lips traveled to her throat that she gulped and scooted away.

"Um, is it okay to drink from the stream?" she asked, though she knew perfectly well that even high mountain water could have contaminants.

"Better not without filtering," Gideon said, his chest heaving. "I'll get our canteens."

Alaina let out a breath. She should have controlled her impulsiveness. When he returned with the water, she gave him a contrite look. "I apologize."

He sat down and handed her a canteen. "Don't apologize. You made me feel like a teenager again. It was nice."

She swallowed a few mouthfuls and capped the bottle. "Then you weren't such a serious guy back in the day?"

"Nope, life of the party. But I grew up and got married to the wrong woman. It was a disaster from the beginning, except I was too proud to admit it. So when Grandpa Colby's foreman retired and I came to run the ranch, I wanted to prove myself. The family plan was for Flynn to eventually get the Carmichael family ranch in Shelton, while I was supposed to inherit the Double Branch, the Westcott family legacy. But I didn't want to take anything for granted."

"That's a whole bunch of history and responsibility to land on your shoulders all at once."

"Yes and no. Grandpa never made me feel as if I had to earn the Double Branch, but ranching in the mountains is different than raising cows at lower elevations, so I needed to learn a good deal. I'm still learning."

Alaina wiggled her toes in her boots. "Life would be boring if we ever stopped learning. But surely he didn't mean for you to stop enjoying other things. You can love what you do, but still see there's more to living than raising cattle."

"Ranching doesn't leave much for anything else," Gideon said wryly. "People get romanticized ideas about it, but this is basically a 24/7 commitment. My having to work outside of a traditional eight-to-five time frame is one of the things my ex-wife resented the most."

"Long work hours are why your marriage broke up?"

"That, along with her hating small towns and not wanting kids, something she kept me from knowing until *after* we were married. We'd barely said I do before she started pushing for us to move to Chicago. I'm a rancher with a degree in animal science. What was I going to do in the city? Anyhow, when it came time for me to run the Double Branch, she said goodbye and had her lawyer send divorce papers."

"She was a fool."

"I should have known better. But when we were dating, I talked about wanting a family and that I'd be moving to Bannister County someday, so I didn't hide anything from her. She even said things like, *that sounds nice* and asked me to tell her about the Double Branch as if she were really interested."

Alaina watched the dappled sunlight on the stream for a long minute. It was inevitable that you discovered things about your partner after getting married, but it shouldn't be something huge, or that they deliberately didn't reveal. She'd always known that Mason's career would continue taking him to wherever wolves were found. Together they'd traveled through North America to Mexico, and Europe to Asia. If she'd gotten him to change, he wouldn't have been the man she'd fallen in love with.

"How about you and children?" Gideon asked at length.

"We wanted a family, but kept putting it off, thinking we had time. Now I don't like putting anything off."

He tucked a damp strand of hair behind her ear. "Such as photographing wolves or having a water fight?"

"Absolutely. When you're old and gray, you're going to remember today and smile."

"I'm going to remember it next week and smile. I suppose after everything—the divorce, then losing-Grandpa Colby and my stepfather—I *have* gotten too grim. Our outings have been a tonic."

Alaina regarded the wet splotches on her jeans from their mock battle. "I'm glad. I've worried the time away would impact the Double Branch too much. I even wanted to volunteer with the haying, but figured it would take more effort for you to teach me what to do than to just leave you alone."

"I noticed you took pictures."

"Hundreds. I don't know if the world needs another book on ranching, but I may give it a shot."

"In addition to your wildlife subjects."

"Naturally. So, how *is* the Double Branch managing without your constant attention?"

"Not badly. I'm letting Nate handle more, which he likes, and I'm able to keep an eye on the herds and check fences while we're out. It would be different if my cows were dropping their calves. I wouldn't dare go anywhere then."

Alaina nodded. Helene and Libby both had described calving season—a backbreaking, unrelenting effort to save lives and keep losses to a minimum. Listening to them made her wonder how anyone managed to make a living at ranching.

"Should we go on?" Gideon asked. "The horses have cooled down by now."

Alaina got up. "Sure."

THAT NIGHT GIDEON lay in his bedroll, arm under his head as he gazed at the sky, trying not to think about the taste and feel of Alaina's lips against his own.

Kissing her again had been the last thing he'd expected. The laughter had been almost as sweet.

The Milky Way was as clear and brilliant as he'd ever seen it, with shooting stars streaking across the darkness every few seconds, some bright, some barely a flicker. He glanced over at Alaina, unsure if she was awake or asleep, and then returned his attention to the celestial display. Normally he didn't have trouble sleeping, but what was normal these days?

The summer was racing by. In some ways, Founders Day always felt like the beginning of the end, so it wasn't unusual to feel that way—winter was their longest season—but Alaina's presence on the Double Branch had complicated everything. She was too appealing for comfort. The image of cuddling with her in front of a winter fire kept intruding into his mind, but while she might appreciate the wild reaches of his world, she wasn't staying. This was her year of adventure and when it was over, she'd find another adventure.

Sensing his wakefulness, Danger rose and padded over to settle down and rest his muzzle on Gideon's chest. It had been good to see him adapting well to the presence of two more dogs on the ranch, treating them as subordinate members of the pack. Clearly he expected to be in charge and the new border collies, Jax and Ollie, had accepted him as their alpha without question.

Subordinates?

Alpha?

Gideon smiled to himself. Alaina's language about wolves and other wildlife was laced with a mix of poetic and scientific terms, and both were creeping into his own thoughts.

An odd contentment filled him as he rubbed behind Danger's ears. He didn't do this sort of thing often—sleeping under the stars felt too much like playing hooky from his duty to the ranch and the Westcott tradition. As a teen he'd roamed all over the mountains alone, staying out for days with little more than food and a blanket—something he had no intention of telling Alaina.

She was an interesting woman, full of contradictions.

Grandpa Colby had once said that life could make you hard, while women made you strong. At the time Gideon had been reeling from his divorce and he'd taken it to mean that women taught men the harshest lessons. But that *couldn't* be what his great-grandfather had intended to say.

A noise across the clearing caught Gideon's attention and he looked over to see a raccoon. Danger was watching it, too, but he knew better than to give chase. Seeming aware of their attention, the animal rose on its hind legs and gave a hiss of warning before continuing.

Gideon faced upward again, still thinking about Grandpa Colby. As Alaina had pointed out, his family had a history of long happy unions. There were a few exceptions, but his great-grandparents had been devoted to each other. Colby had grieved deeply for his wife and spoken of her often in the five years he'd lived on alone. At the end he'd believed she was there in the room, beckoning to him, and his face had lighted with eagerness.

Somehow, it had made saying goodbye a tiny bit easier for the rest of them.

What would it be like to have that kind of

love and devotion…the kind Alaina had felt for her husband?

For the first time in Gideon's life, he truly envied another man. The thought of Alaina looking at him with that much love in her eyes took his breath away.

Beneath his fingers, Danger tensed. An instant later Alaina shuddered in her sleeping bag. A soft moan sounded, followed by a jumble of whispered words.

Danger whined in response.

Gideon's concern escalated as she began twisting back and forth. "Alaina," he called, hoping not to startle her. "It's okay, wake up."

She jerked. "W-what?"

"Sorry, you were having a nightmare."

"No," she muttered, but he didn't think she was denying the nightmare, just the dark images still lingering in her mind.

"Do you want to talk about it?"

Alaina let out a half laugh. "You may be sorry. That's what Libby said when I encouraged her to tell me all she wanted about her dad, not that I ever regretted the invitation."

"She didn't think she could confide in me?" Gideon tried to keep from sounding dismayed.

"There was nothing to confide, she just missed talking about him. You know, telling stories about Stewart and the things he would say. All the little memories you don't want to lose. Mostly she was worried it would upset Helene, so I suggested asking your mom if hearing about him would bother her. Helene must have said it was okay, because I've heard the two of them swapping anecdotes ever since."

Gideon blinked, suddenly realizing that things *were* better, with grief no longer seeming to hang so heavily over his mother and sister. Or him. The loss was still hard, but light finally seemed to be shining through the darkness.

He turned on his side to face Alaina, realizing something else—she'd changed the subject away from herself.

"You learned this stuff the hard way," he murmured. "Was the nightmare about your husband?"

"It's the one I used to have after the accident. Reliving it, over and over in vivid detail. They finally stopped after a few months."

"But now they're back."

"Yeah." Alaina sat up and accepted Danger's anxious attention. "Today was such a nice day I'd hoped it wouldn't be a problem. But something happened in Bannister that stirred things up, and night gremlins *are* persistent."

"What happened?"

She petted Danger for another minute before answering. "Nothing too dramatic. A truck has come up behind my SUV a couple of times, honking and tailgating. Then it passes at a high speed, swerving around as if the driver is intoxicated. My husband died because of a drunk driver, so it's raised some ghosts."

"Have you reported the incidents to the sheriff's office?" Gideon asked. The stillness of the land around them made the threat of a reckless motorist seem far away, but that was an illusion. He lived on the edge of a wilderness with a mechanized world on the other side.

"There isn't any point. I haven't been able to get the license plate number, it was covered with dirt both times, and I'm not even sure it was the same truck. There must be more than one really old red pickup in the area. I've only gone into Bannister once since Founders Day, which is when it happened the second time. That's when I decided to do all my shopping in Bozeman."

"What about having your snow tires installed?"

She shrugged. "Anders Garage called and said they couldn't get them, after all. Mr. Anders recommended a place in Bozeman. They had what I needed in stock, so I've already bought a set. I'll go down in October to have them put on and get the SUV prepped for winter weather."

A peculiar sensation crept across Gideon's shoulders. Bill Anders prided himself on being able to provide for all of Bannister County's vehicular needs, even repairing big rigs. But he couldn't get studded snow tires for a popular SUV model?

"That isn't right. Any of it."

She shrugged. "Mr. Anders has a small business, so he needs to prioritize service for the people who live here permanently. And it's possible the road incidents weren't that bad. I'm just overreacting. The nightmares have settled down before and they will again. I'm sorry I woke you up. I should have suggested doing day trips for a while."

"It's fine. Anyhow, I was still awake," he said, "looking at the sky and thinking I don't take enough time for stargazing. Few people in the world have a finer view."

Alaina settled down again, looking upward. "They're incredible. Countless points of brightness in the distance." From her tone, he could tell she was relieved to talk about something else. "How amazing to think that some of that light traveled years to reach us. A few of those stars burned out eons ago, and yet here we are, still seeing them."

"You don't think that's depressing?"

"How could it be depressing to know that light can continue to shine in the dark, even when the source is gone?" She put a hand over her mouth as she yawned. "It's like memories of the people we've lost. Everyone talks about needing balance, but when it comes to love and grief, I don't care about balance. How Mason lived is more important than how he died. That's why the nightmares frustrate me."

Another shooting star, the largest Gideon had seen that evening, streaked across the sky.

"I'm not making any sense, am I?" Alaina asked after another yawn.

"I'm no philosopher, but I get what you're saying." Curiously Gideon *did* understand. He'd spent months being angry that his stepfather had died at such a relatively young age. But he needed to let it go. There were much better things to remember about Stewart.

Danger was tucked close to Alaina and even in the faint illumination from the stars,

Gideon could see that he'd relaxed into sleep, probably because she had drifted off again, too.

Gideon looked over at Brushfire and Nikko where they were tethered on a hitch line. He considered getting up to check them, but they were quiet and he didn't want to disturb Alaina.

His feelings about her were getting more and more confused. Libby had accused him of comparing her to Celeste, but that wasn't true, even when Alaina had first moved into the foreman's cabin. She was genuine and passionate and cared deeply about both people and animals.

And she had a gift for challenging him. He'd gotten into the habit of just doing his work until he was tired enough to sleep, but she was right, as much as he cared about the ranch, there ought to be room for more. Having responsibility didn't require him to give up everything else he enjoyed.

Did he really expect to spend the rest of his life alone because of a failed marriage? It was a bleak picture. No wife to love and laugh with together. No companionship. No chance of children to cherish and pass the ranch to one day. There would be nothing except long days and longer nights.

He shook his head. No matter what, there was one thing he needed to pay attention to or be sorry… Alaina's feelings about her husband. What had she said, *I can't imagine finding anyone else I'd love as much as Mason*?

He'd be wise to remember those words.

The next morning Alaina took her cue from Gideon, who behaved as if nothing had happened in the middle of the night. In reality, nothing *had* happened except for a drowsy discussion. Still, she'd appreciated being able to talk to someone instead of banishing the nightmare on her own.

Of course, Danger did his best to help when she was camping alone with him. He would lick and snuggle, sharing his warmth. Wolves did the same thing to comfort other members of the pack.

"I've been meaning to ask if the Double Branch has any hot springs or other geothermal features," Alaina said as they ate breakfast. "I've been transcribing Jonah's journals and found the section I thought could be a clue. He mentions a warm water source and seeing an unusually long arrowhead."

Gideon cocked his head. "Unusually long? I wonder if that could be a Clovis point. My stepdad was fascinated by them. He said they were early Paleo-Indian."

"I've heard of both Folsom and Clovis points. Anyhow, I thought the connection was promising since hot springs are an easily identifiable landmark."

Gideon nodded. "As a matter of fact, the Double Branch has two—we just don't let people visit them. Jonah named them Pixie Jump and Dragon's Tooth, of all things. It makes sense that an early human settlement would find a geothermal feature useful. We can ride up there next week. Libby and her friends won't be here before then. They're moving her into a new apartment."

"It sounds as if she's planning to be at the ranch a lot."

"Yeah, well, I suspect Deke has something to do with that," Gideon muttered.

Alaina tried not to smile. She didn't think he would be thrilled to see his sister dating *any*body, but plainly it was an even bigger challenge to see her dating one of his friends.

"She and her pals will keep coming until the weather gets too bad, then start again next spring," he explained. "Searching if they haven't found anything by then, or digging if they have."

"You must be pleased Libby is finally letting you do something for her. On top of everything else, her friends are going to spend their weekends at the ranch, dig on your land and ride your horses."

Initially Alaina had worried the college students would want to use ATVs for their search, but instead they were going out on horseback. It was why Libby had wanted her own horse, Ladybug, brought down from the Carmichael ranch in Shelton.

Gideon laughed. "Yeah, it's a first since she turned twelve. You complain about your brothers. Can you explain how I went from being someone she counted on to becoming the enemy who's trying to take her independence away?"

"Because you are."

"I don't see that."

Alaina just smiled and shook her head. While Gideon behaved like an overprotective big brother, Libby had learned at a young age to push back and defend herself. Now it mostly seemed to be a game they played.

Maybe that was also true of Alaina's own brothers and she just hadn't recognized it.

"By the way," Gideon said more seriously, "you'll be happy to know I've limited the search area for Libby and her friends. They're required to stay within certain GPS coordinates, which excludes the Wind Singer territory. Wolves and archeology students aren't a mix I'm eager to see."

"You weren't eager to see a mix of wolves and a photographer, either."

"I'm still not that thrilled about it."

Alaina pushed her hat down more firmly on her head. "You *do* understand how shy wolves are, right? They'll protect their young and their kills, but for the most part, they avoid humans. Bear spray is primarily intended to deter bears."

He laughed again. "You don't worry about bears, either."

"I respect and love them, just as much as wolves. Several years ago I even had a Native American artisan walk up to me and announce that the bear was my animal spirit guide. It came out of the blue, for seemingly no reason except that he wanted to be certain I understood."

"You believe in animal spirit guides?" Gideon's tone was predictably dry.

"I believe more than I doubt," she said. "There's so much we don't understand in the world around us, it would be arrogant to think it wasn't possible. I've had an affinity for bears since before I can remember. Besides, a lot of people believe in guardian angels, why couldn't some of them be animals?"

"Maybe."

"And look, he gave me a gift." Alaina took off the pendant she always wore and handed it to Gideon. It was a silver bear, with an intricate pattern of inlaid turquoise and coral. "See the symbol on the back?"

Gideon turned the pendent over and his eyebrows rose. "The artist's mark is a wolf?" He held it out to her. "Interesting coincidence."

"That depends on how you look at it." She dropped the necklace over her head again. "Maybe it was chance, or maybe the artist perceived something beyond our normal senses. I'm willing to take some things on faith."

Gideon didn't appear convinced, but he didn't argue the point. He got up and finished packing his sleeping bag.

Alaina saddled Nikko, feeling calm and content despite the broken night of sleep. How could she feel otherwise, she mused, filling her lungs with the cool morning air. She was high in the mountains in one of the most beautiful places on the planet.

"Ready to go?" Gideon asked as he finished.

Alaina nodded and got into the saddle, marveling at how relaxed she was on Nikko. It wasn't just that her muscles no longer screamed in protest after a long day's ride, it was feeling at ease while riding him. She even trusted Nikko enough now to take photographs while mounted on his back, though she was careful. A horse could always bolt if startled.

They headed west toward the Wind Singer territory in comfortable silence.

Gideon drove her to distraction with some of his attitudes, but she kept seeing depths in him that she hadn't expected. He was intelligent and devoted to his family. Though he'd fundamentally disagreed with Colby Westcott on various issues, he'd loved and valued his great-grandfather. And those endearing hints of whimsy kept appearing at the oddest times.

Suddenly a low warning sound came from Danger and Alaina reined in Nikko. In the distance she saw a grizzly tearing apart a rotten log in search of grubs.

She turned on her camera and began taking shots. It would have been great to use one of her super-telephoto lenses, but they were best for work at an established observation point, where she could set up her equipment and be focused for hours.

Finally she let the camera rest around her neck. She wrinkled her nose at Gideon, who was waiting. "Sorry."

"I'm used to it by now, but I'm glad you have Danger on your hikes. You get totally absorbed. At least he keeps watch and will alert you if an animal approaches."

Alaina shrugged and let the comment rest. She was more watchful when she was alone; it was Gideon's presence that made her feel secure enough to simply focus on getting pictures.

There were pluses and minuses to their tours. They were leaving supplies in various caches around the ranch, which included enough cold weather gear to get by in an emergency. She had also seen a good deal of the ranch and high backcountry. Amazingly Gideon didn't need to graze cattle on every inch of his acreage, some of which was over eight thousand feet high. Instead he was able to move his herds around the lower elevations to ensure they had the best forage.

But the downside of their tours was the way she kept dropping her guard, both physically and emotionally. Gideon was at one with the land, understanding its rhythms and creatures. She felt safe with him at a time she needed to be taking care of herself.

She wouldn't always have a Gideon Carmichael to conduct tours and keep watch... which brought her to another persistent thought. *Danger.* He was a remarkable dog, but he didn't belong to her and there wasn't any question of being able to buy him. He was a member of Gideon's family, after all.

The bear moved to another section of the log and began rooting in it. Plainly he wasn't going anywhere soon. Fattening for winter hibernation was his priority.

Alaina looked over at Gideon. "We'd have to detour well around that grizzly to avoid disturbing him, so maybe we should just go back to the ranch. I get my backpack food online, and some recent orders are overdue. If we return earlier, rather than later, I can check on the status."

He agreed and they turned the horses.

Truth be told, she needed time alone to reflect. She hadn't told Gideon the entire story about her encounters in Bannister. The reckless driver had swerved so wildly the second time she'd gone off the road to avoid being hit. That was the most disturbing, but things had also gotten weird at the small grocery store. She didn't know if the owner and his wife had deliberately turned hostile or if they were just wary about a newcomer. Regardless, it was uncomfortable.

The counter clerk at the post office had been nice, though. And Nels Hewitt came out to say hello whenever he saw her, even when the hardware store was busy with customers.

Still, it wasn't just the tensions in Bannister that bothered Alaina. Gideon and the way he made her feel were more unsettling than everything else put together.

CHAPTER THIRTEEN

"DOES ALAINA THINK it was the same driver on both occasions?" Deke asked. When Gideon had called, saying they needed to talk, he'd expected it to be about Libby, not a traffic report.

"She wasn't sure. Apparently it was an old red truck each time, but she couldn't read the license plate because it was covered with dirt."

"Did the incidents occur during daylight hours?"

"I assume so. She was going into town to shop, so it must have been before 5:00 p.m. Nothing in Bannister is open later except the Made Right Pizza Parlor and Good Drinks Tavern."

Deke tapped his pencil on the desk, trying to recall who owned an old red truck in Bannister County. He could think of several. "You realize that if she'd wanted an official report, she would have done it herself."

An exasperated sound came over the telephone line. "Alaina is a nice person and willing to believe she overreacted, but I don't think she did. Whether this is someone being aggressive or a drunk driver, it's a problem for all of us. I live in this county and I don't like it. You should be concerned, too, since your family drives in the area."

Deke's back straightened. "Slow down, pal. I'm concerned about everyone who lives here. I happen to agree with you. I just want to be careful about treading on Alaina's toes."

"You're just worried she'll tell Libby that we tread on her toes, and then Libby will be annoyed with you," Gideon retorted.

"I'm no fool. Your sister is both independent and strong-willed."

"You don't need to tell me."

Deke choked down a laugh. "She just doesn't like you getting in her way."

"How can I get in her way? I don't even know where she *is* most of the time." His buddy couldn't hide the humor in his voice.

Deke grinned. It *was* hard keeping up with Libby. It should bother him more than it did, given that whatever was brewing between them was still in the air.

"I understand. *Completely*," he said. "Now, about what happened to Alaina, we're always on the lookout for drunk or aggressive drivers, but I'll tell the other deputies to be particularly vigilant. I won't bring her name into it. We can also run extra patrols around the Good Drinks Tavern."

"Glad to hear it."

Deke leaned back in his chair. "I've heard the new owner is putting in a restaurant and plans to change the name to Good Eats Bar and Grill. That should help in more ways than one. Bannister needs more restaurants than just a pizza parlor and the deli at the grocery store."

"You're forgetting the Sunrise Earth natural food store."

Deke laughed. "True. Have you ever tried their Earth Special Burger? It's tofu on gluten-free bread, piled with alfalfa sprouts and drizzled with tahini sauce."

A startled noise sounded over the phone. "You've eaten there?"

"My mom likes the place and that's her favorite sandwich. Every now and then she gets the urge to be motherly and visits with lunch. The Earth Special Burger wouldn't be my first choice, but if someone is nice enough to feed me, I won't question what it is."

"To each their own. They've stayed in business for twenty years, so they must have more customers than your mother."

"That's a fact. I'll talk to you later."

Deke hung up the phone and frowned at the notes he'd made. They occasionally caught someone driving under the influence, but repeat offenders were rare.

As for the possibility Alaina had overreacted? Gideon was right—it was unlikely. Deke didn't know Alaina well, but she seemed levelheaded.

Though concerned, Deke was also amused by his friend's involvement with his tenant. Taking her around the ranch and backcountry had made sense, but they must be beyond the need for guided tours by now.

Yet Deke's humor faded as he wondered if Gideon was falling for the wildlife photographer. Alaina was beautiful and intelligent, but while he'd like to see his friend happily married, he was concerned about Gideon getting put through another emotional wringer.

Like Libby, Alaina had a career that could take her all over the world.

Deke took out his smartphone and looked at the picture he'd taken of Libby on Founders Day, right after the three-legged race. Though she'd declared a determination to win, she had spent more time teasing him than making a real effort to get across the finish line.

He closed his eyes, remembering how they'd tripped and he'd kissed her. Or maybe she'd made the first move. He didn't know. What he couldn't get out of his head was the faint scent of her perfume, teasing his senses. Or the lingering flavor of vanilla on her lips. She made him laugh and feel good, even when he was uptight about work or whether he should be involved with her in the first place.

He cared about Libby, more than he'd ever cared about a woman, but that didn't make their problems go away.

Deke shook himself and sent a notification to his fellow officers about reports of a drunk or aggressive driver in the vicinity of the Good Drinks Tavern. He'd also speak with the new owner of the bar and see if they had any suspicions. If a customer had a habit of revving their motor and spinning gravel as they left the parking lot, the same person might be just as aggressive on the road.

Another deputy arrived to relieve him in the office, so he eagerly went out on patrol. None of them enjoyed desk duty and he'd spent long weeks riding a desk chair while recovering from his gunshot wound. On top of that, his father was making noises about him becoming a shift supervisor. It was a logical step toward him running for sheriff, but it meant more paperwork and less action.

Deke rubbed his shoulder, more with the memory of pain than anything real. He hadn't planned to tell Libby about getting shot, but it was better that she knew. Her reaction had been typical—concern, with a period of withdrawal. He didn't blame her. He'd rather have her decide sooner rather than later whether she could handle being involved with someone in law enforcement. A lot of people couldn't.

They wouldn't be seeing each other for a few days, which was just as well. Libby's classes were starting soon and she needed to get settled into her college routine. She might even lose interest once she resumed her normal life.

Summer romance had a habit of falling apart once time and distance offered perspective.

GIDEON KEPT THINKING about his call to Deke. Even though it needed to be done, Alaina wouldn't appreciate him interfering. Had she acted that way with her husband or was it something new?

That's none of your business, the sensible

half of his brain reminded him. The other half, the one that liked her too much, kept chewing on the question.

He'd made the call in the horse barn to prevent his mother from overhearing. He didn't want her to worry, especially since she was driving into Bannister more often. Of course, now *he* was going to worry whenever she or Libby went into town.

"Hi, Gideon." Alaina's greeting made him jump, partly out of guilt. He would have to tell her that he'd contacted Deke.

"Uh, hi. Do you need something?"

She looked at him quizzically. "Just getting carrots for Griz. I'm going to sit by the paddock and work on my computer."

"Did you track down your missing supply shipments?"

Alaina frowned. "Yes, but it's strange. Apparently they were returned with the notation *address unknown*."

"Surely it wasn't the post office that messed up."

"No." She took several carrots out of the sack. "My supplier is using a start-up shipping company, but the drivers haven't had trouble finding the Double Branch before now. Maybe it's a glitch in their computer system. I found a store in Bozeman that carries the brands I like, so I'll stock up there. I want a big supply on hand for the winter."

"That's good. Er, I should tell you that I spoke to Deke about the problem you had near the tavern. He'll alert the other deputies, but keep your name out of it. I had to tell him. After all, a drunk or aggressive driver affects everyone's safety."

ALAINA WANTED TO scold Gideon for his presumption, but he looked so guilty that she was more amused than annoyed. "I understand."

"Look," he said, "I get monthly shipments of both dog and cat food, but I don't want to risk running short in case a similar shipping issue crops up. I'll feel better about it if I drive into Bozeman today to get a truckload as backup. Why don't we go together?"

"Aren't you sick of my company after spending the last two days together?"

"I wouldn't have offered if that were true. You could work on your photos when we get back."

Alaina wavered. She enjoyed her time with Gideon a little too much. He was complicated, interesting, fun to debate with…and fun to tease. While he didn't laugh often, when he did it was wholehearted.

"How about it?" Gideon prompted.

"All right. Are you leaving right away?"

"I just want to see if Mom needs anything. She may decide to go with us."

Alaina nodded, wryly amused at herself. Thank goodness he couldn't read minds; to him this was just a shopping trip, not a contrived social outing.

"Then I'll meet you at the truck."

She stopped to feed carrots to Grizzly and give him a minute of special attention. It was great to see him getting friendlier with the other horses in the paddock, so he wasn't as lonely through the day. He didn't even move aside when Nikko came over for a treat.

"I have to go," she told them finally.

They whinnied as she rushed to the cabin for her purse, then went to wait by Gideon's large pickup. He came out a few minutes later. Danger, Jax and Ollie were sitting on the porch, tails waving as they watched, probably hoping for an invitation to come along.

"Sorry, guys, you're staying here," he told them, giving each a pat. He came down the steps, tucking a piece of paper into a pocket. "Mom is in the middle of baking, but she gave me a list," he explained.

Alaina accepted his assistance into the high truck seat without objection. She was more and more conflicted about Gideon. He was a decent man, walking a tightrope between the traditions of the past and the realities of the present, so it wouldn't destroy her independence to compromise with him sometimes. Compromise was important in any relationship, even one between a tenant and landlord. He'd reminded her of that.

Except a tenant and landlord usually didn't kiss each other. Still, both occasions had been a fluke, a moment outside of time. Surely that sort of kiss didn't count in the real world.

And if she kept telling herself that, she might actually start to believe it. Thinking less about it would also help.

"You mentioned the possibility of doing a book on ranches. How would that work?" Gideon asked as he started the engine.

"Actually, I have a publisher who's interested, but it doesn't mean a book is feasible."

"Why not? People are fascinated by ranching. That's why my ex moved to Montana from Chicago. She had the idea that a ranch community would be wildly romantic. Then she discovered it isn't all roundups, barn dances and barbecues, and that Shelton doesn't have a boutique and designer coffeehouse on every corner. It's just as well she went back home when I moved down here. The Double Branch is no place for someone who isn't tough enough to handle what nature deals out."

Alaina focused on the view ahead, not wanting to seem too curious about his ex-wife. "You've said she didn't like your long working hours."

"Celeste was pretty unhappy when things didn't turn out the way she expected. Marrying me could have been a last-ditch effort to prove she hadn't made a mistake by moving to Montana."

"That's insightful."

Gideon laughed. "Don't sound so surprised. It's amazing what you come up with when you stop being angry. To give credit where credit is due, I kind of learned that from you."

"Have we ever talked about being angry?"

"It's more of a general thing. Tell about the problem with your book. Not enough variety? That shouldn't be an issue. We're moving the herds down to lower pastures before long and getting ready for the October market. You'll also be here for spring calving and branding. Lots more chances to take pictures."

"It's more about needing releases in order to publish."

"The amendment to our agreement—"

"Doesn't cover individuals," Alaina said quickly. "I'll need a release signed by anybody in the photographs."

"I'm sure my ranch hands will be happy to cooperate."

Alaina swallowed uncomfortably. Janet had shown a client the photos of Gideon carrying the calf…a client who owned a nonfiction publishing house. She'd loved the pictures and wanted them to be the centerpiece of a book on western ranching. It was understandable. He was sexy, photogenic and the embodiment of pure masculinity. But whether he'd be willing to have his bare torso displayed in a book was another matter. He wasn't an exhibitionist.

"Your ranch hands have already signed releases for me, but I'd need one from you, too. I'll show you the photographs and you can decide. Some people are self-conscious about seeing themselves in print." While she expected him to refuse, there was always a chance.

"I suppose."

They chatted pleasantly for the remainder of the drive. Once in Bozeman, she suggested he drop her off at the sport supply company to shop, while he went down the street to get what he needed for the dogs and barn cats.

Alaina moved around the store, selecting a large supply of freeze-dried food, along with fuel for her camp stove and other items. The manager asked if he could help, and after hearing her story, explained that they remained fully stocked throughout the year due to the popularity of winter sports in the state.

"I'm sorry you had a problem with your regular supplier," he told her. "But you shouldn't have any trouble getting what you need in Bozeman, even during the winter. We usually aren't snowed in for extended periods."

"That's good to hear."

She was pushing her cart outside as Gideon arrived. He helped stack everything on the floor and back seat of the truck and then they went to a warehouse store for groceries. They were on their way to the checkout when Alaina stopped to look at Christmas decorations. She'd already bought solar light strings and other holiday decor off the internet, but the sparkle and appeal of the displays were impossible to resist.

"Is there room in the truck for a Christmas tree and some other stuff?" she asked Gideon.

"I brought a tarp and rope to tie everything down, so get whatever you want. But you don't need a tree. I'll cut a fresh one when we get close to the holiday. There's always a few near the house that need clearing."

"I'd love that, but I still want one of these to put up on Thanksgiving. A fresh tree would dry out too quickly. A second on the cabin porch would be great, too."

"You want *three* trees?"

Alaina grinned. "Just making up for lost time. Mason and I spent most of our holidays in the field on research projects. Christmas doesn't require lights and ornaments, but I enjoy the festive trappings."

"Surely wolf biologists don't have to be in the field every minute."

She shrugged. "It varies, but Mason was determined to study wolf populations all over the world. Even when he was on one project, he was writing grant proposals for the next."

"Is that what *you* wanted? You said you chose to be part of his research, but that doesn't mean you enjoyed living that way."

Alaina hesitated, recalling her thoughts the day she and Gideon had talked about their plans for the future.

"In the beginning I was thrilled to be part of those studies," she said slowly. "But

I admit it got old for me. That's one of the reasons I wanted to rent the cabin, so I could come back from a hike and have a place that felt like home."

"And why you want so many Christmas decorations."

"Of course. Making up for lost time, remember?"

"Then how about that one?" Gideon asked, pointing to a tree on display. "It's tall, but doesn't spread out as much at the bottom, so it wouldn't take as much floor space."

Alaina regarded the tree, picturing it in the cabin. "Perfect," she pronounced, then gestured to a shorter version. "And I'll get that one for the porch." She didn't want to confess she had already gotten a tree for the loft. As a kid she'd loved falling asleep in the light of a Christmas tree and hoped to recreate the magical feeling it had once given her.

Gideon loaded the various boxes, including evergreen-style swag on a flatbed dolly, and they managed to direct it, along with their shopping carts, to the checkout. Creativity was required to fit everything into the truck, but they managed, securely tying everything down with the tarp and ropes so nothing would be lost on the return trip home.

"This didn't take very long. If you aren't

in a hurry, maybe we could run over and see Libby's new apartment before heading back," Gideon suggested as he drove onto the street.

"I'm sure she'd prefer to get everything unpacked before family visits," Alaina advised. She could imagine Libby's annoyed expression if her brother showed up in the middle of her friends helping her move.

"You mean she'd think I was checking up on her."

"As if you didn't already call the police department to see if there are any law enforcement concerns around the apartment she rented."

Red crept up Gideon's throat. "How do you know I did that?"

"Because it's what my father and brothers did when I moved out of the dorms and into my own place. Did you think you were inventing the wheel?" Alaina teased.

"Do you think she guessed?"

"Probably. Look, it'll soon be lunchtime and Libby said she was going to get pizza for the crew. If it makes you feel better, we could order food to be delivered. Even if they've already eaten, they'll be hungry again soon enough."

Gideon's face brightened. "That's a great idea."

They stopped at a restaurant near the college where he ordered ten large pizzas to be delivered. It seemed excessive, but he shrugged and said the students could split the leftovers between them.

"How about adding some family-sized Greek salads?" she suggested.

Gideon agreed and wrote, *Hope the move is going well, Alaina and Gideon* on the delivery ticket. Then he refused to let her contribute.

"You shouldn't have added my name if you weren't going to let me help pay," she scolded as they drove out of town.

"The idea was worth a million bucks and you kept me from upsetting Libby by going over there in person."

Alaina shook her head. It was educational to see the struggle for autonomy from a brother's perspective. She unwrapped one of the calzones they'd gotten for their own lunch and handed it to him.

Gideon's phone buzzed when they were halfway home. He pulled it from his pocket and handed it to her. "That's an incoming text message. Would you read it for me? Just swipe upward to unlock the screen. But please don't tell Libby there's no password or she'll question which century I'm living in."

Alaina chuckled and accessed the message. "It's Libby, so at least she believes you're technical enough to retrieve texts. If I'm deciphering her abbreviations correctly, she says thanks for the food and that she's coming up Tuesday afternoon. She and Deke are going to ride to the hot springs on Wednesday to check for artifacts. He'll be off duty and she doesn't have any classes that day."

"But we were going up there next week."

"She knows what I found in Jonah's journals and I'm sure she'd prefer locating a potential site on her own."

Gideon still didn't look happy and Alaina grinned. "Don't be grumpy. They aren't eloping, just going for a horseback ride."

"Life was easier when she was four and looked up to me as her hero," he grumbled.

"You top her by eight inches. She still looks up to you."

He glared. "That isn't funny. Libby just got out of a bad relationship. What if this is one of those ugly rebound things that hurts both her and Deke?"

Alaina sobered instantly. She understood Gideon's concern and tried to think of a way to reassure him without revealing something Libby had told her in confidence. Basically

Libby's only unresolved emotion toward her old boyfriend was irritation that he'd attempted to sabotage her internship. It was natural, even though everything had turned out for the best.

"Um, I wouldn't be too concerned about the rebound thing," Alaina said finally. "It's just a guess, but I don't think her ex-boyfriend was ever that important to her."

GIDEON CAST A glance at Alaina, realizing he trusted her judgment about the situation. It didn't mean Libby or Deke couldn't get hurt, but it was less likely if his sister didn't have lingering feelings for someone else.

"I'm glad to hear it. What do you think about the age difference?"

Alaina smiled faintly. "The same thing I *always* think when you bring it up. They have to figure out where they're going. You can't do it for them. Deke is a good man. You wouldn't be friends with him otherwise."

Gideon nodded. He enjoyed having his sister around so much. And while his mom hadn't made a decision about moving to the Double Branch, she was talking about staying until next spring, which was promising. Life was falling into a pattern that felt more normal than it had in the bleak period after Stewart's death.

A new normal.

They'd never forget Dad, but at least the happy memories were coming before the memory of loss. For his part, he gave a lot of the credit to Alaina. Despite her husband's tragic death, she was moving forward, refusing to let sorrow have too much power over her life.

"I should have asked before, but did you find everything you needed at the sporting goods store?" Gideon asked. "We could go back and look somewhere else."

"It's fine. I wasn't sure if I should keep bringing Danger with me once it starts snowing, so I also picked up a few things for him, just in case."

"You'd have trouble keeping him from going," Gideon assured quickly. "He isn't amenable to dog boots, but I put an ointment on his feet to help protect them from the ice."

"Oh, good, I got some of that."

While the trees hadn't started changing color yet, Gideon's instincts said it would be an early, shorter autumn than usual. There was a feel to the air, a sense that winter could arrive at any minute. And now that Alaina had talked about going out in the snow, his concern for her had instantly exploded again. Bears wouldn't be an issue once they were in hibernation, but the weather would be a greater threat than wolves *or* bears put together.

"The food and gear we cached at your different observation points hasn't been disturbed, right?" he asked.

"It's all fine, and I'll still carry enough to get by whenever I go out," she assured.

In some aspects a rancher's work was lighter during the winter, but Gideon knew he wouldn't always have the time to go with her. It was an idea he'd be reluctant to propose, regardless. She was so stubborn it might make her push even harder to prove herself.

Honesty forced him to acknowledge, if only to himself, that she'd *never* needed to prove anything. He felt better when Alaina had Danger with her or he was there as well, but that was his issue, not hers. It was something he also needed to keep in mind with Libby.

"By the way, do you remember that last entry in Jonah Westcott's journals?" he asked to change the discussion.

"Yes, the one where he says he's finally beginning to understand Theodore. I've compared the letters from President Roosevelt and the journals, nothing seems to relate."

"That's because it's the date that Jonah's wife passed away."

Alaina was silent for a long while and Gideon was concerned that he'd upset her. She sighed finally. "Theodore Roosevelt's mother and first wife died within hours of each other and he wrote in his journal that the light had gone out of his life. If only he'd known what an extraordinary future of love and adventure was ahead of him."

An odd sensation caught Gideon by surprise.

He wasn't entirely sure what it meant, but it felt a little like hope.

CHAPTER FOURTEEN

THAT THURSDAY ALAINA took picture after picture around the Dragon's Tooth hot spring, which Libby had temporarily designated as Site A in hopes it would be one of many.

Gideon assisted by holding branches and undergrowth to one side when needed, sometimes at an extreme arm's length to keep from blocking natural light. But they'd yet to locate the artifact Libby had left intact where she'd spotted it, so her student team could do proper documentation. She was anxious to ensure that no one could claim they hadn't followed the most rigorous archeological methodology.

"You aren't Libby's personal photographer," he commented. "She shouldn't treat you that way."

Alaina flashed him a grin. "I don't mind. I'm honored she trusts me to take pictures without grabbing a souvenir at the same time."

"She'd better trust you. She wouldn't have

even *started* looking for artifacts on the ranch except for something you said."

"I'm still honored. And the photographs are a onetime thing. They'll take their own pictures during the excavation."

Though Alaina had been camping away from the ranch for several days, she'd come home early on Wednesday in anticipation of hearing good news. When Libby had returned from her ride with Deke, she'd been ecstatic, convinced the area around one of the Double Branch hot springs showed promise as a Paleo-Indian settlement.

Yet she'd also been on edge, the tension so thick between her and Deke it was palpable.

Men, she'd mouthed at Alaina, rolling her eyes in the deputy's direction. But aside from a request that Alaina do an initial photo survey of the area, they hadn't found time to talk.

"Here's the artifact Libby told us about," Gideon called.

Alaina went over to photograph the stone, partially exposed by eroded earth. Enough was visible to see where the edges and point had been knapped. An echo of Libby's excitement charged through Alaina's body. She might not be an archeologist, but she was awed by the history and age of the artifact.

"That's much larger than the arrowheads in the Bannister Museum," she said.

Gideon nodded. "It's promising. No wonder Libby is so pleased."

"You're happy, too. If this area turns out to be a Paleo-Indian settlement, she'll be working close to home for years to come." Alaina grinned again.

"Sue me, I enjoy having her around."

After Alaina was satisfied she'd shot enough pictures, they continued their ride. Gideon was taking her above the tree line and they needed to be especially watchful; this was the time of year when bears climbed to high elevations to forage for army cutworm moths in the loose rocks.

So far she'd found little opportunity to work that high, but she had packed extra supplies, hoping to stay and hike back to the ranch in a few days, while Gideon rode back sooner with the horses.

But when she made the suggestion during their late lunch, Gideon refused. "There's no way I'm just leaving you."

"I want to photograph some of the smaller mammals and they might be easier to spot up here. It'll take time and you have work back at the ranch."

"Do you know how far we are from the Double Branch?"

Alaina sighed. "It's mostly downhill."

"Is that supposed to make me feel better? I'll leave Nikko with you. It's the least I can do."

It was still a generous offer, but Alaina was uncomfortable about taking sole responsibility for Nikko. Danger was one thing, he could handle himself in the wild, a horse was another story.

Perhaps that was how Gideon saw things with her. He had a vast amount of experience in the wild, while hers was much more limited. Yet understanding his position didn't mean she was going to completely capitulate.

"Nikko would hate being by himself while I'm working. You know how social he is."

Gideon frowned and patted Danger, who'd sensed they were disagreeing once more. The German shepherd preferred the human members of his pack to be in accord.

"Then I'll stay," he grumbled. "However long it takes."

Alaina gritted her teeth. She couldn't keep Gideon from his responsibilities to the Double Branch, which meant she'd have to go back with him as planned, then go out again.

It would be a full day's return hike just to reach the location where she wanted to work.

Compromise, she reminded herself.

"Fine. Then we won't ride any higher. Instead I'll look for a good observation area," Alaina said. "A place where we can also camp for the one night we planned. We'll stay until midafternoon tomorrow, and then ride back."

It was more capitulation than compromise on her part, but while he couldn't force her to return with him, she also couldn't make him leave alone. He was a man accustomed to action and would quickly grow weary of sitting for hours and hours, doing nothing while she worked.

"You're just going to hike right back up here, aren't you?" Gideon asked suspiciously.

"We've already established that I'm going to go exactly where I want on my own time."

Though he muttered something under his breath, they began scouting for an observation post. A spot was quickly located and she settled down with her camera to watch for movement while Gideon tethered the horses on a hitch line below them. Soon he was sitting nearby with his binoculars and a can of bear spray set conspicuously on a nearby rock. Danger sat between them, ears and nose up, equally attentive. He knew his job was to watch for threats.

Alaina gave him a hug and returned to her camera.

One thing she hadn't anticipated about her year in Montana was falling in love with a dog and two horses. Leaving the Double Branch next May was going to be even harder than she'd thought. The animals wouldn't understand if she stopped giving them attention…but maybe she should consider putting some distance between her and Gideon.

He might not give her another thought after she'd moved out of the foreman's cabin—aside from a sigh of relief—but she doubted it would be as easy for her. Something about Gideon turned her inside out, whether she liked it or not.

"I think it's time to stop doing our tours," she said, keeping her focus on the terrain beyond their vantage point. "You're going into another exceptionally busy season and I've seen enough of the ranch and surrounding area that I'm pretty well set."

From the corner of her eye, she saw Gideon put his binoculars down. "There's more to show you."

"But I've seen a good deal, and I won't be

hiking as far during the winter months, regardless. I doubt I can move as fast on snowshoes and pulling a sled."

"We'll talk about it."

"We just did."

"I mean when you aren't annoyed because I won't leave you here to hike down by yourself."

Alaina made a scoffing sound. "That has nothing to do with it. Your attention should be on the ranch."

"Don't you need pictures of us moving the herds and separating the cows to be sold?" Gideon asked. "I signed the release, so you can go ahead with the book."

She continued gazing through her camera. She'd shown Gideon the pictures she'd taken so far of ranch operations, including the ones of him carrying the calf. He hadn't objected to them being used, probably because he'd simply seen them as a rancher doing whatever was needed, no more, no less. There *was* a gritty, authentic realism to all the photos she'd taken of him, but his masculine appeal couldn't be denied.

"My agent is finalizing the details with the publisher," Alaina murmured.

"That's great."

"I'll also be doing the captions and other

text because they want the book to be an out-sider's view of ranching. I cowrote two books with my husband, so I have publishing cre-dentials. A mix of my wildlife photos will be included to show how close many Montana ranchers live to the wilderness."

"Any of the Wind Singer pack?"

"No way. I don't want anybody to know where they are."

A movement at the edge of the lens caught her attention, so she shifted and refocused. It was an American pika harvesting plants for the winter. She took a burst of photos, following the small animal as it darted here and there through the low growth, diving into a group of rocks to deposit its collection for drying, then reappearing to get more. At one point it stopped and opened its mouth to make a series of calls. They were too far away to hear its squeaky "eek, eek," but she'd heard it often enough in the past that the sound echoed in her memory.

"Busy little guy," Gideon said as he gazed through his binoculars. "It won't be long be-fore snow covers his home again."

Alaina looked at Gideon. "He has a precar-ious life up here. Some might say the same about the Double Branch, at least in the early days."

"We still have our challenges, but it's nothing compared to what Grandpa Jonah faced. His father made a fortune mining gold, but Jonah was interested in cattle. He was in the Dakotas working as a ranch hand the winter of 1886 to 1887, when thousands of cows froze to death. That winter was a nightmare."

Alaina shivered. "Jonah talks about it in his journals. He learned his father was dying, but couldn't get back. It was just too dangerous."

"He returned in the late spring of 1887 and got his brothers together, convincing them to settle up here. Despite what had happened, he still saw ranching as the future. They bought existing ranches with their inheritance and homesteaded what they could. The ranchers around Bannister had lost everything and were eager to sell. But Jonah was the one who kept buying more and more property as the years passed, leasing what he couldn't buy outright. His son and grandson did the same."

A fluke of timing, Alaina thought. The Westcott brothers had received their inheritance in a period when Montana ranchers were going under. They'd taken the chance to become ranchers themselves, though the previous winter had shown it was risky to raise cattle in the northern territories.

"Everything seemed to work out in the end," she said.

"It was a good life for the Westcotts. Montana became a state soon afterward. The Hewitt family moved here and dedicated their lives to upholding the law. We've had setbacks, but we're survivors."

Pride resonated in his voice and the old longing to know more about her roots filled Alaina. If her mother didn't do some research soon, she would give it a try herself.

"Why didn't Colby and his wife have a bigger family?" she asked, turning back to her camera.

"Well, he was overseas a long time during World War II. They had a son, Arthur, but after that, my great-grandmother had several miscarriages. When Grandma Claire finally came along, they called her their Easter blessing. Sadly, Arthur caught measles when he was twenty and died from pneumonia."

"Were they upset when their daughter married out of the area?"

"They probably weren't thrilled, but she visited often and sent my mom here each summer when she was old enough. Mom did the same with us kids."

"That's nice." Alaina shot pictures of a chipmunk, then a hoary marmot lumbered into view and she took another burst of photos. "Did you know as a kid that you'd inherit the Double Branch?" she asked.

"I didn't think much about it, but I loved the ranch and the mountains, while Flynn wasn't as enthusiastic. It could be why my grandparents and great-grandparents arranged things the way they did. Sometimes I feel guilty that I can be my own man, while Flynn is still running the Carmichael ranch in Shelton for Grandpa Joe."

"There's no reason to feel guilty," Alaina said. "I'm sure you both prefer your grandparents to be in such good health. Besides, Libby says that Flynn has full autonomy."

"For the most part. Grandpa Joe helps out during busy periods and can't resist offering his opinion when he thinks it's needed. But he does the same with me, too."

"Once a rancher, always a rancher?"

"Something like that."

Alaina tried to stay focused on the area beyond, hoping to get more pictures of the marmot. They were appealing animals that used high-pitched whistles to communicate with their colony or warn them.

But her thoughts kept getting dragged

back to Gideon. How could she have let him get under her skin this much? She didn't *want* to have feelings for him or any other man.

Or did she?

Gideon was making her rethink herself. She'd loved Mason, but he wouldn't have wanted her to bury her heart with him. He'd believed in living to the fullest, and that love was an essential part of living. In fact, he'd be upset that she'd rejected any thought of falling in love and getting married again. And, while Mason had never blamed ranchers for worrying about their herds, he would have appreciated Gideon and his efforts to coexist with predators.

Still, happily-ever-after seemed improbable with Gideon. Though he claimed to be less angry about his ex-wife, it didn't mean he'd changed his mind about marriage or sharing his life with someone.

Alaina let out a breath.

Okay, just because Gideon wasn't a likely possibility, she shouldn't close her heart and mind to the idea of meeting someone in the future. She just had to stop thinking about him so much, and put up some of the emotional barriers he was so good at erecting himself.

Anyway, her feelings were so muddled she

wasn't sure what she really felt. It was one thing to contemplate the possibility of love, another to decide where to go with it.

A FEW WEEKS later Libby walked out of the Made Right Pizza Parlor with Deke, a stiff breeze scattering leaves at their feet. Her friends had already left for Bozeman and she needed to drive down herself, but she'd wanted to eat dinner with him first.

The group had chosen her as the excavation leader to thank her for getting them involved, which was awfully nice of them. She was lucky; archeologists could wait years for this kind of opportunity.

"Cold?" Deke asked as she zipped her jacket.

"Some. Gideon must be right about an early winter. We've already had two early snows, though it melted quickly."

They reached her SUV and Libby let Cookie out to run around before the trip down out of the mountains.

She sighed.

It was getting harder and harder to leave Deke. But while they'd shared an enthusiastic kiss after finding an artifact at the Dragon's Tooth hot spring, he'd kept his distance ever since.

She knew her own feelings—she loved him. And she was certain he loved her. But how did she convince him that their differences weren't insurmountable?

Things didn't seem to be any better with Gideon and Alaina, either. They were polite to each other, which seemed less promising than when they'd argued often. Worse, they had stopped going on their tours. Of course, Gideon and his ranch hands were frantically busy moving the cattle and sorting the animals to be sold. It was the same with Flynn at the Carmichael family ranch in Shelton.

Alaina sometimes rode out with the ranch hands, staying on the periphery to get the pictures she needed, but Gideon didn't make any special effort to be near her.

There was an urgency to Gideon's preparations for winter. He'd increased his order of protein cake for the cattle and was splitting logs until late into the evening, putting up more firewood than usual in case the ranch lost power during a storm. So maybe he and Alaina weren't having a problem. Gideon had tunnel vision when he needed to do something for the Double Branch.

"Hey, you're frowning," Deke said. "Is something wrong?"

"No. But it's going to be hard to stop working on the site when winter arrives. We sent a camera up on a balloon and saw a large number of circular patterns in the tree growth. It doesn't necessarily mean anything, but we know Paleo-Indians built round lodges with stone-lined platforms."

"It's amazing those patterns could exist after so long."

"And lucky for archeologists."

Deke chuckled. "That's right. I foresee a great career in your future. A doctorate and maybe a book or two or three."

"Gee, thanks," she said, snuggling close to him.

A truck pulled into the restaurant parking lot next to them, but she didn't care if they had an audience.

"Is your team coming up next weekend?" Deke asked.

"If it doesn't snow too much. We're going to—"

"Hey, I want to talk to you," a harsh voice interrupted.

Deke looked up. It was Yancy Felder, who owned a ranch on the eastern edge of Bannister County. Felder wasn't too bad most of the time, but he had a big mouth, especially when he'd been drinking.

"What do you want?" Deke asked calmly.

"Not you, *her*." Yancy pointed at Libby.

"What could you want with me?"

Cookie raced over, offering a warning growl, and the rancher took a wary step backward. "Your brother is letting that woman stay at the Double Branch. I don't like it."

"If you're talking about Alaina Wright, she's a wildlife photographer and none of your concern," Deke told him.

While Yancy had driven up in a white truck, Deke recalled he had a battered red pickup that he mostly used for moving hay around his property.

"She's more than that." Yancy pulled some paper from his pocket and held it out while keeping a cautious watch on Cookie. "She was married to a famous wolf guy."

Deke unfolded the crumpled pages and saw a magazine article titled, "Scientific World Stunned by Loss of Wolf Biologist." The picture below was of an older man, but Alaina was recognizable in the background. She was the kind of woman who'd be hard to miss. Deke scanned the text to pick out the pertinent facts, Libby leaning against his shoulder to read it, as well.

Dr. Mason Wright, 58. Respected wolf biologist killed in head-on collision with a drunk driver. Leaves a widow, fellow scien-tist Alaina Wright, 27. Also survived by his parents and a sister. A prominent voice in wolf conservation...

It went on to explain that Mason Wright was one of the experts who'd advocated for the reintroduction of wolves to Yellowstone National Park, listing his degrees and the ti-tles of his books, including two that he and Alaina had coauthored. Deke refolded the article and returned it to Yancy.

"So?"

"So we don't want her in Bannister."

"We? You mean *you*. Don't speak for the rest of us." Deke struggled to keep the anger out of his voice. "This is a free coun-try. Alaina has every right to do her work and be left alone. And if the sheriff's office learns you've made trouble or threatened her in any way, you could be facing criminal charges. I'll be looking into it *personally*."

Yancy went pale. "But...but her hus-band helped bring wolves back. What was he doing with a gal young enough to be his daughter, anyhow?"

"That isn't any of your business. Now go home and remember what I said."

When Yancy had driven away, Deke turned to Libby. Her eyes sparked furiously.

"I'll bet he's the one responsible for Alaina being treated so badly in town," she snapped.

"I've only heard about two encounters with an aggressive driver. Is there more?"

LIBBY NODDED. "THE second time she was forced off the road. I just found out about it a few days ago. We wanted her to come into Bannister and have pizza with us on Friday, but she wouldn't go. I kept asking and she finally told me."

Deke gazed in the direction that Yancy's truck had disappeared, his eyes cold with restrained anger. "I should have arrested him."

"You don't have evidence it was Yancy."

"Not yet. But if there is some, I'll find it. What else can you tell me?"

A quiver crept through Libby. She'd never seen *this* side of Deke; it was both sexy and disconcerting. "Um, that was the worst thing, but Alaina stopped shopping at the grocery store because they were so unfriendly. Then in August, Bill Anders canceled her order for snow tires. I bought the same tires from him a week later. And I'll bet Yancy is somehow responsible for Alaina's supply orders being returned, too."

Cookie was looking at her anxiously, so she gave him a comforting pat.

Deke sighed. "I'd hoped Alaina's interest in photographing wolves wouldn't become common knowledge, but no one seems to know about it. The concern is her marriage to Dr. Wright. Funny, I would never have pictured her with an older guy."

Libby winced, recalling the way she'd fumed to Alaina about Dr. Barstow's young wife. Plainly Alaina had been much younger than her husband, but really, what difference had it made?

"Alaina was in love with her husband, that's all that matters," Libby said firmly. "Besides, you saw Mason Wright's photo. That guy was *hot*. He didn't need to prove anything to himself or anyone else."

"Uh, no comment. But I'll phone Gideon and explain what's going on."

"I can call him."

Deke shook his head. "Nah, he'll probably use language he doesn't want you to hear. Regardless, you have to get back to Bozeman for class tomorrow and shouldn't drive angry."

"Too late for that," Libby muttered.

"At least let me know when you get there. Not because I'm checking up on you, because I'm concerned."

"Then I get something from you in return." She looped her arms around Deke's neck and gave him a long kiss. When she stepped away, she was glad to see he looked as discombobulated as she felt. "See you on Friday."

Libby opened the SUV door and Cookie jumped in ahead of her. She waved at Deke as she drove out of the lot.

The man was impossible. A small part of her remained old-fashioned enough to want *him* to be the one to propose, but she might have to bite the bullet and do it herself.

Otherwise they might never get together.

CHAPTER FIFTEEN

GIDEON THANKED DEKE for the heads-up and hung up the phone, struggling with a mix of anger and disappointment. How could his neighbors behave that way toward anyone, much less a guest on the Double Branch? And what would have happened if Yancy had confronted Libby when she was alone?

"What's wrong?" his mom asked as he paced the kitchen.

"Nothing for you to worry about," he said automatically.

She put her hands on her hips and gave him a stern look. "I may have had trouble coping after Stewart died, but I'm past that. Now stop trying to protect me and start talking."

Despite his churning emotions, Gideon smiled. "All right. What do you know about Yancy Felder?"

"Not much except Grandpa Colby tried to buy him out once, saying he was a poor rancher and a worse neighbor to everyone in the area."

"He got that part right."

Gideon quickly gave her a rundown of what Deke had told him.

Helene's eyes turned bright with anger. "How could Bill Anders go along with that sort of thing? I would have expected better of him."

"There's a family connection."

"That's no excuse. Wrong is wrong."

Gideon agreed. A decent man was participating in Yancy's misconduct and it was a bitter pill to swallow.

"So what are we going to do?" she asked.

"I'm not sure yet. I'll have to talk with Alaina and then go from there. Right now I need to work off my tension, so I'm going out to chop wood. Thanks for a great dinner. Your huckleberry pie was amazing as always."

"Thank the kids who had the patience to pick the berries," she retorted.

His mother had stayed busy all summer and fall, making jam and freezing gallon after gallon of wild huckleberries in July and August, all picked by the local Scouts.

She and Grandma Claire had divided the fruit from the orchard, putting some aside for the horses and canning and freezing the rest. Helene had even collected the volunteer pumpkins discovered growing in the ranch's old vegetable garden.

"I found the original family recipe for pumpkin pie and bread," she'd told Gideon a few weeks earlier. "So we're well set for winter and the holidays."

He'd teased, saying she was returning to her pioneer roots in canning and preserving, but it had reassured him, as well. Her search for family keepsakes now seemed more like a treasure hunt, with calls back and forth with Grandma Claire to uncover the history of items like a sturdy handmade cradle and a cedar chest.

Outside Gideon checked his phone for the latest weather updates, along with the application that tracked Alaina's GPS location. It told him she was at the first wolf observation point she'd found.

He was trying not to worry about her as much, though it wasn't easy. Ironically she was probably much safer up there than around a loose cannon like Yancy Felder.

Gideon put the phone away and swung his ax down on a chunk of wood. An hour later he'd thrown off his coat and was dripping with sweat, but he couldn't escape his churning thoughts.

Why hadn't Alaina told him about the problems Yancy was causing? She hadn't mentioned having issues at the grocery store or even how serious the road incidents had been, and he distinctly remembered her saying Anders Garage couldn't get the tires she'd needed, not that her order had been canceled.

They'd had their disagreements, but surely she knew he wouldn't take Yancy's side in the matter.

Just then Nate came around the side of the barn with one of the barn cats draped contentedly around his neck. Bongo's tail was waving and he was licking a paw.

"Evening, boss. The boys wanted me to thank you for the new easy chairs you got for the bunkhouse. They're a treat."

"I'm glad you like them."

"One of us could work on the firewood," Nate said, gesturing at the oversized logs that still needed to be split with wedges and a maul. "You don't have to do it all."

"You've got plenty else to handle." Gideon didn't ask the ranch hands to do chores around the house. He'd hired them to work the Double Branch, not take care of his household needs. Besides, they were already splitting wood for the bunkhouse. "Thanks for stepping up while I was showing Alaina around."

"She's a nice lady." Nate scratched Bongo's neck and the feline's purr rumbled, audible from several feet away. Of all the ranch hands, Nate appreciated the barn cats the most and made special friends with them. "You paid me extra, but I would have done it anyway. Besides, you rode fences and watched the herds on the days you were gone. Somebody had to do that."

"I just want to be fair."

"We like workin' for the Double Branch," Nate said after another minute, a curiously intent expression on his weathered face. "So if there's ever anything that you and yours ever need, just say the word."

"Thanks."

He left, still stroking Bongo, and Gideon frowned, wondering if his employees already knew that Yancy Felder was spreading his spite around town.

AFTER A SLEEPLESS NIGHT, Gideon saddled Brushfire and rode out to speak with Alaina. Thick frost coated the grass and the aspens had turned a brilliant gold against the blue sky.

He tied Brushfire to a tree near the spring, unhooked a bag from the saddle and climbed as silently as possible to where Alaina was camped.

"Hi," she murmured when he came close. "What are you doing up here?" Though her tent and sleeping bag were already tucked away, she was heavily bundled against the cold and sitting on an insulated pad to watch for her wolves.

He rubbed Danger's neck. "Just visiting. Would you like coffee? Mom made a thermos."

"Sure." She accepted a cup and sipped appreciatively. "Mmm, freeze-dried coffee tastes nothing like what Helene makes."

"Yeah, Mom must have been a barista in another life."

Gideon poured a cup for himself and capped the thermos. He wanted to find the right moment to ask about the problems Alaina had encountered in Bannister, so he sat next to her where they could watch the river valley in comfortable silence.

"Have the Wind Singers shown up this morning?" he asked finally.

"Not so far. I think they're hunting up the valley. There was a group howl that could have initiated a chase, but nothing since, so they may not have been successful. Wolves often howl to celebrate."

"Did you learn that from those field studies you worked on or in college?" Gideon asked casually.

Around 2:00 a.m. he'd finally given up the attempt to sleep and gone to the computer to research Alaina and her husband. He'd found quite a bit. Deke had said there was a substantial difference in their ages, but when Gideon had seen the pictures of Dr. Wright, he'd become more discouraged than ever.

Mason Wright hadn't been an aging scientist with little to offer a woman except intellectual stimulation; he'd been healthy and dynamic. Energy leaped from his photographs and he'd looked as if there was nothing he couldn't have accomplished. The pictures of him with Alaina had shown a devoted couple, often smiling or laughing.

Gideon's hand tightened on his cup. Did he have any hope of competing with Mason Wright's memory or Alaina's new career? And what about the possibility that he'd have to shoot a bear or wolf someday? She might never forgive him.

"I have a degree in environmental science, which naturally included classes on botany and wildlife biology," Alaina explained after a moment. "I was one of those overachievers who skipped grades in school to start college early."

"From what you've told me about your childhood, you must have been eager to get out on your own so you wouldn't feel so stifled. What about your master's degree?"

She blinked, looking surprised. "I was doing postgraduate work when I met Mason. To be honest, I only finished my thesis because of the insinuations that I'd married my way onto his research team. Not that I ever told him it was the reason."

Gideon felt a guilty elation at the admission. If she'd kept something from her husband, it was less surprising she'd keep things from other people. "Why is that?"

"He wouldn't have understood. And he would have been right. I shouldn't have let it get to me. I was qualified and worked hard, but it's difficult to escape petty jealousies. In particular, two of Mason's longtime associates felt displaced as his confidant when I came along." Her face held a wry acceptance. "Research teams can be like families, resenting a newcomer because the dynamics have changed."

"Not *all* families. I had a hard time accepting my stepdad, but I was old enough to see that my grandparents welcomed him from the very beginning."

"You're right, not all families. And by the time I earned my degree, the issues had resolved. People learn and grow. I still hear from them, asking how I am and if I'm coming back."

"Is that something you've considered?" he asked, drawing a harsh breath.

"No. In fact, I've decided to concentrate my work on the wildlife in Montana and around Yellowstone."

"What about Antarctica and the other places you talked about?"

"I'm happiest here," she said simply.

It was a relief to hear, even if it didn't answer all of his questions.

The truth he couldn't escape any longer was how deeply he'd fallen in love with Alaina. She was the only future that mattered to him.

ALAINA BENT TO look through her camera, wondering why Gideon was so curious about the past. *Her* past, no less. He would tell her, sooner or later. Probably sooner if she didn't push.

The approach of winter was no less thrilling or interesting because she'd studied the science behind it. The wolves were magnificent. Elk, deer and other animals were eating every bite of food they could find before snow covered the ground. And the deciduous trees had turned glorious autumn colors, a forerunner of the approaching winter.

A sense of anticipation filled the air.

Autumn was her favorite time of year and she'd taken picture after picture, trying to capture the changing season. Before long she'd have to use snowshoes to reach her various observation posts. Just the other day she'd photographed a standoff between the Wind Singer pack and a grizzly over possession of a kill. The wolves had ultimately surrendered; bears were so powerful, it was unlikely the pack would risk their small number fighting one. But by the end of November, the bears would be in hibernation and wolves would be on top.

Next to her, Gideon cleared his throat. "I've heard you've had more trouble in Bannister than you told me about."

Oh. *That* was why he'd ridden up to see her.

Alaina straightened and made a face. "It doesn't matter. I'm driving to Bozeman for everything now. Better selection, better prices, so it worked out."

"It matters to me," he insisted. "I expect more of my neighbors."

"It isn't everyone. And perhaps I just caught a few people on bad days."

"That may be true for the most part," Gideon said flatly. "But one of our strongest anti-wolf ranchers recognized you from an article about your husband. Yancy has a big mouth and relatives in town. He's never stopped resenting wolves being introduced to Yellowstone, and he knows Mason Wright was one of the scientists who advocated for the government's decision."

That explained a lot. Yancy was the old guy she'd met in the post office; she remembered the postal clerk calling him by name.

"These things blow over," Alaina said.

"He should be in jail for running you off the road."

She let out an exasperated breath. "And I shouldn't have told Libby what happened. We don't know it was him."

"An old red truck splattered with mud? Angry, aggressive driver? Sounds like Yancy. Deke seems certain, too."

"It's a moot point since I couldn't read the license plate. Honestly, Gideon, this isn't worth getting uptight over. A few people are still unhappy about something that happened a long time ago. So what? I should have realized that was the reason for things getting a little weird."

"You should be outraged. *I'm* outraged."

Alaina sighed. "Hey, I've heard my share of grumbling, and not just from Mason's team. Before long the emotions settle down and things go back to normal. Besides, I don't blame ranchers for being concerned about their herds. Wolves and grizzlies are a real threat."

"Regardless, Yancy needs to be put on notice."

"And I'm sure Deke has already done that. Please, it wouldn't be right for you to get on bad terms with your neighbors because of me."

"I can't—"

"I appreciate the concern," Alaina said quickly. "But things were a lot touchier when wolf reintroduction was first proposed. I've heard stories."

"Stories are *all* you could have heard. Why didn't you tell me your husband was so much older?" Gideon asked. "You were obviously happy with him. I might have felt better about Libby and Deke dating if I'd known."

Alaina shook her head. "Age is just a small part of who Mason and I were as a couple.

No matter what, you were going to keep finding things to worry about Libby and Deke because it's hard for you to let go of being a protective big brother."

"Am I really that bad?"

She finished her coffee and handed him the cup. "I think because your marriage was a mistake, you're worried that Libby will make the same one. But have you stopped to consider that keeping her and Deke apart could be just as much of a mistake?"

Gideon's brow creased. "No."

"Then it's fortunate Libby is too strong-minded to let anyone get in her way," Alaina said with a reassuring smile. She longed to kiss him again, but he might get the wrong idea. *Or the right one*, her heart suggested. But it wasn't easy to throw her inhibitions aside. Kissing him now had higher stakes than when they'd kissed after their playful water fight. Over the past few weeks, she may have accepted she was ready to love again, but the risks she'd taken with Mason had been different and she had already lost so much. It had been much easier to fling herself into romance when she was twenty-one and didn't know how badly a shattered heart could hurt.

"Are you still generally opposed to marriage?" Alaina asked lightly, hoping Gideon would give her a hint about his feelings.

"I was never opposed, exactly. I just had a bad experience. Actually, I've been giving marriage a fair amount of consideration lately."

Their gazes met briefly and Alaina's pulse jumped. He undoubtedly felt something for her. Warmth, definitely. Love, maybe.

Perhaps she *should* have told him about the issues in town, but she'd hated the idea of adding to his worries.

Alaina was suddenly struck by irony. How many times had she objected to Gideon trying to protect her? Now she'd done the same thing. Was there any real difference between him being protective of her physical safety and her wanting to safeguard him from stress?

Relationships required give and take. Not that she was 100 percent sure this *was* a relationship yet, though she was becoming more optimistic.

A wolf howl echoed through the air, saving her from having to say anything. Together they leaned over to look into the river valley. No wolves were in sight, but that wasn't unexpected since a howl could carry for miles.

"Why *do* wolves howl?" Gideon asked after a moment.

"Mmm, lots of reasons. Affection, for one. And to help gather the pack or find each other. Sometimes to rev themselves up for a hunt or celebrate success afterward. It also warns rival packs away. But mostly I think they enjoy it, especially when they're together. Wouldn't you howl if you could?"

He grinned. "Probably. Are you staying up here another night?"

"Another *several* nights."

While a tight expression flickered across Gideon's face, he didn't object. Whether he'd be so accepting once winter arrived was another matter. Still, she was resolved to be more understanding about it...especially if he was concerned because he cared about her.

BY OF THE third week in November, Gideon's convictions about an early winter had been proven right. Snow lay in drifts around the ranch center and got deeper with each hundred-foot rise in elevation. Daytime temperatures were barely above freezing and the thermometer sank much lower at night.

At first Alaina had day-hiked to become accustomed to her snowshoes while pulling a loaded sled. It was both easier and harder than she'd expected. But soon she was going on overnight excursions, sometimes accompanied by Gideon. They still took the horses when they went together, which wouldn't be feasible once the snow got much deeper.

Alaina enjoyed his company, though she felt guilty about taking him away from the ranch. Nonetheless, there was a peaceful simplicity to being alone with Gideon in the frozen wild.

And it brought clarity. As it turned out, the whole time her head had been worried about her heart getting torn apart again, her heart had already taken the leap.

She loved Gideon, wholly and completely.

"Libby tells me it isn't unusual to see elk in the ranch compound during bad storms," she said as they rode back from their latest outing.

"There's more shelter between the buildings and they can find bits of hay. But they move back up the valley when anyone comes out."

A smile played on Alaina's lips. She was sure Gideon deliberately put hay out for the elk, at least during the worst weather.

How could she not adore someone who tried to protect wolves, elk and cattle, all at the same time?

And right now the cattle needed protecting.

She and Gideon had been up by 4:00 a.m., breaking camp. He was convinced a bad storm was on the way, much worse than predicted. He'd spoken to Nate on the satellite phone before light, telling him to start putting hay and protein cake out for the herds and that he'd be there to help as soon as possible.

"We could lose electricity," Gideon said. He looked up as they approached the ranch. The sky was a leaden gray and the temperature was sinking rapidly. "Why don't you stay in the main house until the storm blows over? We have a generator that keeps lights and refrigeration going when power is lost. You'd be more comfortable."

"Thanks, but I'll be fine in the cabin. If the storm lightens up enough, I'll visit Rita in the calving barn." Rita and her fellow orphans each weighed hundreds of pounds now, but Alaina still saw them as defenseless babies.

"She'll be all right with the other calves," he said gently.

"I know."

Gideon hadn't sold any of the motherless calves in October, which made Alaina happy. She would have hated seeing them leave.

They rode to the horse barn so he could

unload the camping supplies Brushfire carried, where they were greeted by Jax and Ollie. Flakes of snow blew in through the open door and Alaina's stomach twisted.

A whole day out in this?

Yet Gideon's cowhands were already feeding the herds and he would never leave them to work alone.

"I know how this will sound after everything I've said…but be careful out there," she urged.

Gideon pulled her into a tight embrace. "It sounds fine to me. And don't worry. I have every intention of being around for a very long time."

A moment later he and the dogs were gone and Alaina's heart ached. Someday she would have the skill to help feed the cattle, but right now she'd just be in the way.

Determined to be useful, she unsaddled and groomed Nikko, then put a heavy padded blanket over him. She brought the other horses in and dried them off before putting blankets on them, as well. Then she went to the cowhand's barn and did the same for their spare horses, making sure all the feed buckets were full and that they had fresh water.

While the snow was still light, Gideon's urgency about the weather had communicated itself to her, so back at the cabin she brought armloads of firewood inside and stacked more on the porch by the door.

Her mother called shortly after she'd finished. "Hi, Mom, what's up?"

"Unfortunately, nothing. We were going to surprise you for Thanksgiving, but the airline just canceled our flight. I'm so sorry. We wanted the family to be together for the holiday."

Alaina's eyes widened. "You were going to drop in from Connecticut?"

"Not exactly. We've had our tickets since August and I would have bought groceries before driving up there."

Phew.

Alaina dropped onto a chair by the woodburning stove. She'd forgotten it would be Thanksgiving in a couple of days.

"Um, that's too bad," she murmured, wincing at the idea of hosting her parents and brothers in the tiny cabin.

"Your father and I can't get away at Christmas, or we would have switched our trip to then," her mother said regretfully.

"That's all right," Alaina assured her. "We can do a video call for both holidays."

"It isn't the same as being together."

"I spent both Thanksgiving and Christmas in Port Coopersmith last year," Alaina pointed out.

"I know, but we missed so many together when you…that is…when you and Mason were working. We thought that maybe, you know, eventually everything might get back to normal."

Normal?

Alaina pressed a finger to her aching temple. "Mom, I love you, but my life isn't in Connecticut any longer, and it hasn't been for a long time. Things won't ever be the way they were before I got married."

"I didn't mean… That isn't what I meant."

"I think it is. You want the old days back, before I grew up. But I'm a different person now, and I'm doing what makes me happy. I'm sorry you're disappointed and I don't want to hurt you, but please accept what I'm saying."

A long silence followed, then her mother sighed. "I'm the one who's sorry. What happened with Mason was so awful. It's hard not to remember we could have lost you both. It made us want to hold on that much harder."

"I understand, more than you know," Alaina said gently. "But you *didn't* lose me. Look, I should get off. I have things to do before the weather gets worse."

They said goodbye and she breathed a sigh of relief. She loved her family and understood they worried, but she couldn't return to being their coddled little girl.

Alaina shook the thought away and pulled out her Christmas decorations. Yet it was a restless energy that drove her rather than the desire to decorate.

All she could think about was Gideon out in the cold and how much she loved him, heart and soul and everything in between.

She looked across at the large ranch house. It had been built for a family and she wanted to spend the rest of her life there raising kids and taking pictures of Montana…if those kids belonged to Gideon, too.

SNOW SWIRLED AROUND Gideon and his employees as they rode up to the ranch, the dogs trailing along tiredly. It was almost dark, but the cheerful display at the far end of the property sent a murmur of appreciation through the weary group.

Gideon had rolled his eyes when Alaina put out white Christmas lights in June. Now he smiled, warmth washing over him at the sight.

Twinkling multicolored light strings decorated the porch roof and lighted evergreen swags adorned the railings. What must be battery-powered candles flickered a welcome in the windows and a brightly lit Christmas tree sat on one side of the door covered with shiny ornaments.

"Hey, and somebody brought the horses in," Jeremy said, brightening even more. "I bet it was Alaina."

"Does she know about the meeting, boss?" Nate asked worriedly.

"No, and don't say anything to her."

The others nodded. An underlying tension remained in Bannister about Alaina's presence on the Double Branch. She might believe everything would blow over, but Gideon wasn't convinced. He planned to address it at the next ranch association meeting.

Nate and the other hands were attending in support, though they all agreed it was just a few people involved. Unfortunately those few people had made Alaina feel so unwelcome she wouldn't go anywhere near the town.

The dogs settled on piles of straw in the barn, waiting while Gideon took care of Brushfire and checked on the rest of the horses. Griz woke, looked at him and snorted in apparent disgust, likely hoping it had been Alaina visiting.

"Sorry, pal." He gave the horse a carrot.

He put Danger, Jax and Ollie in the house and said hello to his mom as he ran a towel over each dog and encouraged them to lie in their beds by the fireplace.

"Are you ready for dinner?" Helene asked. "I have stew and corn bread ready."

"Sounds great, I just want to check on Alaina first."

Gideon kissed her and then walked down to the foreman's cabin. The door opened before he could knock and he saw relief in Alaina's eyes.

"Thank goodness you're done," she exclaimed, urging him inside and handing him a steaming mug of coffee. "You *are* done, right?"

"For now. I wanted to thank you for bringing the horses in," he said before taking a long welcome swallow.

She shrugged. "It wasn't much."

"It's a lot to me, and to the men."

The Christmas tree Alaina had gotten on their trip to Bozeman stood by the staircase, arrayed with nature-themed decorations and silver balls. As Gideon looked closer, a feline paw reached between the stair railings to swat an ornament.

"It looks as if you had help with those decorations," he said with a chuckle. The bone-deep exhaustion in his body was easing, just from seeing Alaina, and he would have loved to snuggle with her in front of the stove for the next several hours.

Soon, he hoped.

Alaina ran up the stairs and returned with the gray tabby who usually resided in the main horse barn. "Merlin likes to visit. I know the barn cats have warm places to sleep, but the wind was so strong I couldn't bear to put him out."

"He can stay whenever he likes. I'll bring cat supplies over."

A faint pink brightened her cheeks. "I already have a litter box and food for him," she confessed.

He grinned. There was no doubt about it, Alaina was an animal charmer. He just wished that Yancy Felder had allowed himself to be charmed as well, or he wouldn't still be causing problems.

Gideon was anxious to clear the air in town before speaking to Alaina about the future. Surely his friends and neighbors would help put a stop to what Yancy and his few supporters were doing.

He loved Alaina more than anything else in the world and would do whatever he could to make her happy.

CHAPTER SIXTEEN

FOLLOWING A SUCCESSFUL Thanksgiving video call with her family, Alaina settled down to work on the narrative for her ranch book project.

Everything was going well professionally. Her agent had sold a number of her wildlife photographs, in addition to the ranch book deal. She had even more choices now than she'd had before. But none of that seemed terribly important at the moment.

"Mrrreow," Merlin trilled as he jumped onto her lap, nearly sending her computer to the floor. She put it to one side and cuddled him. The storm had finally passed, but he showed no interest in returning to his life in the barn.

"You're leaving all your pest control responsibilities to the other cats," she scolded him. "You'll have to go back when I go out again. You can't stay alone in the cabin."

He yawned and put his head on her arm, purring loudly.

A knock on the door startled them both and he leaped away. It was Helene. She'd called during the storm with an invitation to the holiday meal, but Alaina had made an excuse, saying she needed to focus on her ranch book project.

"Happy Thanksgiving," Helene said brightly. "I know what you said, but I won't take no for answer. You have to share our meal," she said in a tone reminiscent of her pleas to attend the Founders Day celebration. "You had all that time during the storm to work. You can spend part of the day with us."

"But I don't have anything to contribute," Alaina protested, albeit half-heartedly.

"We don't need anything except your company. Libby is here with Deke, but I can't cook a Thanksgiving feast for less than twenty people. Food will be coming out of our ears."

"What about Nate and the other ranch hands?"

"Their families are local. Please come."

A home-cooked Thanksgiving dinner sounded better than the lasagna Alaina had in the fridge, so she put on her coat and went with Helene.

Alaina stepped into the main house and looked around, instantly imagining it decorated for Christmas. It was a perfect canvas for the bright, welcoming warmth of the upcoming holiday. Not that she had anything against Thanksgiving; it would be wonderful to decorate for that, as well.

You're getting ahead of yourself, her brain warned.

"Great, Mom talked you into coming," Libby exclaimed. "The food is almost done. I can't cook, but Deke claims to know his way around a stove, so I sent him to help in my place."

Alaina grinned. She knew Gideon's sister planned to propose to Deke this trip and was looking forward to seeing the deputy sheriff's reaction to Hurricane Libby.

Gideon nodded a greeting and went back to dozing on the couch. She knew he'd been out working since before dawn, so she and Libby sat by the fireplace and talked quietly, trying not to disturb him.

Libby was philosophical that the early winter had shortened her team's dig time at the hot spring, even before they could confirm the value of the site.

"My biggest concern is that Dragon's Tooth is relatively close to Victor Reese's spread. Once we're there a lot, he might realize what we're doing. I don't want news leaking out early."

"Victor is the rancher who lets his cattle stray onto the Double Branch to graze, right?" Alaina asked.

"That's right. He's okay, but he might say something in town about students digging."

"You can stop worrying, I bought Victor's ranch a month ago," Gideon said, startling them as he sat up. "He's retiring to Arizona where his son and daughter live."

Libby blinked. "How did you swing that?"

"The money is from a trust fund that Grandpa Colby created to buy ranches in the area. I'm the trustee, but the land won't be part of the Double Branch unless I'm able to purchase it later."

"Then who does it belong to?"

"All of us. You, me, Flynn, Mom and Grandma Claire. I didn't want to mortgage the Double Branch, so I tapped the trust fund. Under the rules Grandpa set up, I'll run the ranch and profits will go back into the fund until any expenditures are recovered."

Libby's jaw dropped. "But that's more work for you."

"It'll be fine. Nate is moving over there and he'll be the foreman." Gideon's jaw tightened. "I've named it the Westcott Memorial Ranch. I considered calling it the Westcott Wolf Preserve, but cooler heads prevailed."

Deke had come in and he whistled. "Westcott Wolf Preserve? You aren't serious. Your great-grandfather would spin in his grave."

"Dead serious. I'm sick of the attitude around here. Don't forget there are a few things he disliked more than wolves."

A look passed between Deke and Gideon that made Alaina uneasy. Surely he wasn't still uptight about the issues she'd encountered in Bannister.

"Come and eat," Helene called from the dining room.

The meal was delicious, but Alaina had trouble enjoying the food. She was too concerned about what Gideon might be thinking. He was a good man and she didn't want him to overreact to an issue that would probably go away on its own.

Or was he thinking enough about the future that he wanted it to be resolved for both their sakes?

WHEN THE OTHERS settled down to play a word game, Deke let Libby drag him out for a walk.

The storm had ended in time for crews to

plow the roads and allow holiday travel. He was on call in case a problem cropped up, but with any luck, he'd have the rest of the evening to spend with Libby and her family.

"Isn't it beautiful?" Libby asked, gazing at the stars.

Deke had trouble looking at anything except her face, but he nodded. "Yeah, though there's a nice glow from Alaina's cabin, as well."

Libby laughed. "We love it. Mom said that she could see Alaina's Christmas lights even during the blizzard. She wants to decorate the main house, but the light strings from Great-Grandma's day are so old they're a fire hazard. I'll get more in town and bring them the next time I come. We'll have a decorating party."

"Gideon won't mind?"

"He won't object to anything Mom wants." Libby stopped and pulled him around to face her. "Okay, we need to talk."

"Isn't that what we were doing?"

She gave him an impatient look. "I don't know how to build up to something serious, so I'm just going to say what I want to say. I love you, and I know you love me. Let's get married next summer after I graduate from college."

Deke stared. He was head over heels in love with Libby, but they hadn't begun to resolve their problems.

"You're right, I love you, too," he said finally. "But there are too many reasons why we shouldn't be together. The difference in our ages and my job are two of the biggest. You can't deny being uncomfortable that I'm in law enforcement."

Libby made a scoffing noise. "What kind of person wouldn't worry about her husband taking risks? So, yes, you're older than me, and, yes, you're a deputy sheriff, but a much greater age gap didn't keep Alaina and her husband apart. Life is uncertain. My dad didn't die in the line of duty and Alaina lost her husband in an accident. If the past year has taught me anything, it's to grab on to what's good and never let go."

"But we don't know if Site A will turn out to be worth excavating," Deke argued. "I can't let you make a commitment you might regret."

"Listen to what I'm saying," Libby said firmly. "You aren't allowed to use the I'm-older-and-more-experienced argument with me, now or ever."

"Can I say something?"

"As long as it isn't too dumb."

Deke was exasperated . "If I don't agree with you, you'll say it's dumb."

She kissed his chin. "You're cute, so maybe I can forgive you for saying something not so smart."

It was hard to think straight with her looking at him like that. "You were the one who told me that Alaina sacrificed being a wildlife photographer to marry her husband."

"She never regretted it. And you can't compare us. We're two different people. I want you to know, beyond any doubt, that it doesn't matter if an archeological site is conveniently located nearby. Oh, and in case you're wondering, I want kids and I don't want to wait too long to have them. Is that how you feel?"

"Um, yeah, but—"

"No buts, unless you want a large family. We'll have to negotiate if you're hoping for more than two."

A smile grew on Deke's face. Libby was a woman who knew her own heart…a heart he wanted with every atom in his body. How could he resist her any longer?

"Two will be perfect. And I accept your proposal," he said, gathering her close for a kiss. They might still face family opposition or other challenges, but together they could get through anything.

GIDEON WALKED ALAINA to her cabin later that evening carrying the leftovers that Helene had insisted on sending.

"Your mom sure made a mountain of food," she said.

"She and Grandma Claire usually cook the Thanksgiving meal together in Shelton. I go when the weather isn't too bad, but it wouldn't have been possible this year with the early snow."

Alaina made a face. "On Tuesday I found out my parents and brothers had gotten plane tickets to Bozeman. They were going to surprise me, but the airline canceled their flight at the last minute. I admit to being relieved."

"If it was a question of needing beds, they could have stayed at the house. And heaven knows Mom made enough food."

"And let them drive *you* crazy? Not a chance. Supposedly my parents can't come at Christmas, but I wouldn't put it past them to finagle a trip to Montana, regardless."

Maybe for their daughter's wedding?

Gideon had to restrain himself from saying it aloud. Alaina was the light that had been missing from his life. Just having her

there had helped ease the absence of his stepfather, though they'd still encountered a few
tough moments...like when Libby and Deke
had announced their engagement.

In the midst of accepting everyone's con-
gratulations, tears had begun pouring down
Libby's face and she'd sobbed something
about wishing Dad were there.

"You look sad all of a sudden," Alaina
said.

"I was thinking how much my stepfather
would have enjoyed today. He was a sentimental guy."

"Would he approve of his daughter marrying Deke?" Alaina asked as she opened
the cabin door.

Gideon thought about it while he carried
the box of leftovers into the kitchen and
began handing Alaina the various contain-
ers to put in the fridge.

"Dad would have approved," he said finally. "And it's funny, there was a moment
when I could have sworn his arm was around
my shoulder while Libby made her announce-
ment. That's how he used to hug me, but..."
Gideon stopped, feeling ridiculous.

"I don't believe the people we love are ever
truly gone," Alaina said seriously.

"Your husband?"

"I still feel him sometimes. Not the way I used to, but occasionally." She cocked her head and smiled. "Maybe he's come back as a wolf."

Gideon didn't know if that was reassuring or not, and he knew it wasn't just the air in Bannister that needed clearing. As much as he hoped Alaina cared for him, Mason Wright remained a ghost between them. Gideon didn't begrudge the love she'd felt for her husband; he just wanted to be certain he was loved as deeply.

He cleared his throat. "I need to check on the horses and take care of other chores. When are you going out to work again?"

"Sunday, unless another storm moves in, but I'm not taking Danger this time," she said firmly.

"He isn't going to like that."

"The snow is too deep now for a dog to easily travel. It isn't as if I can strap snowshoes on his feet."

Danger wasn't the only one who wouldn't like her going alone, but the ranch association meeting was on Wednesday, and Gideon knew if he went with Alaina, he couldn't be sure of getting back in time.

"All right. I'll keep Danger inside until you're well away from the house," he said reluctantly. "That's the only way to keep him from following you."

ALAINA CLOSED THE cabin door behind Gideon, wondering what was going on with him. He'd been far too amenable about her going out alone. Still, he had grown accustomed to her solitary hikes during the summer and fall, so maybe he was starting to feel the same about her winter treks.

Yet the conviction that something wasn't right kept bothering her over the next couple of days.

Danger visited each evening, sometimes bringing Jax or Ollie with him. Merlin was especially fond of Danger and they would lie together next to the woodstove, soaking up the heat.

"What do you think?" she mused to Danger on Saturday night. "Am I being unreasonable? After all my determination to be independent, now I'm uptight because Gideon didn't argue about me going out on my own. Not very much, at least."

Danger raised his head and let out a small "Rrffff."

"I know, you don't have the answers. But neither do I. The thing is, I'm pretty sure he loves me, but he hasn't actually said so. Of course, neither have I. Maybe we both have too much pride for our own good."

Danger yawned and she laughed.

"You're right. Humans are totally illogical."

EARLY THE NEXT morning Alaina took Merlin to the horse barn and fed carrots to Griz and Nikko. The feline seemed philosophical about returning to his pest-controller duties, promptly going to investigate a rustle in a corner.

Then Alaina headed up to her favorite observation point. Watching the Wind Singers over the next few days soothed some of her edginess; winter was their most active season and they were often in evidence. But when she got into her tent at night, there were too many hours of darkness to just sleep and she kept turning everything over in her mind.

Something was up.

Alaina understood why Gideon had bought his neighbor's ranch. His frustration with the overgrazing issue was understandable, and he also wanted to help protect his sister's archeological interests. But why consider calling it the Westcott Wolf Preserve? The name alone would raise a huge amount of ire.

Finally Alaina called Libby. "What's going on with Gideon?" she asked bluntly.

"Oh, well, I'm not supposed to…"

"Tell me what's up."

"I wanted to tell you sooner, but Gideon is confronting Yancy and his buddies at the ranch association meeting tonight. He says things haven't settled down about your husband and he won't let it go any further."

"But it takes months for something like this to cool off. It doesn't happen in a few weeks."

"You know my brother."

Alaina looked at the time and did some fast calculations in her head. "I'm coming down. If I hurry, I can get there before it's over."

"You'll have company. I left Bozeman an hour ago. I couldn't let him do it without me. I'll meet you at the house."

"Thanks."

Alaina's habit of breaking down camp each morning stood her well. She mostly needed to fill her backpack and get moving. Adrenaline and frustration gave her extra speed and she got to the cabin earlier than expected. After a quick shower and a change into clean clothes, she raced outside to find both Helene and Libby.

"I'm going, too," Helene said obstinately.

Alaina saw the determination in their faces and nodded. They got into her SUV and headed for Bannister. Since the meeting had started by the time they arrived, she stayed in the rear to assess the best moment to speak up.

The Double Branch ranch hands were standing in front with Gideon, along with Deke in his uniform and an older man who looked exactly like him. They were a visible show of support and dismay gathered in Alaina's stomach. It wasn't right that Gideon was having trouble because of her background, and now Libby's fiancé and future father-in-law were being drawn into the conflict.

"The question of wolves was settled a long time ago and I won't allow anyone on my ranch to be harassed because of it," Gideon was saying.

"Ah, you're just in love with the woman," yelled an older man. It was Yancy, the man from the post office.

"That doesn't change what's right, as you well know," Gideon declared. "Not only that, Alaina is no threat to you or your cattle."

"Your great-grandfather would be ashamed of you."

Though Alaina's pulse had leaped when Gideon didn't deny his feelings for her, she tried to focus on the moment. She stepped forward, determined to face Yancy down herself.

Gideon caught her gaze and shook his head.

She hesitated.

Perhaps this was one of the compromises she'd have to make if they were going to have a future together. Sometimes Gideon would need to handle things; it didn't mean she wasn't holding up her end. She'd find a moment to speak up, but she needed to let him have his say now.

"You're dead wrong," Gideon said, his calm voice more quelling than if it was louder. "Colby Westcott would have let wolves live in his house before he'd treat anyone unfairly."

A faint murmur ran around the room.

"Have you forgotten my great-grandfather hosted a team of wolf scientists at the Double Branch?" he continued. "Grandpa Colby understood the difference between disagreeing with an opinion and respecting the person who *held* that opinion. If he were here today, he wouldn't tolerate anyone who gave Alaina such a poor reception in town, even to the point of forcing her off the road in his *old red truck*."

This time the murmur that went through the meeting hall was distinctly appalled and almost every attendee's head swiveled to look at Yancy.

He sat abruptly.

Another man stood, saying that he'd been trying to live with wolves on his spread; he'd even consulted with Yellowstone scientists about ways to make it easier. Others rose in agreement. None were thrilled about the predators, which was understandable, but quite a number seemed to feel wolves and bears had a place. And while any lost cow or calf was a concern, having compensation available to recoup those losses was a help.

"We also don't make questionable claims about predator kills," one rancher declared, again looking pointedly at Yancy. "At least *most* of us don't."

Yancy's face had sunk deep between the lapels of his coat and his gaze seemed permanently affixed to the floor.

When Alaina was recognized, another murmur rippled through the air, this time of surprise. But she didn't sense hostility in their expressions; it seemed more like curiosity.

She stepped forward again. "I understand you're concerned about your cattle. And that's completely valid. One thing I've learned over the past few months is that ranching isn't easy. You do it because you love this amazing place and the lives you've made here. But please don't be angry at Gideon. He's an incredibly good and decent man who I really…really care about. He's just trying to do the right thing."

She'd almost confessed to being in love with Gideon, too, but it was hard to bare her heart in front of strangers.

Following the meeting, a group of ranchers came over and apologized, saying they'd allowed old attitudes to have too much influence.

"Don't worry," the president of the ranch association said grimly. "After Gideon explained what was happening, I spoke to Bill Anders at the garage and the folks at the grocery store. They're related to Yancy, but that's a shoddy excuse for going against conscience, which is exactly what I told them. They seem pretty ashamed of themselves. I'll also get everyone else straightened out who needs it. We might be behind the times in this county, but we're decent folks."

Alaina thanked them, though she wondered if she'd ever be comfortable in Bannister again.

Then one of the ranchers held up the last book she and Mason had written together. "Um, could I get your autograph?" he asked. "We never had a real writer here before."

Alaina laughed and signed the title page. Perhaps feeling comfortable again wouldn't be as hard as she'd thought.

GIDEON WATCHED YANCY FELDER leave after getting a stern lecture from Deke and Sheriff Hewitt. He looked contrite and more than a little alarmed. Like so many bullies, he was a coward at heart. With the entire community watching him now, Gideon was confident that he'd stay in line. He might even be willing to sell his ranch to the Westcott Trust.

As for Alaina?

It was plain that the ranchers crowding around her had succumbed to her appeal. Hardly a surprise—she'd banished most of *his* doubts. They also had to admire her nerve at being willing to face them.

Gideon admired it himself, though nothing would stop him from wanting to protect her, that's what you did when you loved someone. You wanted to take care of them. Alaina even seemed to be accepting that about herself. He'd always cherish the moment when she'd urged him to be careful in the storm.

"She's really something, isn't she?" Helene said.

"Don't get your hopes up, Mom."

"I've had my hopes up since the first day Alaina came to the ranch and you couldn't stop reading the paperwork she'd left."

"You didn't even get a good look at her."

"But I saw your face."

Gideon didn't know if his feelings for Alaina had been a foregone conclusion, but he couldn't deny the way she'd impacted him from the very beginning. It wasn't just her beauty and talent. She also made him a better person. How many people could do that? He and Celeste had been terrible as a couple, bringing out the worst in each other. But he liked the man he was with Alaina. Even though he had a long way to go, he knew he could get there if she was at his side.

"I still wouldn't start hoping," he advised his mother. "Remember, Alaina was deeply in love with her husband. The love of her life, you called him."

Helene smiled determinedly. "Loving one person doesn't mean she can't love someone else, just as deeply. I saw her face when Yancy accused you of being in love with her and you didn't deny it. She started glowing. And she admitted to caring about you, too. Love was all over her face."

Gideon had seen it, too, and his heart had begun pounding so hard he'd had trouble catching his breath.

Libby came over as the ranchers began leaving and looked at him defensively. "Alaina called me. I couldn't lie when she started asking questions about what was up, could I?"

"No, but I hope you didn't break the speed limit getting up here. You're engaged to a lawman now and wouldn't want to compromise him."

She grinned. "Compromise him? How very old West."

Gideon made a gesture of mock surrender. "I don't know what old West is supposed to mean, but it can't be any worse than anything else you've accused me of as your big brother."

"Wrong, you're the best big brother and you've finally caught up to someone from the nineteenth century. I'd call that progress."

Alaina shook hands with the last rancher and came over to them. "I *had* to come when I found out what was going on," she said. "Are you upset?"

Gideon shook his head. "It worked out for the best. You earned their respect by showing up. I should have taken that into account."

"Good. Your mom, Libby and I drove in together, so we'd better get going. Will I see you back at the Double Branch?"

The mysterious glow was still in her blue-green eyes and it was all he could do not to declare himself immediately. But they needed to return home and he had a truck-load of ranch hands waiting.

"Yes," he told her, his voice hoarse.

Back at the Double Branch, Gideon crunched through the snow to Alaina's cheerfully lit cabin. It felt more like home than the big ranch house, but that had nothing to do with the holiday lights bedecking the smaller structure—it was because she lived there.

Alaina opened the door at his first knock.

"I love you," he blurted, unable to stay quiet any longer. "Though I suppose that isn't a secret after what happened at the meeting. The problem is I don't know if I can deal with coming second to a memory."

ALAINA THREW HER arms around Gideon's neck and kissed him with a giddy joy.

"I love you, too, and you could never come second."

"But you said you couldn't imagine loving someone as much as you loved Mason."

Alaina kissed Gideon again, an I'm-going-to-be-with-you-forever kind of kiss, reveling in the freedom to touch him. Then she dropped her head back to look into his eyes.

"Listen to me," she said intently. "I'm a different person now than when Mason was alive. It doesn't mean what I felt for him wasn't strong and real, but I've changed."

"I want to believe you."

"You can. You're the love of my *new* life, and it's more powerful and intense than I could have imagined. If you're going to trust me about anything, trust that. Love has no limits."

Alaina saw the struggle to believe in his eyes.

"Do you remember what else I said?" she asked. "I told you that I could never marry somebody without being completely in love with them. I think even then I was aware that something had started between us."

"It had."

"Well, I meant every word," she murmured. "I'm an utter romantic when it comes to love and marriage. And I'm not talking about the trappings of candlelight and flowers. I don't believe in marrying someone for practical reasons. I believe in loving to the absolute depths of my soul, through all the good and bad."

"That's how I see it, too. I think that's why my divorce was such a shock. Even though things weren't good between us, a part of me thought we'd work through it, because that's what you're supposed to do."

Alaina tugged him inside the cabin. She'd only just started a fire in the stove so it wasn't warm yet, but at least it was out of the wind.

"Were you genuinely in love with Celeste?" she asked.

Gideon sighed. "No, I just thought so at the time. And it turned out there wasn't anything to work through because we didn't value any of the same things. Or even cared that much about each other."

"I'm sorry."

"I'm not. If I was still with Celeste, I'd be miserable. And I wouldn't be here with you right now. You see, I'm old-fashioned about commitment. Even when things were bad with her, I never looked at another woman that way."

His sweet, endearing tone made Alaina's heart ache.

"I'm old-fashioned about commitment, too," she said. "And however much of a romantic I might be, I know that a good marriage takes work and meeting each other halfway."

A wry smile grew on Gideon's face. "That's going to be hard when it comes to you taking risks for your photography."

"It will be just as hard for me," she said seriously. "You take risks, too, every single day on the ranch. You just aren't used to seeing it like that. I was afraid when you went out to work in the storm and I couldn't help asking you to be careful, even though I knew you would be. But if we live our lives afraid for each other, we won't really be living."

GIDEON KNEW ALAINA was right.

"What if I have to shoot a bear or wolf someday? Could you ever forgive me?"

It was a hard question to ask, but he needed to ask it. She'd talked about accepting the balance of nature, but she might not see protecting the Double Branch's herds the same as he did.

Alaina smiled sadly. "I know you wouldn't do it unless you had no other choice. So while I'd grieve that something so beautiful was gone, there wouldn't be anything to forgive."

Gideon saw the sincerity in her eyes and certainty swept through him.

To really love Alaina, he'd have to let go sometimes, to let her be the wildlife photographer who trekked into the mountains for her photographs, even when it gave him heart failure to think of her so far from safety. But then he was starting to believe that bears *were* her guardian angels, along with wolves and dogs and all other living creatures.

They all seemed to adore her.

"Well?" Alaina prompted.

"I guess there's only one thing left to ask—how about a Christmas wedding?"

Christmas, the following year...

"HOW IS DADDY'S ANGEL?" Gideon asked his daughter as he changed her diaper.

Helen Noelle cooed and kicked her tiny legs. The doctor claimed her smiles were still just a reflex, but Gideon knew better. Noelle knew exactly who he was and had twined him around her little finger as effectively as her mother had.

He wrapped Noelle in the baby quilt Grandma Claire had made and carried her to the loveseat, illuminated by the flickering light from the fireplace and the bright Christmas tree in front of the window.

"She's almost asleep," he said, laying her in Alaina's arms.

"Then maybe you should use the quiet and get some rest, too."

"Nah." Gideon sat next to his wife and put his arm around her and the baby. This was their time, with the house quiet and their holiday guests settled down for the night.

With his mother, Alaina had decorated every single room for Christmas and outside, as well. Nearby trees, along with the barns, were outlined by strings of lights. The night sky was crisp and clear, the thermometer below zero, with stars sparkling against the snow in a merry competition with the Christmas cheer. Even the old foreman's cabin—where Alaina's brothers were sleeping—was decorated.

She'd filled his world with light and love and he adored it. The grinding work on the ranch hadn't lessened, but having Alaina in his life made the load easier.

ALAINA PUT HER head on Gideon's shoulder, gazing dreamily at the fire and the dogs and cats asleep in front of it. "It's a full house," she murmured.

"Yeah. You would have brought Griz

and Nikko inside if there had been enough room," Gideon teased.

"Ha. You only married me so your great-grandfather's horse wouldn't be lonely."

"He's your horse now," Gideon murmured. "Griz loves you almost as much as I do. But not quite."

Alaina smiled. She finally had the big family she'd always wanted, and it included wonderful animals like Grizzly, Nikko, Danger and Merlin, who had promptly moved indoors after the wedding, abandoning his life as a barn cat. Gideon had also welcomed Mason's sister, saying she was as a much a member of the family as anyone else. Mason's parents remained wary and distant, but with time they might be able to see Noelle as a surrogate grandchild.

Deke and Libby had gotten married in August and were living on the Westcott Memorial Ranch since it was closer to Libby's archeological site than the Double Branch. They were debating the best time to try for a family, but Alaina suspected they'd wait awhile longer.

Alaina snuggled closer to her husband, happy and grateful. She'd given up thoughts of marriage and children, only to find them when she wasn't looking. She adored Gideon more each day, and now they had a beautiful daughter. In the years to come, she hoped there would be more children to share their lives.

She was right.

Love had no limits.

* * * * *

If you missed Twins for the Rodeo Star, *the first charming romance in this series from Julianna Morris,* *visit www.Harlequin.com today!*

Get 4 FREE REWARDS!

We'll send you 2 FREE Books plus 2 FREE Mystery Gifts.

Love Inspired Suspense books showcase how courage and optimism unite in stories of faith and love in the face of danger.

FREE Value Over $20

THE 2020 CHRISTMAS ROMANCE COLLECTION!

NEW YORK TIMES BESTSELLING AUTHOR
RaeAnne Thayne
Christmas at Holiday House

MAISEY YATES
The Last Christmas

brenda novak
A California Christmas

'Tis the season for romance!

You're sure to fall in love with these tenderhearted love stories from some of your favorite bestselling authors!

Visit ReaderService.com Today!

As a valued member of the Harlequin Reader Service, you'll find these benefits and more at ReaderService.com:

- Try 2 free books from any series
- Access risk-free special offers
- View your account history & manage payments
- Browse the latest Bonus Bucks catalog

Don't miss out!

If you want to stay up-to-date on the latest at the Harlequin Reader Service and enjoy more content, make sure you've signed up for our monthly News & Notes email newsletter. Sign up online at ReaderService.com or by calling Customer Service at 1-800-873-8635.

RS20